There was only the sound
of their breat...

"Ma'moiselle," he whispered, and not once did the intensity of his gaze falter. His eyes had darkened to a smolder that held her so completely that she could not look away. It seemed as if she were transfixed by him, unable to move, unaware of anything save him and the strange tension that seemed to bind them together.

Her eyes flickered over the harsh, lean angles of his face. She was acutely conscious of the hardness of his chest and hip and, against her, the long length of his legs. Her breath wavered, and she was sure that he would hear its loud raggedness.

"Josephine," he said, and she could hear the hoarse strain within his voice. "God help me, but you tempt me to lose my very soul."

His hand moved around to cradle her head. His face lowered toward hers, and she knew that he was going to kiss her. Slowly Josie tilted her face up in response, and the blanket slipped from her shoulders to fall upon the groundsheet.

A noise sounded from outside—a noisy tread over the grass, a man clearing his throat.

They froze.

"Captain Dammartin," a man's voice said.

The spell was broken.

* * *

The Captain's Forbidden Miss
Harlequin® Historical #1061—October 2011

The Captain's Forbidden Miss

MARGARET McPHEE

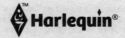

TORONTO NEW YORK LONDON
AMSTERDAM PARIS SYDNEY HAMBURG
STOCKHOLM ATHENS TOKYO MILAN MADRID
PRAGUE WARSAW BUDAPEST AUCKLAND

Recycling programs
for this product may
not exist in your area.

ISBN-13: 978-0-373-29661-3

THE CAPTAIN'S FORBIDDEN MISS

Copyright © 2008 by Margaret McPhee

First North American Publication 2011

Available from Harlequin® Historical and
MARGARET McPHEE

The Captain's Lady #785
Mistaken Mistress #815
The Wicked Earl #843
Christmas Wedding Belles #871
"A Smuggler's Tale"
Untouched Mistress #921
*Unlacing the Innocent Miss #1016

*Part of Silk & Scandal miniseries

**Look for this roguish Regency duet
from Margaret McPhee**

Gentlemen of Disrepute
Unmasking the Duke's Mistress
A Dark and Brooding Gentleman

Coming soon

Author Note

I was reading a book on the Peninsular War when, instead of concentrating on all the facts and figures, my mind wandered off (as it is wont to do!) and I began imagining the meeting between a handsome French Dragoon captain and the rather brave daughter of a British Lieutenant Colonel. They are enemies simply because one is French and the other English. Could love overcome that? Probably so, I thought, particularly if he was wickedly attractive! But what if there was more to it than that? What if there was a more personal grudge that lay between them? Whether love would flourish in such hostile circumstances is a much trickier question, to which Pierre and Josie's story provides the answer.

Just a very brief note on the history: General Foy's mission across Portugal and his large escort of protective troops are fact, although it is not certain that the 8th Dragoons formed a part of the convoy. The fifth battalion of the 60th Regiment of Foot were deployed in the region at the time, but the village of Telemos and the confrontation between these specialist riflemen and Foy's escort belong only with Pierre and Josie.

I am indebted to Professor Tony Payne for all the wonderful information he supplied on the Peninsular War in general and specifically on the details of military uniforms and Napoleonic armies, although any mistakes are, of course, my own. I hope that he will forgive me the certain liberties I have taken with accuracy for the sake of the story. My thanks also go to Carole Verastegui for her kind help with French language translations.

Pierre and Josie's is a story of love against all odds and I really do hope that you enjoy reading it.

Chapter One

Central Portugal—31 October 1810

High up in the deserted village of Telemos in the mountains north of Punhete, Josephine Mallington was desperately trying to staunch the young rifleman's bleeding when the French began their charge. She stayed where she was, kneeling by the soldier on the dusty stone floor of the old monastery in which her father and his men had taken refuge. The French hail of bullets through the holes where windows had once stood continued as the French dragoon troopers began to surge forwards in a great mass, the sound of their *pas de charge* loud even above the roar of gunpowder.

'En avant! En avant! Vive la République!' She heard their cries.

All around was the acrid stench of gunpowder and of fresh spilt blood. Stones that had for three hundred years sheltered monks and priests and holy Mass now witnessed carnage. Most of her father's men were dead, Sarah and Mary too. The remaining men began to run.

The rifleman's hand within hers jerked and then went limp. Josie looked down and saw that life had left him, and, for all the surrounding chaos, the horror of it so shocked her that for a moment she could not shift her stare from his lifeless eyes.

'Josie! For God's sake, get over here, girl!'

Her father's voice shook her from the daze, and she heard the thudding of the French axes as they struck again and again against the thick heavy wood of the monastery's front door. She uncurled her fingers from those of the dead soldier and, slipping the shawl from her shoulders, she draped it to cover his face.

'Papa?' Her eyes roved over the bloody ruins.

Bodies lay dead and dying throughout the hall. Men that Josie had known in life lay still and grotesque in death—her father's men—the men of the Fifth Battalion of the British 60th Regiment of Foot. Josie had seen death before, more death than any young woman should see, but never death like this.

'Stay low and move quickly, Josie. And hurry—we do not have much time.'

On her hands and knees she crawled to where her father and a small group of his men crouched. Dirt and blood smeared their faces and showed as dark patches against the deep green of their jackets and the blue of their trousers.

She felt her father's arms around her, pulling her into the huddle of men.

'Are you hurt?'

'I am fine,' she said, even though *'fine'* was hardly the word to describe how she was feeling.

He nodded and set her from him. She heard her father speak again, but this time his words were not for her. 'The door will not hold them much longer. We must make for the uppermost floor. Follow me.'

She did as her father instructed, responding to the strength and authority in his voice as much as any of his men would have done, pausing only to collect the rifle, cartridges and powder horn from a dead rifleman, and taking care to keep her eyes averted from the gaping wound in his chest. Clutching the rifle and ammunition to her, she fled with the men, following her father out of the hall, past the door through which the French axes had almost hacked, and up the wide stone staircase.

They ran up two flights of stairs and into a room at the front of the building. Miraculously the key was still in the lock of the door. As it turned beneath her father's hand, she heard the resounding thud of the front door being thrown open and knew that the French were in. They heard the sound of many French feet below running into the great hall and then the booted footfalls began to climb the stairs that would lead them to the room that housed the few remaining riflemen.

There was little to mark Lieutenant Colonel Mallington from his riflemen save his bearing and the innate authority that he emanated. His jacket was of the same dark green, with black frogging, scarlet facings and silver buttons, but on his shoulder was a silver thread wing and around his waist was the red sash of rank. His riding boots were easily unnoticed and his fur-trimmed pelisse lay abandoned somewhere in the great hall below.

Within their hiding place, Josie listened while her father spoke to his men. 'We need to draw this out as long as we possibly can, to give our messengers the best chance of reaching General Lord Wellington with the news.' Lieutenant Colonel Mallington's face was strong and fearless. He looked each one of his men in the eye.

Josie saw the respect on the riflemen's faces.

Her father continued, 'The French force are marching through these hills on a secret mission. General Foy, who leads the column of French infantry and its cavalry detachment, is taking a message from General Massena to Napoleon Bonaparte himself. He will travel first to Ciudad Rodrigo in Spain and then to Paris.'

The men stood quiet and listened to what their lieutenant colonel was saying.

'Massena is requesting reinforcements.'

'And General Lord Wellington knows nothing of it,' added Sergeant Braun. 'And if Massena gets his reinforcements…'

'That is why it is imperative that Wellington is forewarned of this,' said Lieutenant Colonel Mallington. 'It is only half an hour since our men left with the message. If Foy and his army realise that we have despatched messengers, then they will go after them. We must ensure that does not happen. We must buy Captain Hartmann and Lieutenant Meyer enough time to get clear of these hills.'

The men nodded, thin-lipped, narrow-eyed, determined in their conviction.

'And that is why we will not surrender this day,' the Lieutenant Colonel said, 'but fight to the death. Our sacrifice will ensure that Wellington will not be taken unawares by a reinforced French army, thus saving the lives of many of our men. Our six lives for our messengers.' He paused and looked solemnly at his men. 'Our six lives to save many.'

Within the room was silence, and beyond rang the clatter of French boots.

'Six men to win a war,' he finished.

'Six men and one sharpshooting woman,' said Josie, meeting her father's gaze and indicating her rifle.

And then one by one the men began cheer. 'For victory!' they shouted.

'For the King and for freedom!' boomed Lieutenant Colonel Mallington.

A raucous hurrah sounded in response.

'No man shall come through that door alive,' said Sergeant Braun.

Another cheer. And one by one the men positioned themselves at either side of the door and readied their weapons.

'Josie.' Her father's voice had quietened and softened in tone.

She came to him, stood beside him, knowing that this was it, knowing that there were no more escapes to be had. For all the men's bravado, Josie was well aware what her father's order would cost them all.

A single touch of his fingers against her cheek. 'Forgive me,' he said.

She kissed his hand. 'There is nothing to forgive.'

'I never should have brought you back here.'

'I wanted to come,' she said, 'you know how I hated it in England. I've been happy here.'

'Josie, I wish—'

But Lieutenant Colonel Mallington's words were cut short. There was no more time to talk. A French voice sounded from beyond the door, demanding surrender.

Lieutenant Colonel Mallington drew Josie a grim smile. 'We will not surrender!' he bellowed in English.

Twice more the French voice asked that they yield, and twice more Lieutenant Colonel Mallington refused.

'Then you have sealed your fate,' said the highly accented voice in English.

Josie cut the paper of a cartridge with the gunflint to release the bullet, poured the gunpowder into the rifle's barrel and rammed the bullet home before priming the lock. Her father gestured her to crouch closest to the corner farthest from the door. He signed for the men to hunker down and aim their weapons.

The French unleashed their musket fire, their bullets thudding into the thick wooden door.

Wait, instructed the Lieutenant Colonel's hand signal.

For Josie that was the hardest time, crouched there in the small room, her finger poised by the trigger, her heart racing somewhere near the base of her throat, knowing that they were all going to die, and disbelieving it all the same. Never had the minutes stretched so long. Her mouth was so dry she could not swallow, and still her father would not let them fire. He wanted one last stand, one last blaze of glory that would hold the Frenchmen at bay until the very last moment. And still the bullets kept on coming, and still the six men and Josie waited, until at last the door began to weaken and great chunks of wood fell from it, exposing holes through which Josie could see the mass of men crammed into the corridor outside, their uniforms so similar in colour to that of her father and his men that she could have imagined they were British riflemen just the same.

'Now!' came the order.

And what remained of their section of the Fifth Battalion of the 60th Foot let loose their shots.

Josie could never be sure how long the mêlée lasted. It might have been seconds; it seemed like hours. Her arms and shoulders ached from firing and reloading the rifle, yet still she kept going. It was an impossible cause, and one by one the riflemen went down fighting, until there was only Sergeant Braun, Josie and her father. Then Lieutenant Colonel Mallington gave a grunt, clutched a hand to his chest, and through his fingers Josie could see the stain of spreading blood. He staggered backwards until he slumped against the wall, the blade of his sword clattering uselessly to the floor. As Lieutenant Colonel Mallington's strength failed, he slithered down the wall to land half sitting, half lying at its base.

'Papa!' In two steps she had reached him and was pressing the sword back into his hand where he lay.

His breathing was laboured and the blood was spreading across his coat.

Sergeant Braun heard her cry, and positioned himself in front of the Lieutenant Colonel and his daughter, firing shot after shot, and reloading his rifle so fast as to make Josie's paltry efforts seem laughable, and all the while roaring his defiance at the French force that had not yet crossed the threshold where the skeleton of the door still balanced. It seemed that he stood there an eternity, that one man holding back the full force of the French 8th Dragoons, until at last his body jerked with the impact of one bullet and then another and another, and he crumpled to the ground to lie in a crimson pool.

There was no more musket fire.

Josie moved to stand defensively in front of her father, aiming her rifle through the gun smoke, her breathing ragged and loud in the sudden silence.

The holed and splintered wood that had been the door fell inwards suddenly, landing with a crash upon the floor of the barren room that housed the bodies of the riflemen. There was silence as the smoke cleared to show Josie exactly what she faced.

The French had not moved. They still stood clustered outside around the doorway, in their green coats so reminiscent of the 60th's. Even the facings on their coats were of a similar red coloration; the difference lay in their white breeches and black riding boots, their brass buttons and single white crossbelts and most of all in the brass helmets with black horsehair crests that they wore upon their heads. Even across the distance she could see their faces beneath those helmets—lean and hard and ruthless—and she saw the disbelief that flitted across them when they realised whom it was that they faced.

She heard the command, *'Ne tirez pas!'* and knew that they would hold their fire. And then the man who had issued that command stepped through the doorway into the room.

He was dressed in a similar green jacket to that of his men, but with the white epaulettes upon his shoulders and a leopardskin band around his helmet that was given only to officers. He looked too young to wear the small, silver grenades in the carmine turnbacks in the tail of his jacket. He was tall and well muscled. Beneath the polish of his helmet his hair was short and dark, and down the length of his left cheek he carried a scar. In his hand was a beautifully weighted sabre, from the hilt of which hung a long, golden tassel.

When he spoke his voice was hard and flinty and highly accented. 'Lieutenant Colonel Mallington.'

Josie heard her father's gasp of shock and she raised the rifle higher, aiming it at the Frenchman.

'Dammartin?' She could hear the incredulity in her father's voice.

'You recognise me from my father, Major Jean Dammartin, perhaps. I understand that you knew him. I am Captain Pierre Dammartin and I have waited a long time to meet you, Lieutenant Colonel Mallington,' said the Frenchman.

'Good Lord!' said her father. 'You are his very image.'

The Frenchman's smile was cold and hard. He made no move, just stood there, seemingly relishing the moment.

'Josie,' her father called with urgency.

Josie kept the rifle trained on the French Captain, but she glanced down at her father. He was pale and weak with lines of pain etched around his eyes.

'Papa?'

'Let him approach. I must speak with him.'

Her gaze swung back to the Frenchman, whose eyes were dark and stony. They watched one another across the small distance.

'Josie,' her father said again. 'Do as I say.'

She was loathed to let the enemy any closer to her father, but she knew that she had little choice. Perhaps her father had a trick up his sleeve, a small pistol or a knife with which to turn the situation to their advantage. If they could but capture the French Captain and bargain for just a little more time....

Josie stepped to the side, leaving the approach to her father free, yet never taking her eyes from the Frenchman's face.

The French Captain's sabre sat easily in his hand as if it were an old friend with which he was so comfortable that he ceased to notice it. He advanced forwards to stand before the Lieutenant Colonel, taking the place that Josie had just vacated, waiting with a closed expression for what the older man would say.

And all the while Josie kept the rifle trained upon the Frenchman's heart, and the French soldiers kept their muskets trained upon her.

'Captain Dammartin.' Her father beckoned him closer.

The Frenchman did not move.

Lieutenant Colonel Mallington managed to smile at the young man's resistance. 'You are of the same mould as your father. He was a most worthy opponent.'

'Thank you, Lieutenant Colonel.' Dammartin's mouth was grim. 'A compliment indeed.'

The Lieutenant Colonel's eyes slid to Josie. 'She is my daughter, all that I have left in this world.' Then his gaze was back fixed on Dammartin. 'I do not need to ask that you treat her honourably. I already know that, as Jean Dammartin's son, you will do nothing other.' He coughed and blood flecked red and fresh upon his lips.

Dammartin's eyes glittered dangerously. 'Do you indeed, Lieutenant Colonel?' He slowly extended his sword arm until the edge of the blade was only inches from the Lieutenant Colonel's face. 'You are very certain for a man in your position.'

The French dragoons in the background smiled and sniggered. Dammartin held up a hand to silence them.

Josie took a step closer to the French Captain, the weight of the raised rifle pulling at her arms. She showed no weakness, just tightened her finger slightly against the trigger and took another step closer, keeping the rifle's muzzle aimed at Dammartin's chest. 'Lower your sword, sir,' she said, 'or I shall put a bullet through you.'

'No, Josie!' came her father's strained voice.

'Think of what my men will do if you pull the trigger,' Dammartin said.

'I think of what you will do if I do not,' she replied.

Their gazes locked, each refusing to look away, as if that would determine whether the sabre blade or the rifle trigger moved first.

'Josie!' Her father coughed again, and she heard his gasp of pain. 'Lay down your weapon.'

Her eyes darted to her father's face, unable to believe his words. 'We will not surrender,' she said in a parody of his earlier words.

'Josie.' His bloodstained fingers beckoned her down, their movement weak and fluttering with a control that was fast ebbing.

One last look at Dammartin, who let his blade fall back a little, and, keeping the rifle pointed in his direction, she crouched lower to hear what her father would say.

'Our fight is done. We can do no more this day.'

'No—' she started to protest, but he silenced her with a touch of his hand.

'I am dying.'

'No, Papa,' she whispered, but she knew from the blood that soaked his jacket and the glistening pallor of his face that what he said was true.

'Give up your weapon, Josie. Captain Dammartin is an honourable man. He will keep you safe.'

'No! How can you say such a thing? He is the enemy. I will not do it, Papa!'

'Defiance of an order is insubordination,' he said, and tried to laugh, but the smile on his face was a grimace, and the effort only brought on a fresh coughing fit.

The sight of the blood dribbling from the corner of his mouth brought a cry to Josie's lips. 'Papa!' Without so much as a glance as Dammartin, she abandoned the rifle on the floor, and clutched one hand to her father's. The other touched gently to his face.

The light was fading from his eyes. 'Trust him, Josie,' he whispered so quietly that she had to bend low to catch his words. 'Enemy or not, the Dammartins are good men.'

She stared at him, unable to comprehend why he would say such a thing of the man who looked at them with such hatred in his eyes.

'Promise me that you will yield to him.'

She felt the tremble in her lower lip and bit down hard upon it to hide the weakness.

'Promise me, Josie,' her father whispered, and she could hear the plea in his failing voice.

She said the only words that she could. 'I promise, Papa.' And she pressed a kiss to his cheek.

'That's my girl.' His words were the faintest whisper.

Josie's tears rolled, warm and wet.

'Captain Dammartin,' Lieutenant Colonel Mallington commanded, and it seemed that something of the old power was back in his voice.

Josie's heart leapt. Perhaps he would not die after all. She felt him move her fingers to his other hand, watched him reach out towards Dammartin, saw the strength of his hand as he gripped the Frenchman's fingers.

'I commend Josephine to your care. See that she is kept safe until you can return her to the British lines.'

Her father's gaze held the Frenchman's. It was the last sight Lieutenant Colonel Mallington saw. A sigh sounded within the cold stone room of the Portuguese monastery, and then there was silence, and her father's hand was limp and lifeless within Josie's.

'Papa?' she whispered.

His eyes still stared unseeing at the Frenchman.

'Papa!' The realisation of what had just happened cracked her voice. She pressed her cheek to his, wrapped her arms around his bloodstained body, and the sob that tore from her was to those that had heard a thousand cries and screams of pain and death still terrible to hear. Outside the room men that had both perpetrated and suffered injury for the past hour stood silent with respect.

When at last she let her father's body go and moved her face from his, it was Dammartin's fingers that swept a shutting of the Lieutenant Colonel's eyes, and Dammartin's hand that took hers to raise her to her feet. She barely heard the order that he snapped to his men, or noticed the parting of the sea of men to let her through. Neither did she notice Captain Dammartin's grim expression as he led her from the room.

The French camped that night in the same deserted village in which they had fought, the men sleeping within the shells of the buildings, their campfires peppering light across the darkness of the rocky landscape. The smell of cooking lingered in the air even though the meagre stew had long since been devoured.

Pierre Dammartin, Captain of the 8th Dragoons in Napoleon's Army of Portugal, had wanted the English Lieutenant Colonel taken alive. The only reason that he had tempered his assault against the riflemen hiding in the empty monastery was because he had heard that it was Mallington who commanded them. He wanted Mallington alive because he wanted the pleasure of personally dispatching the Lieutenant Colonel to his maker.

For a year and a half Dammartin had wanted to meet Mallington across a battlefield. He had dreamt of looking into Mallington's eyes while he told him who he was. He wanted to ask the Englishman the question he had been asking himself for the past eighteen months. Barely an hour ago it had seemed that his prayers had been answered and Mallington delivered into his hands in the most unlikely of places.

Mallington had not been easily beaten despite the difference in numbers, one section of a British company against one hundred and twenty mounted men backed by a whole battalion of infantry. Indeed, Mallington's men had fought to the death rather than let themselves be taken, refusing Dammartin's offers that they surrender. The fight had lasted longer than Dammartin could have anticipated. And even at its conclusion, when Dammartin had walked into that blood-splattered room in the monastery, he had not been satisfied. True, Dammartin had looked into Mallington's face and revealed his identity. But Mallington's reaction had not been what he expected, and there had been no time for questions. The moment for which the Captain had so longed had left him unexpectedly disgruntled. Especially because of Mallington's daughter.

He stood by the window in the dilapidated cottage that was situated at the foot of the road that led up to the monastery. A few men still drifted around the place. He could hear the soft murmur of their voices and see their dark shapes by the light of the fires. Soon they would be bedding down for the night, just as the thousands of men in the canonments around Santarém not so far away to the south would be doing. Above, the sky was a spread of deep, dark, inky blue studded with the brilliance of diamond stars. And he knew that the temperature was dropping and that the cold would be biting. Tomorrow General Foy would lead them across the mountains towards Ciudad Rodrigo and they would leave behind the ruined monastery at Telemos and the dead riflemen and Mallington. He heard Lamont move behind him.

'Your coffee, Pierre.'

He accepted the tin mug from his sergeant's hands. 'Thank you.' The brown liquid was bitter, but warming. 'Has Major La Roque sent for me yet?'

'No.' Lamont smiled, revealing his crooked teeth. 'He is too busy with his dinner and his drink.'

'He is making me wait until morning then,' said Dammartin, 'to haul me over the coals.'

Lamont shrugged his shoulders. He was a small, wiry man with eyes so dark as to appear black. His skin was lined and weatherbeaten, his hair a dark, grizzled grey. Lamont knew how to handle a musket better than any man in Dammartin's company. Despite the fact he had grown up the son of a fishmonger and Dammartin the son of a distinguished military major, the two had become close friends.

'The riflemen refused the option of surrender. They were like demons. Never before have I seen the British fight until there is not a man left alive. It was no easy task to overcome them. The Major must know that.'

Dammartin met his gaze, knowing that his sergeant understood very well that the fight had been unnecessarily prolonged by Dammartin's refusal to storm the monastery until the last. 'The Major will only be concerned with the delay this has cost us. General Foy will not be pleased. One day of marching and we do not even make it past Abrantes.'

Lamont sniffed and wiped his nose with the back of his hand. 'The cost was worth it. You wanted the English Lieutenant Colonel alive so that you might watch him die.'

Dammartin said nothing.

'You have waited a long time to kill him, and now he is dead.'

'But not by my hand.'

'Does it make any difference? He is dead just the same.'

'I wanted to look into his eyes while I killed him. I wanted to watch his reaction when I told him who I was, to see that he understood, to feel his fear.'

'And today that is what you did. This Mallington looked upon you with his dying breath. It is done, Captain. Your father is avenged.'

The line of Dammartin's mouth was hard. He said nothing. It was true that Dammartin had looked into Mallington's face and revealed his identity. But thereafter nothing had been as the French Captain anticipated, and he was left feeling cheated.

Lamont fetched his own battered tin mug and sat down

on his pack by the fire he had lit on the hearth. Steam rose in wisps from the steaming-hot coffee. Lamont wrapped his hands around the mug, seemingly impervious to the scald of the heat, and gazed into the flames. 'Perhaps my ears deceived me, Captain, but I thought the Englishman said the girl was his daughter.'

'He did.'

'Sacré bleu!' cursed the Sergeant. 'It shows the nature of this Lieutenant Colonel Mallington. Only a crazy Englishman would bring his daughter with him to war.' The Sergeant drilled a forefinger against the side of his head. 'Crazy.'

'So it would seem,' said Dammartin, remembering the image of the girl standing alone and seemingly unafraid before the men of the 8th Dragoons to defend her father.

'She is so young, so fragile looking. It does not seem possible that she could have survived this hell of a country.'

'So fragile that her bullets are lodged in half our men,' said Dammartin sourly.

'That is the truth,' Lamont said soberly, and took a gulp of his coffee.

Dammartin retrieved a small, silver hip flask from his pocket and loosened the cap. 'Brandy? To keep the damp from your bones tonight.'

Lamont gave a grin and nodded, holding the still-steaming tin mug up.

Dammartin poured a liberal dousing of the amber liquid into the proffered mug before doing likewise with his own. 'Why should Mallington have sacrificed his men over a deserted village in the middle of nowhere? It makes no sense. Wellington's forces are all down at the lines of Torres Vedras and Lisbon. What was Mallington even doing up here?'

The sergeant shrugged. 'A scouting party? They were riflemen after all.'

'Perhaps—' Dammartin sipped his coffee '—Mademoiselle Mallington may be able to shed some light on her father's actions.'

Lamont glanced up quickly at the young captain. 'You mean to interrogate her?'

'She is the only one still alive. Who else can tell us?' Dammartin's expression was unyielding.

'The English Lieutenant Colonel gave her into your care,' protested Lamont. 'She's only a girl.'

Dammartin glared unconvinced.

'She's the daughter of a gentleman, and today she watched her father die.'

'She is the daughter of a scoundrel, and an English scoundrel at that,' Dammartin corrected. 'She handled that rifle as good as any man and she is not to be trusted. Where is Mademoiselle Mallington now?'

'Locked in the cellar below.'

Dammartin drained his mug and set it down. 'Then it would seem that I have work to do this evening.'

Lamont stopped nursing his coffee to look at Dammartin. 'I pray, my friend and captain, that you are certain as to what you are about to do.'

'Never more so,' said Dammartin, and walked from the room.

Chapter Two

Josie sat perched on one of the dusty wooden crates, hugging her arms around her body, trying to keep out the worst of the damp chill. Wherever she looked, it seemed that she saw not the darkness of the cellar in which the French soldiers had locked her, but her father's face so pale and still in death, the blood seeping from his mouth to stain his lips and dribble down his chin. Even when she squeezed her eyes shut, she could not dislodge that image. All around in the dulled silence she heard again the crack and bang of rifles and muskets and the cries of dying men. She stoppered her hands to her ears, trying to block out the terrible sounds, but it did not make any difference, no matter how hard she pressed.

That morning she had been part of a section of twenty-five men and three women. She had collected the water from the spring behind the monastery and boiled it up to make her father's tea, taking the place of his batman for that short time as was her habit. They had laughed and drunk the brew and eaten the porridge oats that were so warming against the cold.

She remembered just those few hours ago in the afternoon when her father had told her of the column of Frenchmen marching through these hills and how he would have to go in closer to discover what they were about. Papa and a handful of men had gone, leaving Josie and the others in the old monastery, cooking up a stew of rabbit for the evening meal. But the small party's return had been panicked and hurried, retreating from the pursuit of the French, scrambling to send their captain and first lieutenant with news to General Lord Wellington. And then Josie's world had exploded. Papa would not laugh again. He was gone. They were all gone. All except Josie.

Even though she had seen their broken bodies and heard her father's last drawn breath, she could not really believe that it was so. It was like some horrific nightmare from which she would awaken. None of it seemed real. Yet Josie knew that it was, and the knowledge curdled a sourness in her stomach. And still the images flashed before her eyes, like illustrations of Dante's *Inferno*, and still the racket roared in her ears, and her throat tightened and her stomach revolted, and she stumbled through the blackness to the corner of the cellar and bent over to be as sick as a dog. Only when her stomach had been thoroughly emptied did she experience some respite from the torture.

She wiped her mouth on her handkerchief and steadied herself against the wall. Taking a deep breath, she felt her way back to the wooden box on which she had been seated.

It seemed that she sat there an eternity in the chilled darkness before the footfalls sounded: booted soles coming down the same stairs over which the French soldiers had dragged her. One set only, heading towards the cellar. Josie braced herself, stifling the fear that crept through her belly, and waited for what was to come. There was the scrape of metal as the key was turned in the lock, and the door was thrown open.

The light of the lantern dazzled her. She turned her face away, squinting her eyes. Then the lantern moved to the side; as her eyes began to adjust to the light, Josie found herself looking at the French captain whom her father had called Dammartin.

'Mademoiselle Mallington,' he said, and crossed the threshold into the cellar. His lantern illuminated the dark, dismal prison as he came to stand before her.

He seemed much bigger than she remembered. The dust and dirt had been brushed from the green of his jacket, and its red collar and cuffs stood bright and proud. The jacket's single, central line of brass buttons gleamed within the flickering light. His white breeches met knee-high, black leather boots and, unlike the last time they had met, he was not wearing the brass helmet of the dragoons. Beneath the light of the lantern his hair was shorn short and looked as dark as his mood. She could see that the stare in his eyes was stony and the line of his mouth was hard and arrogant. In that, at least, her memory served her well.

'Captain Dammartin.' She got to her feet.

'Sit down,' he commanded in English.

She felt her hackles rise. There was something in the quietness of his tone that smacked of danger. She thought she would defy him, but it seemed in that moment that she heard again her father's voice, *Trust him, Josie.* Trust him, when her every instinct screamed to do otherwise? She hesitated, torn between obeying her father and her own instinct.

He shrugged a nonchalant shoulder. 'Stand, then, if you prefer. It makes no difference to me.' There was a silence while he studied her, his eyes intense and scrutinising.

Josie's heart was thrashing madly within her chest, but

she made no show of her discomfort; she met his gaze and held it.

Each stared at the other in a contest of wills, as if to look away would be to admit weakness.

'I have some questions that I wish to ask you,' Dammartin said, still not breaking his gaze.

Josie felt her legs begin to shake and she wished that she had sat down, but she could not very well do so now. She curled her toes tight within her boots, and pressed her knees firmly together, tensing her muscles, forcing her legs to stay still. 'As I have of you, sir.'

He did not even look surprised. 'Then we shall take it in turns,' he said. '*Ladies* first.' And there was an emphasis on the word *'ladies'* that suggested she was no such thing.

'My father's body… Is he… Have you…?'

'Your father lies where he fell,' he said harshly.

'You have not given him a burial?'

'Did Lieutenant Colonel Mallington take time to bury Frenchmen? Each side buries its own.'

'In a battle situation, but this is different!'

'Is it?' he asked, and still their gazes held. 'I was under the impression, *mademoiselle*, that we were engaged in battle this day.'

She averted her gaze down to the floor, suddenly afraid that she would betray the grief and pain and shock that threatened to overwhelm her. *'Battle'* was too plain, too ordinary a word to describe what had taken place that day in the deserted village of Telemos. Twenty-seven lives had been lost, her father's among them. Only when she knew that the weakness had passed did she glance back up at him. 'But there is no one left to bury him.'

'So it would seem.'

His answer seemed to echo between them.

'I would request that you give him a decent burial.'

'No.'

She felt her breath rush in a gasp of disbelief. 'No?'

'No,' he affirmed.

She stared at him with angry, defiant eyes. 'My father told me that you were an honourable man. It appears that he was grossly mistaken in his opinion.'

He raised an eyebrow at that, but said nothing.

'You will leave him as carrion for wild animals to feed upon?'

'It is the normal course of things upon a battlefield.'

She took a single step towards him, her fingers curled to fists by her sides. 'You are despicable!'

'You are the first to tell me so,' he said.

She glared at him, seeing the dislike in his eyes, the hard determination in his mouth, this loathsome man to whom her father had entrusted her. 'Then give me a spade and I will dig his grave myself.'

'That is not possible, *mademoiselle*.'

Her mouth gaped at his refusal.

'You wish Lieutenant Colonel Mallington's body to be buried? It is a simple matter. It shall be done—'

'But you said—'

'It shall be done,' he repeated, 'as soon as you answer my questions.'

Fear prickled at the back of Josie's neck, and trickled down her spine. She shivered, suspecting all too well the nature of the French captain's questions. Carefully and deliberately, she fixed a bland expression upon her face and prayed for courage.

Pierre Dammartin watched the girl closely and knew then that he had not been wrong in his supposition. 'So tell me, Mademoiselle Mallington, what were riflemen of the Fifth Battalion of the 60th Regiment doing in Telemos?'

'I do not know.'

'Come now, *mademoiselle*. I find that hard to believe.'

'Why so? Surely you do not think my father would discuss such things with me? I assure you that it is not the done thing for British army officers to discuss their orders with their daughters.'

He smiled a small, tight smile at that. 'But is it the done thing for British army officers to take their daughters on campaign with them? To have them fight alongside their men?'

'It is not so unusual for officers to take their families, and as for fighting, I did so only at the end and out of necessity.'

He ignored her last comment. 'What of your mother, where is she?'

The girl looked at him defiantly. 'She is dead, sir.'

He said nothing. She was Mallington's daughter. What had Mallington cared for Major Dammartin's wife or family? The simple answer was nothing.

'Tell me of your father's men.'

'There is nothing to tell.' Her voice was light and fearless, almost taunting in its tone.

'From where did you march?'

'I cannot recall.'

He raised an eyebrow at that. The girl was either stupid or brave, and from what he had seen of Mademoiselle Mallington so far, he was willing to bet on the latter. 'When did you arrive in Telemos?'

She glanced away. 'A few days ago.'

'Which day precisely?'

'I cannot remember.'

'Think harder, *mademoiselle*…' he stepped closer, knowing that his proximity would intimidate her '…and I am sure that the answer will come to you.'

She took a step back. 'It might have been Monday.'

She was lying. Everything about her proclaimed it to be so: the way her gaze flitted away before coming back to meet his too boldly, too defiantly; her posture; the flutter of her hands to touch nervously against her mouth.

'Monday?'

'Yes.'

'How many men?'

'I am not sure.'

'Hazard a guess.' Another step forward.

And again she edged back. 'A hundred,' she uttered with angry defiance.

'A large number.' He raised an eyebrow, knowing from the scattering of corpses that there had been nowhere near that number of men.

'Yes.'

He watched her. 'Did you ride with your father, or walk with the men, *mademoiselle*?'

She looked up at him, and he could see the puzzlement beneath the thick suspicion. There was the shortest of pauses before she said, 'I rode a donkey, the same as the other women.'

'You are telling me that the unmarried daughter of the Lieutenant Colonel rode with the company's whores?'

'They were not whores,' she said hotly. 'They were wives to the men.'

'And your father was happy to leave you with them while he rode ahead with his officers on horseback? How very caring of him,' he ridiculed.

'Do not dare to judge him. You are not fit to speak his name!'

'Only fit to kill the bastard,' he murmured in French.

'Scoundrel!' she cursed him.

He smiled. 'Who took the horses?'

All of the anger drained from her in an instant. She

froze, caught unawares. He saw the tiny flicker of fear in her eyes and knew that he had guessed right.

'I do not know what you mean,' she said, but the words were measured and careful.

'There are only two horses stabled at the monastery. Where are the others?'

Beneath the glow of the lantern her face paled. There was a pause. 'We shot the others for food.'

'Really,' he said, 'you shot the horses and left the donkeys?'

'Yes.' One hand slid to encase the other and she stood there facing him, with her head held high, as demure as any lady, and lying through her teeth.

'I see.' He watched her grip tighten until the knuckles shone white. He looked directly into her eyes and stepped closer until only the lantern separated them.

She tried to back away, but her legs caught against the wooden crate positioned behind her and she would have fallen had he not steadied her. Quite deliberately, he left his hand where it was, curled around her upper arm.

'You would do better to tell me the truth, Mademoiselle Mallington,' he said quietly. He saw the pulse jump in her neck, could almost hear the skittering thud of her heart within the silence of the cellar. Her eyes were wide and her skin so pale as to appear that it had been carved from alabaster. She was smaller than he remembered from the shoot-out in the room in the monastery, the top of her head reaching only to his shoulder. Perhaps it was the rifle that had lent her the illusion of height. They were standing so close that he could see the long lashes that fanned her eyes and hear the shallowness of her breath.

'Do you want to start again?' The softness of his words did not hide the steel beneath them.

She shook her head, and he noticed the fair tendrils of

hair that had escaped her pins curl around her neck. 'No, sir.' Her words were as quiet as his, and Dammartin could only admire her courage.

'Very well.' He knew what he must do. The task was not pleasant, but it would give him the answers that the girl would not. Yet still he stood there, staring at her, as much as she stared at him, until he stepped abruptly away. 'We shall continue our conversation at a later time.' And he was gone, leaving her once more in the dark solitude of the cellar.

Josie still glared at the door long after it had closed behind him. Her heart was racing so fast that she thought she might faint, but still she did not move to sit down. Her eyes strained through the darkness, seeing nothing, her ears hearing the steady climb of his feet back up the stairs. Her arm throbbed where his hand had been even though his grip had been so light as to barely be a restraint.

She pressed her fingers hard to her lips as if to catch back all of the words she had spoken.

What had she revealed? Nothing that he would not already have known, yet Josie knew that was not true. The Frenchman's face had told her it was so. He knew about the horses, and if he knew about that, then it would not be so very long before he knew the rest.

Her lies had been feeble, obvious and pathetic. Dammartin did not believe her, that much was evident. And he would be back. Her stomach turned over at the thought.

It had taken an hour for twenty-seven men and women to die so that General Lord Wellington might be warned of Massena's scheme. In the space of a matter of minutes Josie had almost negated their sacrifice if Captain Hartmann and Lieutenant Meyer had not yet reached Wellington. How much time would it take the two men to weave their way back to Lisbon? The future of the British army at the lines of Torres Vedras rested on that and Josie's ability to prevent, or at least delay, Dammartin's discovery that the messengers had been sent. And that was not something in which she had the slightest degree of confidence.

Not for the first time Josie wondered if her father would have done better to let her die with him in the monastery. For all Papa's assurance of Pierre Dammartin's honour, she had a feeling that the French Captain was going to prove a most determined enemy.

It took almost half an hour for Dammartin, his lieutenant, Molyneux, and his sergeant, Lamont, to finish the gruesome activity that the girl's reticence to talk had forced them to. The night was dark, the moon a thin, defined crescent. They worked by the light of flambeaux, moving from corpse to corpse, examining the uniforms that garbed the stiffened, cold bodies that had once been a formidable fighting force for Britain, noting down what they found. And with each one Dammartin felt the futility of the loss. As prisoners of war they would have lost no honour. They had fought bravely, and the French had acknowledged that. Yet they had laid down their lives seemingly in a pointless gesture of defiance.

Three times Dammartin had given them the opportunity to surrender, and three times Mallington had rejected it. Time had been running out. Dammartin knew he had already delayed too long, that General Foy and Major La Roque would arrive to take over if Dammartin did not bring the matter to a close, and Dammartin's chance would have been lost. In the end he had been forced to storm the monastery, just as La Roque had ordered.

He pushed such thoughts from his mind and forced himself to concentrate on the task before him. It seemed a long time before they had finally been able to rinse the blood from their hands and make for the stables.

With the flambeaux held low, they scrutinised the marks and patterns of feet and hooves impressed upon the ground.

'What do you think?' Dammartin asked of his lieutenant. Molyneux had been trained in tracking, and when it came to his expertise in this field, there was no one's opinion that Dammartin trusted more.

'Two men and two horses heading off in the direction of the track over there. Prints are still fairly fresh. They probably left some time this afternoon.'

'It is as I thought,' said Dammartin. 'We have found what we were looking for.' It all made sense. Now he understood why Mallington had fought so hard for so long. Not for Telemos. The village was of little importance to the British regiment. But time was, and time was what they had bought for their messengers, and paid for with their lives. He gave a sigh and moved to instruct a pursuit team.

Josie was in the midst of a dream in which the battle of Telemos was being fought again. She shouted the warning to her father, snatching up the dead man's weapon, running up the staircase, loading and firing at the pursuing French. Her bullet travelled down the gun's rifled barrel, cutting with a deadly accuracy through the air to land within the Frenchman's chest. Smoke from the gunpowder drifted across her face, filling her nose with its stench, catching in her throat, drawing a curtain before her eyes so that she could not see. She heard the stagger of his footsteps, and then he was there, falling to his knees before her, his blood so rich and red spilling on to the hem of her dress. She looked down as the enemy soldier turned his face up to hers and the horror caught in her throat, for the face was that of Captain Pierre Dammartin.

She opened her eyes and the nightmare was gone, leaving behind only its sickening dread. Her heart was thumping in her chest, and, despite the icy temperature of the cellar, the sheen of sweat was slick upon her forehead and upper lip. She caught her breath, sat up from her awkward slump against the stack of wooden boxes, and rubbed at the ache in her back. As she did so, she heard the step of boots upon the stairs and knew that he was coming back, and her heart raced all the faster.

She struggled up to her feet, ignoring the sudden dizziness that it brought, felt herself sway in the darkness and sat rapidly back down. The last thing she wanted Dammartin to see was her faint.

And then he was there, through the door before she was even aware that the key had turned within the lock.

He looked tired and there was fresh dust upon his coat and a smear of dirt upon his cheek. The expression on his face was impassive, and she wondered what he had been doing. How much time had passed since he had questioned her? Minutes, hours? Josie did not know.

He set the lantern down upon a box at the side of the room and moved to stand before her. Josie knew that this time there was a difference in his attitude. His eyes were filled with such darkness and determination that she remembered the stories of interrogation and torture and felt the fear squirm deep in the pit of her stomach. Tales of bravery and singular distinction, men who had defied all to withhold the information that their enemy sought. And something in Josie quailed because she knew that she had not a fraction of that bravery and that just the prospect of what Dammartin could do to her made her feel nauseous. She swallowed and wetted the dryness of her lips.

If Dammartin noticed that she had forsaken her defiance of refusing to remain seated, he made no mention of it. Instead he drew up a crate and sat down before her, adjusting the long sabre that hung by his side as he did so.

She waited for what he would do.

'Do you wish to tell me of the horses, Mademoiselle Mallington?'

'I have told you what I know,' she said, feigning a calmness, and looked down to the darkness of the soil below her feet.

'No, *mademoiselle*, you have told me very little of that.'

In the silence that followed, the scrabble of rodents could be heard from the corner of the cellar.

'Your father sent two men to warn your General Wellington of our march.'

She felt the shock widen her eyes, freeze her into position upon the discomfort of the hard wooden crate. He could not know. It was not possible. Not unless... She stayed as she was, head bent, so that he would not see the fear in her eyes.

'Have you nothing to say, *mademoiselle*? Nothing to ask me?'

The breath was lodged, unmoving in her throat at the thought that Hartmann and Meyer might be captured. She forced its release and slowly raised her head until she could look into his eyes. There she saw ruthlessness and such certainty as to make her shiver.

'No,' she said. 'There is nothing.' Her voice was gritty with the strain of emotion.

His eyes were black in the lantern light as her gaze met his. They stared at each other with only the sound of their breath in the dampness of the cellar, and the tightness of tension winding around them.

'Denial is pointless. I know already the truth. Make this easier for us both, *mademoiselle*.'

She could hear the chilling determination in those few words so quietly uttered. The worst of imaginings were already crowding in her mind.

He was still looking at her and the distance between them seemed to shrink, so that the implacable resolution of the man was almost overwhelming.

It was as if there was something heavy crushing against her chest, making it hard to pull the breath into her lungs and she could feel a slight tremble throughout her body. She curled her fingers tight and pressed her knees together so that the Frenchman would not see it. She swallowed down the lump in her throat, praying that her voice would not shake as much as the rest of her.

Part of her argued that there was no point in lying any-more. Dammartin knew about the messengers already. And the other part of her, the small part that had kept her going throughout that nightmare year in England, refused to yield.

'I will not.' Her words seemed to echo in the silence and she felt her teeth begin to chatter.

'What would you say if I told you that we have captured your messengers?'

She got to her feet, ignoring the way that the cellar seemed to spin around her and the sudden lightness in her head that made her feel that she would faint. 'You are lying!'

Dammartin stood too. He smiled, and his smile was wicked and cold. 'Am I?'

They faced each other across the small space, the tension stretched between them.

'If you wish to know of the messengers, *mademoiselle*,

you will tell me what your father and his men were doing in these hills.'

From somewhere she found the strength to keep standing, to keep looking him in the eye. All of the fear was crowding in around her, pressing down on her, choking her. If the French had captured Hartmann and Meyer, all hope was gone. Her father's message would never reach Wellington. It had all been in vain. All of today. All of the sacrifice.

'I am not privy to my father's orders.' Her gaze held his, refusing to look away, angry disbelief vying with grief and misery and wretchedness.

A terrible desolation swept through her. The tremble had progressed so that her legs were shaking in earnest now, and the cold sweat of fear prickled beneath her arms. She thought again of what it would mean if the French truly had captured her father's messengers. A fresh wave of hopelessness swept over her at the thought, and as the moisture welled in her eyes she squeezed them shut to prevent the tears that threatened to fall. Yet, all of her effort was not enough. To her mortification, a single tear escaped to roll down her cheek. She snatched it away, praying that Dammartin had not noticed, and opened her eyes to stare her defiance.

'Are you crying, *mademoiselle*?' And she thought she could hear the undertone of mockery in his words. He looked at her with his dark eyes and harsh, inscrutable expression.

She glared at him. 'I will tell you nothing, nothing,' she cried. 'You may do what you will.'

'*Mademoiselle*, you have not yet begun to realise the possibilities of what I may do to you.' He leaned his face down close to hers. 'And when you do realise, then you will tell me everything that I want to know.'

Her heart ceased to beat, her lungs did not breathe as she looked up into the dark promise in his eyes.

His hand was around her arm, and he pulled her forwards and began to guide her towards the door.

'No!' She struggled against him, panicked at where he might be taking her and felt him grab her other arm, forcing her round to look at him once more.

'Mademoiselle Mallington,' he said harshly. 'The hour grows late and the ice forms in the air. If I leave you here, without warmth, without food or water, it is likely that you will be dead by morning.'

'Why would you care?' she demanded.

He paused and then spoke with slow deliberation, 'Because you have not yet answered my questions.'

Josie shivered. She did not know if he was lying about Hartmann and Meyer, but she did know that despite all of her fear and despair she had no wish to die. She ceased her struggle and let him lead her out of the cellar and up the creaking staircase into the heart of the little cottage.

The room into which he took her was small and spartan, its floor clean but littered with makeshift blanket beds and army baggage. A fire was roaring in the fireplace at which a small, grizzled man in a French sergeant's uniform was toasting bread and brewing coffee. His small, black eyes registered no surprise at her appearance.

'*Capitaine,*' the man uttered, and gave a nod in Dammartin's direction.

She sat down warily on the edge of the blanket that Dammartin indicated, trying to clear the fog of exhaustion from her brain, trying to remain alert for the first hint of a trap. There was nothing.

The small sergeant placed some toasted bread and raisins and a cup of coffee on the floor by her side before he and Dammartin busied themselves with their own bread.

Josie looked at the food set before her. The smell of the toasted bread coaxed a hunger in her stomach that had not been there before. Slowly, without casting a single glance in the Frenchmen's direction, she ate the bread and drank the coffee. And all the while she was aware of every move that the enemy made and the quiet words that they spoke to one another, thinking that she could not understand.

The logs on the fire cracked and gradually the room grew warm and no matter how hard she fought against it, Josie felt the exhaustion of all that had happened that day begin to claim her. She struggled, forcing her eyes open, forcing herself to stay upright, to stay aware of Captain Dammartin until, at last, she could fight it no more, and the French Captain faded as she succumbed to the black nothingness of sleep.

It was late and yet Pierre Dammartin sat by the fire, despite the fatigue that pulled upon his muscles and stung at his eyes. His gaze wandered from the flicker of the dying flames to the silhouette of the girl lying close by. The blanket rose and fell with the small, rhythmic movement of her breath. Mallington's daughter. Just the thought of who she was brought back all of the bitterness and anger that her father's death ought to have destroyed.

Sergeant Lamont sucked at his long clay pipe and nodded in the girl's direction. 'Did you get what you wanted from her?'

What had he wanted? To know why Mallington had been up here, the details of his men, of his messengers; her realisation that her defiance was useless, that she could not hide the truth from him. 'Unfortunately, my friend, Mademoiselle Mallington proved most unhelpful.'

Lamont's gaze darted in Dammartin's direction, his brow rising in surprise. 'You were gentle with her, then?'

The firelight flickered, casting shadows across Dammartin's face, highlighting his scar and emphasising the strong, harsh line of his jaw. 'Not particularly.'

'Pierre.' Lamont gave a sigh and shook his head.

'Did you really think that she would be in such a hurry to spill the answers we seek? The woman faced us alone with a rifle to defend her father.'

'She is just a girl, Pierre. She must have been afraid.'

'She was frightened, for all she tried to hide it.'

'Yet still she told you nothing?'

'The girl has courage, I will give her that.'

Lamont sucked harder on his pipe and nodded.

Dammartin thought of the girl's single teardrop and the tremble of her lips. Tears and emotion were ever a woman's weapons, he thought dismissively, but even as he thought it, he knew that was not the case with Mademoiselle Mallington. Given half a chance she would have taken a rifle and shot him through the heart, and that knowledge wrung from him a grudging respect.

'Do you mean to question her again tomorrow?'

'Yes. I suspect that she knows more than she is telling.'

Lamont frowned. 'Interrogating women goes against the grain.'

'We must make an exception for Mademoiselle Mallington.'

'Pierre...' admonished the Sergeant.

Dammartin passed Lamont his hip flask of brandy. 'What the hell am I going to do with her, Claude?'

'I do not know,' Lamont shrugged. 'That Mallington entrusted her to you makes me wonder as to the old man's mind. Why else would he give his daughter over to the son of the man that he murdered?'

'To appease his own conscience, leaving her to face the revenge from which he himself fled?' Dammartin's eyes glittered darkly as he received the flask back from Lamont and took a swig. He sat there for a while longer, mulling over all that happened that day, and when finally he slept, the sleep was troubled and dark.

Dammartin slept late, not wakening until the light of morning had dawned, and with a mood that had not improved. Disgruntlement sat upon him as a mantle even though he had reached a decision on what to do with the girl. He rolled over, feeling the chill of the morning air, and cast an eye over at Mademoiselle Mallington. Her blanket lay empty upon the floor. Josephine Mallington was gone.

'Merde!' he swore, and threw aside the thickness of his great coat that had covered him the whole night through. Then he was up and over there, touching his fingers to the blanket, feeling its coldness. Mademoiselle Mallington had not just vacated it, then.

He opened the door from the room, stepped over the two sentries who were dozing.

They blinked and scrabbled to their feet, saluting their captain.

'Where is the girl?'

The men looked sheepish. 'She needed to use the latrine, sir.'

Dammartin could not keep the incredulity from his voice. 'And you let her go unaccompanied?'

'It did not seem right to accompany your woman in such things,' one of the men offered.

'Mademoiselle Mallington is not my woman,' snapped Dammartin. 'She is my prisoner.'

'We thought—'

Dammartin's look said it all.

The sentries fell silent as Dammartin strode off to find Mallington's daughter.

Chapter Three

Josie hitched up her skirts and ran up the worn stone stairs within the monastery. She could not help but remember the last time she had made this journey. Only yesterday afternoon, and already it seemed a lifetime ago. This time she was alone with only the echo of her own footsteps for company. She reached the top of the stairs, and, hesitating there, braced herself to see once more the horror of what lay not so very far beyond. Her hand clutched upon the banister, tracing the bullet-gouged wood. Then she walked slowly and steadily towards the room in which the 60th had made its last stand.

The doorway was open; the wood remnants that had formed the once sturdy door had been tidied to a pile at the side. Blood splatters marked the walls and had dried in pools upon the floor. The smell of it still lingered in the room, despite the great portal of a window within the room and the lack of a door. Of her father and those of his men that had fought so bravely there was no sign. Josie stared, and stared some more. Their bodies were gone. Their weapons were gone. Their pouches of bullets and powder were gone. Only the stain of their blood remained.

She backed out of the room, retraced her steps down the stairs and peeped into the great hall. The rabbit stew still hung in the corner above the blackened ashes of the fire. The stone floor flags were stained with blood. Yet here, as in the room upstairs, there were no bodies. She turned, moving silently, making her way through to the back and the stables. The two horses were no longer there; nor were the donkeys. Of the supplies there was no trace.

Josie's heart began to race. Her feet led her farther out on to the land that had once been the monastery's garden. And there they were.

She stopped, her eyes moving over the mounds of freshly dug earth. At the front, one grave stood on its own, distinct from the others by virtue of its position. She moved forwards without knowing that she did so, coming to stand by that single grave. Only the wind sounded in the silent, sombre greyness of the morning light. For a long time Josie just stood there, unaware of the chill of the air or the first stirrings that had begun to sound from the Frenchmen's camp. And for the first time she wondered if perhaps her father had been right, and that Captain Dammartin was not, after all, a man completely without honour.

It was not difficult to trace Josie's path. Several of his men had seen the girl go into the monastery. No one challenged her. No one accosted her. Some knew that she was the English Lieutenant Colonel's daughter. Others thought, as had the sentries, that she was now their captain's woman. The misconception irked Dammartin, almost as much as the thought of her escape had done. Yet he knew that it was not the prospect of escape that had led her back to the monastery.

He found her kneeling by her father's grave.

Dammartin stood quietly by the stables, watching her.

Her fair hair was plaited roughly in a pigtail that hung down over her back and her skin was pale. Her head was bowed as if in prayer so that he could not see her face. She wore no shawl, and Dammartin could see that her figure was both neat and slender. He supposed she must be cold.

Her dress was dark brown and of good quality, but covered in dirt and dust and the stains of others' blood. The boots on her feet were worn and scuffed, hardly fitting for a Lieutenant Colonel's daughter, but then holding the 8th at bay with a single rifle was hardly fitting for such a woman, either. He watched her, unwilling to interrupt her grieving, knowing what it was to lose a father. So he stood and he waited, and never once did he take his eyes from Josephine Mallington.

Josie felt Captain Dammartin's presence almost as soon as he arrived, but she did not move from her kneeling. She knew that she would not pass this way again and she had come to bid her father and his men goodbye in the only way she knew how, and she was not going to let the French Captain stop her. Only when she was finished did she get to her feet. One last look at the mass expanse of graves, and then she turned and walked towards Captain Dammartin.

She stopped just short of him, looking up to see his face in the dawning daylight. His hair was a deep, dark brown that ruffled beneath the breeze. Despite the winter months, his skin still carried the faint colour of the sun. The ferocity of the weather had not left him unmarked. Dammartin's features were regular, his mouth hard and slim, his nose strong and straight. The daylight showed the scar that ran the length of his left cheek in stark clarity. It lent him a brooding, sinister look and she was glad that she was much more in control of herself this morning.

'Mademoiselle Mallington,' he said, and she could see

that his eyes were not black as she had thought last night, but the colour of clear, rich honey.

'Captain Dammartin.' She glanced away towards the graves, and then back again at him. 'Thank you.' She spoke coolly but politely enough.

A small tilt of his head served as acknowledgement.

'After what you said...I did not think...' Her words trailed off.

'I was always going to have the men buried. They fought like heroes. They deserved an honourable burial. We French respect bravery.' There was an almost mocking tone to his voice, implying that the British had no such respect. 'And as for your father...' He left what he would have said unfinished.

Beyond the monastery she could hear the sound of men moving. French voices murmured and there was the smell of fires being rekindled.

They looked at one another.

'What do you intend to do with me?'

'You are Lieutenant Colonel Mallington's daughter.' His expression did not change and yet it seemed that his eyes grew darker and harder. 'You will be sent to General Massena's camp at Santarém until you can be exchanged for a French prisoner of war.'

She gave a nod of her head.

'You may be assured that, unlike some, we do not ride roughshod over the rules of warfare or the protection that honour should provide.' His face was hard and lean, all angles that smacked of hunger and of bitterness.

It seemed to Josie that Captain Dammartin disliked her very much. 'I am glad to hear it, sir.'

He made some kind of noise of reply that said nothing. 'If you wish to eat, do so quickly. We ride within the hour and you will leave before that, travelling with the escort of Lieutenant Molyneux.'

Side by side, without so much as another word between them, Josephine Mallington and Pierre Dammartin made their way back down into the village and the French soldiers' camp.

'What were you playing at, Pierre?' Major La Roque demanded.

Dammartin faced the Major squarely. 'I wanted his surrender, sir.'

'Foy is asking questions. What am I supposed to tell him? That it took one of my captains almost two hours to overcome twenty-five men, without artillery, holed up in a ramshackle village. Given our fifty dragoons, seventy chasseurs and four hundred infantrymen, it does not look good for you, Pierre. Why did you not just storm the bloody monastery straight away like I told you?'

'I wanted to interrogate him. I would have thought that you, of all people, would understand that.'

'Of course I do, but this mission is vital to the success of the Army of Portugal and we have lost a day's march because of your actions. Not only that, but your men failed to catch the British messengers that were deployed! Only the fact that you are my godson, and Jean Dammartin's son, has saved you from the worst of Foy's temper. Whether it will prevent him from mentioning the *débâcle* to Bonaparte remains to be seen.'

Dammartin gritted his teeth and said nothing.

'I know what you are going through, Pierre. Do you think I am not glad that Mallington is dead? Do you think that I, too, do not wish to know what was going on in that madman's mind? Jean was like a brother to me.'

'I am sorry, sir.'

La Roque clapped his hand against Dammartin's back. 'I know. I know, son. Mallington is now dead. For that at least we should be glad.'

Dammartin nodded.

'What is this I hear about an English girl?'

'She is Mallington's daughter. Lieutenant Molyneux will take her back to General Massena's camp this morning.'

'I will not have any of our men put at risk because of Mallington's brat. These hills are filled with deserters and guerrillas. We cannot afford to lose any of the men. The child will just have to come with us to Ciudad Rodrigo. Once we are there, we can decide what to do with her.'

'Mademoiselle Mallington is not a child, she is—'

But La Roque cut him off, with a wave of the hand. 'It does not matter what she is, Pierre. If you jeopardise this mission any further, Foy will have your head and there will not be a damn thing I can do to save you. See to your men. Emmern will lead through the pass first. Fall in after him. Be ready to leave immediately.' The Major looked at Dammartin. 'Now that Mallington is dead, things will grow easier for you, Pierre, I promise you that.'

Dammartin nodded, but he took little consolation in his godfather's words. Mallington being dead did not make anything better. Indeed, if anything, Dammartin was feeling worse. Now, he would never know why Mallington had done what he did. And there was also the added complication of his daughter.

Whatever he was feeling, Dammartin had no choice but to leave the house that Major La Roque had commandeered in the valley and return to Telemos.

Josie was standing by the side of the window in the little empty room as she watched Dammartin ride back into the village. She knew it was him, could recognise the easy way he sat his horse, the breadth of his shoulders, the arrogant manner in which he held his head. Condensed breath snorted from the beast's nostrils and a light sweat glimmered on its flanks. She wondered what had caused him to ride the animal so hard when it had a full day's travel before it.

He jumped down, leaving the horse in the hands of a trooper who looked to be little more than a boy, and threaded his way through the men that waited hunched in groups, holding their hands to fires that were small and mean and not built to last.

Even from here she could hear his voice issuing its orders.

The men began to move, kicking dust onto the fires, fastening their helmets to their heads and gathering up the baggage in which they had packed away their belongings and over which they had rolled their blankets. He walked purposefully towards the cottage, his face stern as if he carried with him news of the worst kind.

She watched him and it seemed that he sensed her scrutiny, for his gaze suddenly shifted to fix itself upon her. Josie blushed at having being caught staring and drew back, but not before he had seen her. Her cheeks still held their slight wash of colour when he entered the room.

'Mademoiselle Mallington, we are leaving.'

Her hands smoothed down the skirts of her dress in a nervous gesture.

He noticed that the worst of the dirt had been brushed from her dress and that she had combed and re-plaited her hair into a single, long, tidy pigtail that hung down her back. He moved to take up his baggage, then led her out into the sunlight and across the village through which her father and his men had run and fired their rifles and died.

The French dragoons around ceased their murmuring to watch her, wanting to see the woman who had defied the might of the 8th to stand guard over her dying father.

She followed him until they came to the place she had seen him leave his horse. The boy still held the reins. Dammartin handed him the baggage and the boy threw them over the chestnut's rump and strapped them into place. Beside the large chestnut was a smaller grey. He gestured towards it.

'You will find Fleur faster than a donkey.' Dammartin took a dark blue cloak from the boy and handed it to Josie. 'There was a portmanteau of women's clothes alongside Lieutenant Colonel Mallington's. I assumed that they were yours.'

Her fingers clutched at the warmth of the wool. She touched it to her nose, breathing in faint lavender and rosemary, the familiar scent of her own portmanteau and its sachets that she had sown what seemed an eternity ago on sunny days at home in England. The last time she had worn this cloak her father had been alive, and twenty-seven others with him. She still could not believe that they were dead.

'It is my cloak, thank you, Captain Dammartin,' she said stiffly, and draped the material around her.

'We have not a side-saddle.'

'I can ride astride.'

Their eyes held for a heartbeat before she moved quickly to grasp her skirts and, as modestly as she could manage, she placed her foot in the stirrup and pulled herself up on to the grey horse.

The troopers cast appreciative gazes over Josie's ankles and calves, which, no matter how much she pulled at and rearranged her skirts, refused to stay covered. Several whistles sounded from the men, someone uttered a crudity. She felt the heat rise in her cheeks and kept her gaze stubbornly forward.

'Enough,' Dammartin shouted at his men in French. 'Look to your horses. We leave in five minutes.'

Another officer on horseback walked over to join them, his hair a pale wheaty brown beneath the glint of his helmet.

Dammartin gave the man a curt nod of the head before speaking. 'Mademoiselle Mallington, this is Lieutenant Molyneux. Lieutenant, this is Lieutenant Colonel Mallington's daughter.'

Molyneux removed his helmet, and still seated firmly in his saddle, swept her a bow. *'Mademoiselle.'*

Dammartin frowned at his lieutenant.

Josie looked from the open friendliness on the handsome young lieutenant's face to the brooding severity on his captain's, and she was glad that she would be making the journey to Massena's camp in Lieutenant Molyneux's company rather than that of Captain Dammartin. Dammartin looked at her with such dislike beneath his thin veneer of civility that she was under no illusions as to his feelings towards her. Still, there were formalities to be observed in these situations, and she would not disgrace her father's name by ignoring them.

'Goodbye, Captain Dammartin.'

'Unfortunately, *mademoiselle*, this is no goodbye.'

Her eyes widened.

'You travel with us.'

'But you said…' She glanced towards Lieutenant Molyneux.

The lieutenant gave a small, consolatory smile and said, 'I am afraid, *mademoiselle*, that there has been a change of plan.' He dropped back, so that it seemed to Josie that he was abandoning her to Dammartin.

Dammartin's face was unreadable.

'Am I to be exchanged?'

'Eventually,' said Dammartin.

'Eventually? And in the meantime?'

'You are a prisoner of the 8th,' he replied.

A spurt of anger fired within her. 'I will not ride to act against my own country, sir.'

'You have no choice in the matter,' he said curtly.

She stared at him, and the urge to hit him across his arrogant face was very strong. 'I would rather be sent to General Massena's camp.'

'That is my preference also, *mademoiselle*, but it is no longer an option.'

'Then release me. I will make my own way to the lines of Torres Vedras.'

'Tempting though the offer is, I cannot allow you to do so.'

'Why not?' she demanded, feeling more outraged by the minute.

'I have my orders.'

'But—'

A drum sounded, and a second company of French cavalrymen, not dragoons but Hanoverian Chasseurs, began to ride into the village.

Dammartin shouted an order and his men began to form into an orderly column. The chasseur captain, who was dressed in a similar fashion to Dammartin, but with yellow distinctives on the green of his jacket and a dark fur hat upon his head, drew up beside Dammartin, saluting him. His face broke into a grin as he spoke a more informal greeting.

'Emmern.'

For the first time Josie saw Dammartin smile. It was a real smile, a smile of affection, not some distortion of his mouth out of irony or contempt. And it changed his whole face so that he looked devastatingly handsome. Shock jolted through her that she could think such a thing and, pushing the thought aside, she forced herself to concentrate on what the two men were discussing. They spoke in rapid French, discussing the land that lay beyond the village, and the quickest and safest method by which their men might traverse it.

'Foy is like a bear with a sore head this morning.' Captain Emmern laughed. 'The delay has not pleased him.'

'I am aware,' agreed Dammartin. 'I will have the joy of reporting to him this evening.'

'The day has started well, then,' teased the chasseur.

'Indeed,' said Dammartin. 'It could not get much worse.'

Emmern's eyes flicked to Josie and the grey on which she sat. 'I would not look so gloomy if I had spent the night in such pleasant company.' He inclined his head at Josie in greeting. 'Come, Pierre, introduce me. Surely you do not mean to keep her all to yourself? I swear, she is utterly delicious.'

Josie felt the blood scald her cheeks. She ignored the chasseur captain, fidgeted with the grey's reins, and focused on a peculiarly shaped rock high up on the hill to the side.

'She is Lieutenant Colonel Mallington's daughter.' Dammartin's eyes were cold and his jaw rigid.

Captain Emmern's brow lifted slightly with surprise. 'They said there was a woman, but I did not realise that she was his daughter. What the hell could the man have been thinking?'

'Who knows the workings of a madman's mind?' replied Dammartin dryly.

Josie's fists clenched at the Frenchmen's words of insult.

With blazing eyes she glared at them, words of defence
for her father crowding in her mouth for release. Yet the
suspicion that flashed across Dammartin's face served as
a timely reminder that she must feign ignorance of their
conversation.

Dammartin edged his horse closer towards her, his
brows lowered. *'Parlez-vous français, mademoiselle?'*

Even had she not understood his language, there was
no doubting the accusation in his demand. This was dangerous ground, for she realised that by showing her emo-
tions too readily she was in danger of revealing the one
advantage that she had over her captors. The Frenchmen
would let down their guard and talk easily in front of her
if they thought that their words could not be understood by
their prisoner. Any information she could glean might be
of use, for Josie had every intention of passing on all she
could learn to General Lord Wellington. She straightened
her back and, squaring her shoulders, faced Dammartin,
meeting his penetrating gaze directly.

'I have not the slightest idea of what you are saying,
sir. If you would be so good as to speak in English, then
I may be able to answer you.'

Dammartin's face cracked into a cynical disbelieving
smile, yet he switched to English. 'Do not tell me that you
understand not one word of my language, for I will not
believe such a ridiculous assertion.'

Josie did her best to appear outraged. 'Are you suggesting that I am lying?'

'You have been lying all along, *mademoiselle*…about
that which you know, and that which you do not: the details
of your father's men, his purpose in these hills, his messengers…'

She flinched at that and there was no longer any need
for pretence; her outrage was all too real.

'You are the daughter of a senior officer; your father must have arranged your education. I believe that in England even the lowliest of governesses teach the rudiments of French.'

The heat scalded Josie's cheeks, and her chest tightened at his words. She might have been fluent in French, but that had nothing to do with governesses and everything to do with her mother. Mama and Papa had been the best of parents, yet she felt Dammartin's implied criticism as sharp as a knife.

'What time was there for schooling or governesses following my father around the world on campaign? There is more to education than such formality, and besides, my mother and father ensured that both my brother and I were educated in those matters that are of any importance.' She negated to mention the truth of the situation.

Silence followed her inferred insult.

Still she did not drop her gaze from his so that she saw his eyes narrow infinitesimally at her words. He twitched the rein between his fingers and the great chestnut horse brought him round to her side.

'Have a care in what you say, Mademoiselle Mallington. Such words could be construed by some of my countrymen as offensive, and you are hardly in a position to abuse our hospitality.'

'Hospitality?' Her eyebrows raised in exaggerated incredulity, and so caught up in her own anger was Josie that she did not notice the scowl line deepen between Dammartin's brows. 'You kill my father and his men, you lock me in a cellar for hours on end and interrogate me. Forgive me if I am surprised at your notion of hospitality, sir!'

He leaned in closer until his face was only inches above hers. It seemed to Josie that the angles of his jawline grew sharper and the planes of his cheeks harder, and his eyes darkened with undisguised fury. As awareness dawned of how much bigger he was, of his strength, his overwhelming masculinity, all of Josie's anger cooled, leaving in its stead the icy chill of fear.

'I assure you, *mademoiselle*, that I have been most hospitable in my treatment of you...so far.' His voice was the quiet purr of a predator. 'Do you wish me to prove it is so, by demonstrating how very inhospitable I can be?'

Josie's heart was thumping nineteen to the dozen. She wetted the dryness of her lips, and swallowed against the aridity of her throat. 'You are no gentleman, sir.' Still, she forced herself to hold his dark, menacing gaze.

'And you, no lady.'

She could have argued back. She could have called him the scoundrel that he was, but there was something in his eyes that stopped her, something fierce and impassioned and resolute that shook her to her very core.

'I ask you, sir, to release me,' she said, and all of the bravado had gone so that her voice was small and tired. 'You do not want me as your prisoner any more than I wish to be here. It is madness to drag me all the way to Ciudad Rodrigo. Allowing me to walk away now would be the best solution for us both.'

There was a moment's silence in which he made no move to pull back from her, just kept his gaze fixed and intent, locked upon her, as a hunter who has sighted his prey. 'Ciudad Rodrigo?' he said softly.

Her heart gave a shudder at what she had unintentionally revealed.

'What else do you know of General Foy's mission, I wonder?' His question was as gentle as a caress.

Josie dropped her eyes to stare at the ground, an involuntary shiver rippling through her.

He leaned in closer until she could feel the warmth of his breath fanning her cheek.

Her eyelids closed. The breath stalled in her throat and her fingers gripped tight around the reins, bracing herself for what was to come.

'Pierre.' Captain Emmern's voice sounded, shattering the tight tension that had bound her and Dammartin together in a world that excluded all else.

She opened her eyes and blinked at the chasseur captain, allowing herself to breathe once more.

'Captain Dammartin,' said Emmern more formally this time. He looked from Dammartin to Josie and back again with a strange expression upon his face. 'We should get moving, before the General grows impatient.'

Dammartin gave a nod in reply, then, with a small nudge of his boots against the chestnut's flank, he and the horse began to move away.

Relief softened the rigidity throughout Josie's body, so that she felt that she might collapse down against the little mare's neck and cling on for dear life. She caught her fingers into the coarse hair of the mane, stabilising herself once more now that the danger was receding.

'Mademoiselle Mallington,' he called softly.

She froze at the sound of his voice, saw him turn back to look at her.

'We shall finish this conversation later.'

She felt the blood drain from her face, and she stared at him aghast, unable to move, unable to utter a single word in response.

'I promise that most solemnly.' And with a twitch of his reins he was finally gone.

Foy's column with its cavalry detachment travelled far that day, twenty miles across terrain that was rocky and high and inhospitable. The ground was frozen hard beneath their feet and great chunks of ice edged the rivulets of streams that carved passageways down the hillsides. And in all the hours that passed, Josie could not find a way to escape the officers of Bonaparte's 8th Dragoons.

She had hoped that she might be able to fall back or just slip away unnoticed, but there was no chance of that. The 8th Dragoons were neatly sandwiched between Emmern's Hanoverian Chasseurs in front and a whole regiment of French infantry to the rear. And were that not bad enough, Lieutenant Molyneux rode nearby, offering occasional polite conversational words, checking on her welfare and ensuring that she was served the hard bread rolls and wine when they stopped to water the horses. There seemed no way out. Yet when Josie looked in front to where Dammartin rode, she knew that escape was an absolute necessity.

Dammartin did not look back at her and that was something at least for which she felt relief. His attention was focused upon his men, on the ragged drops that fell away from the sides of the narrow rough roads along which they trotted, and the precipices so high above. If a trooper wandered too close to the edge, Dammartin barked a warning for him to get back in column. If they moved too slowly, one look from Dammartin was enough to hurry them onwards.

Throughout the long hours of riding he ignored her, but his promise lay between them as threatening as the man himself. He would interrogate her in earnest. She knew it with a certainty, had seen it in his eyes. She thought of the danger that emanated from him, of the darkness, a formidable force waiting to be unleashed...upon her. She trembled at the prospect of what he might do to her, knowing that for all her bravado, for all her own tenacity, he was far stronger. He would lead her in circles until she no longer knew what she was saying. Hadn't she already inadvertently revealed that her father had known of Foy's destination? What more would she tell the French Captain?

The thoughts whirred in her head, churning her gut with anticipation. No matter her father's instruction or the promise she had made him, she knew that she had to get away, to somehow make her way back towards the British lines. She would be safe from Dammartin there, and she would ensure that the news of Foy's mission had reached Wellington. Papa would have understood, she told herself.

Having made up her mind, Josie no longer looked ahead to the breadth of Dammartin's shoulders or the fit of his green dragoon jacket across his back and, instead, focused every last ounce of her attention on a way of evading her captor.

They had reached the site of their camp in a small valley between Cardigos and Sobreira Formosa before the opportunity that Josie had been waiting for arose. Most of Dammartin's dragoons were busy pitching the tents. The air rang with the sound of small iron-tipped mallets driving narrow iron tent pegs into the frozen soil. Those troopers not helping with the tents, gathered wood and lit fires upon which they placed kettles and pots to boil, cooking that evening's rations. All along the massive camp both cavalrymen and infantrymen were orderly and disciplined and—busy. Even Molyneux seemed to have disappeared.

Josie knew that this was the best chance of escape she would get. She stood were she was, eyes scanning around, seeking the one man above all that she sought to evade, but of Dammartin there was no sign, and that could only be construed as a very good omen.

Slowly, inconspicuously, she edged towards a great clump of scrubby bushes at the side of the camp until she could slip unseen behind them. And then, hitching up her skirts in one hand, Josie started to run.

Dammartin was making his way back from reporting to Major La Roque and all he could think about was the wretched Mallington girl. She was too defiant, too stubborn and too damned courageous. When she looked at him, he saw the same clear blue eyes that had looked out from Mallington's face. A muscle twitched in Dammartn's jaw and he gritted his teeth.

The old man was dead and yet little of Dammartin's anger had dissipated. His father had been avenged, and still Dammartin's heart ached with a ferocity that coloured his every waking thought. All of the hurt, all of the rage at the injustice and loss remained. He knew he had been severe with girl. She was young, and it was not her hand that had fired the bullet into his father's chest. He had seen that she was frightened and the pallor of her face as she realised her mistake over Ciudad Rodrigo, and even then he had not softened. Now that he was away from her he could see that he had been too harsh, but the girl knew much more than she was saying, and if Dammartin was being forced to drag her with him all the way to Ciudad Rodrigo, he was damn well going to get that information—for the sake of his country, for the sake of his mission... for the sake of his father.

The dragoon camp was filled with the aroma of cooking—of boiling meat and toasting bread. Dammartin's stomach began to growl as he strode past the troopers' campfires, his eyes taking in all that was happening in one fell swoop. Lamont had a pot lid in one hand and was stirring at the watery meat with a spoon in the other. Molyneux was sharing a joke with a group of troopers.

The prickle of anticipation whispered down Dammartin's spine, for Josephine Mallington was nowhere to be seen.

'Where is Mademoiselle Mallington?' The stoniness of his voice silenced Molyneux's laughter. Lamont replaced the pot lid and spoon and got to his feet. The troopers glanced around uneasily, noticing the girl's absence for the first time.

A slight flush coloured Molyneux's cheeks. 'She was here but a moment since, I swear.'

'Check the tents,' Dammartin snapped at his lieutenant, before turning to Lamont. 'Have the men search over by the latrines.'

With a nod, the little sergeant was up and shouting orders as he ran.

Dammartin knew instinctively that the girl would not be found in either of these places. He strode purposefully towards the horses. None were missing.

Dante was saddled by the time that Molyneux reappeared.

'The tents are empty, Captain, and Lamont says that there's no sign of her down by the latrines.' He bent to catch his breath, tilting his head up to look at Dammartin. 'Do you want us to organise a search party?'

'No search party,' replied Dammartin, swinging himself up on to Dante's back. 'I go alone.'

'She cannot have got far in such little time. She is on foot and the harshness of this countryside...' Molyneux let the words trail off before dropping his voice. 'Forgive me, but I did not think for a minute that she would escape.'

Dammartin gave a single small nod of his head, acknowledging his lieutenant's apology. 'Mademoiselle Mallington is more resourceful than we have given her credit for.'

'What will happen if you do not find her? Major La Roque did not—'

'If I do not find her,' Dammartin interrupted, 'she will die.' And with a soft dig of his heels against Dante's flank he was gone.

Chapter Four

The wind whispered through the trees, straining at their bare branches until they creaked and rattled. Josie's run had subsided to a half walk, half scurry as she followed the road back along the route the French army had travelled. The track ran along the ridge of a great hill in the middle of even more hills. The surrounding landscape was hostile: jagged rocks, steep slopes and scree, with nothing of cover and nowhere that Josie could see to shelter.

She knew from the day's journey that some miles back there had been the derelict remains of a cottage and it was to this that Josie was heading. All she needed to do was to follow the road back up over the last hill and keep going until she came upon the cottage. She pushed herself on, knowing that it was only a matter of time before her absence was noticed. They might already be after her; *he* might already be after her. Her lungs felt fit to burst and there was a pain in her side. Josie willed her legs to move faster.

The light was rapidly fading and soon everything would be shrouded in darkness, making it impossible to see the rubble and pot-holes littering the road, and more importantly the cliff edge over to her right. Somewhere far away a wolf howled, a haunting sound that made the hairs on the back of Josie's neck stand erect. She knew what it was to be hunted, but it was not the wolf from which she was running.

Her foot twisted suddenly into an unseen dip on the unevenness of the road's surface, tipping her off balance, bringing her down, landing her hard. The fall winded her, but almost immediately she was scrabbling up to keep on going, ignoring the stinging in her hands and knees.

Dammartin cursed the charcoal-streaked sky. Once darkness fell she would be lost to him, and lost to herself too, he thought grimly. Little idiot, without shelter, without warmth, she would die out here. And no matter who her father had been, Dammartin did not want that to happen.

His eyes swept over the surrounding land, before flicking back to the road over the hill that loomed ahead. The French Captain's instinct told him which route the girl had chosen. Taking the spyglass from his pocket, he scanned the road over which they had travelled that day, and as the daylight died Pierre Dammartin felt the wash of satisfaction. He snapped the spyglass away.

A lone wolf's howl rent the air, urging Dammartin to move faster. He had not reached her yet, but he soon would.

Josie stopped and glanced back, her scalp prickling with foreboding, her ears straining to listen. There was only the wind and the ragged panting of her own breath. A noise sounded to her left, a rustling, a rooting. She stared suspiciously through the growing darkness, but there was nothing there save a few spindly bushes at the foot of the great rock wall. To her right a trickle of pebbles slid over the cliff edge, making her jump nervously.

She was being foolish, she told herself, these were the normal noises of the night, nothing more sinister. But as she hurried on, she remembered the stories of the bandits that roamed this land and she pulled her cloak more tightly around herself, only now beginning to see just how very dangerous her predicament was.

Come along, Josie, she told herself sternly, and she was in the middle of reciting the Mallington family motto, *audaces fortuna juvat*—fortune favours the brave—when she heard the gallop of a horse's hooves in the distance.

Dammartin.

She looked back into the deep inky blueness, her eyes examining every shadow, every shape, but seeing nothing through the cover of the night. For a moment Josie was so gripped with panic that she did not move, just stood there staring for a few moments before the sensible part of her brain kicked back into action.

It would be impossible to outrun him, he was coming this way and fast, and the few bushes around were too small to hide her. Glancing swiftly around she realised that just ahead, to the left, the sheer wall of rock and soil seemed to change, relaxing its gradient, leaning back by forty-five degrees to give a climbable slope. Her eyes followed it up to the flat ground at the top, which merged into the darkness of the other hills. Josie did not wait for an invitation; she began to run again.

A thin crescent moon hung in the sky and Dammartin could just about see the small, dark shape moving on the road ahead. He kicked Dante to a gallop to close the distance between them. One more curve in the road and she would be his, but as he rounded that last corner, with Dante blowing hard, the road was deserted.

Dante pulled up, clouds of condensation puffing from his nostrils, the sweat upon his chestnut coat a slick sheen beneath the moonlight. Dammartin was breathing hard too, his heart racing, a sudden fear in his chest that she had gone over the edge of the cliff rather than let herself be taken.

A small noise sounded ahead, somewhere high up on the left, a dislodged pebble cascading down. Dammartin's gaze swivelled towards the sound, and what he saw made his mouth curve to a wicked smile.

Josie heard the horse draw up below. Just a single horse. She could hear the rider dismount and begin to climb.

One man.

She had to know. Her head turned. She dared a glance below… and gasped aloud.

The thin sliver of moon lit the face of Captain Dammartin as he scaled the rock face at a frightening speed.

Josie redoubled her efforts, clambering up as fast as she could.

She could hear him getting closer. Her arms and legs were aching and she could feel the trickle of sweat between her breasts and down her back, but still she kept going, puffing her breathy exertion like smoke into the chill of the night air.

'Mademoiselle Mallington.'

She heard his voice too close. *Keep going, Josie, keep going*, she willed herself on, climbing and climbing, and still, he came after her, closing the gap between them.

'Cease this madness, before you break your neck.'

She glanced back and saw that he was right below her.

'No!' she cried in panic, and pulling off her hat, she threw it at him.

A hand closed around her ankle—firm, warm fingers. She felt the gentle tug.

'No!' she yelled again. 'Release me!' And she tried to kick out at him with her foot, but it was too late; Josie's grip was lost and she slid helplessly down over the rock and the dirt, towards her enemy.

Dammartin leaned out, away from the slope, so that the girl's body slid neatly in beneath his. Her back was flush against his chest, her buttocks against his groin. The wind whipped her hair to tickle against his chin. She seemed to freeze, gripping for dear life to the rock face, before she realised that he had caught her, that she was safe. He heard her gasp of shock as she became aware of her position, and braced himself.

'Unhand me at once!' She bucked against him.

He pressed into her, gripping tighter. 'Continue as you are, *mademoiselle*, and you will send us both to our deaths,' he said into her ear.

She ceased her struggles. 'What are you going to do?' Her words were quiet.

'Save your life.'

Only the wind whispered in return, but he could feel the rapidity of her breathing beneath his chest, and the tremor that ran through her slight frame.

'It is not in need of saving. Leave me be, sir. I will not return with you to the camp.'

'Then you will be clinging to this rock face beneath me all damn night, for I have no intention of returning without my prisoner,' he said savagely.

She tried to turn her head, as if to glance at what lay beyond, but her cheek touched against his chest, and he knew she could see nothing other than him.

'I do not think you so foolish as to throw your life away, Mademoiselle Mallington, no matter how tempting it may be to dispense with mine.'

There was a silence before she said, 'You climb down first and I will follow.'

His mouth curved cynically. 'We climb down together, or not at all. You cannot answer my questions with a broken neck.'

He felt her tense beneath him. 'You are wasting your time, Captain, for I will never answer your questions, no matter how many times you ask them. I would rather take my chances here on this rock face.'

Dammartin understood then why Mademoiselle Mallington had run. The lavender scent of her hair drifted up to fill his nose. 'And if I tell you there will be no questions tonight, will you come down then?'

Another silence, as if she were contemplating his words, reaching a decision, just a few moments, but time enough for his awareness of the soft curves moulded against him to grow.

She gave a reluctant nod of the head.

They stood like two spoons nestled together, the entire length of their bodies touching. And it was not anger at her escape, or the jubilation of her recapture of which Dammartin was thinking; it was not even the difficulty of the descent they had no choice but to make. For the first time, Dammartin saw Josie not as Mallington's daughter, but as a woman, and a woman that stirred his blood.

She glanced directly down, looking to see the rock face below. Her body tensed further and she clung all the harder to the rocks, laying her face against them.

He started to move.

'No, I cannot!' she said, and he could hear the slight note of panic underlying her words.

'Mademoiselle Mallington…'

'It is too high, we cannot…'

'Just do as I say.'

'I cannot…please…'

There was just the sound of the wind and the rise and fall of her breathing and the feel of her body beneath his.

'I will help you and we will reach the ground safely enough.' He became conscious of where her hips nestled so snugly and felt the stirrings of his body response.

She hesitated before giving a tiny nod.

Josie had thought of nothing other than escape on her way up the cliff, but now she was aware of how very far the ground seemed below, of the loose, insecure surface of the rocks and the wind that pulled at both her and Dammartin. In the darkness she could not see what was safe to grip with her hands, and the skirt of her dress hid her view of her feet and where she might place them. A wave of panic swept through her and she thought that she might be stuck there, unable to move either up or down, but then the French Captain said that he would help her. He edged her to movement and the panic was gone. Slowly they began to descend the rock face.

The warm press of his body and the clean masculine smell of him pulled her mind from the danger of the rocks beneath. He was gentle, encouraging her with quiet words when she struggled to place her feet, coaxing her to keep moving when she thought she could move no more. There was no anger, no harshness, no danger, and, ironically, as they risked their lives to reach the ground, she felt safer with him now than she had ever done. It did not make sense. She did not know this new Dammartin.

She heard his exhalation of breath as they made it to the ground. The cold rushed in against her back as he moved away, opening the space between them. She turned, and was able to see him properly for the first time. Words of gratitude hovered on her lips, but she bit them back, not understanding why she wanted to thank him for saving her, when in truth he was the enemy who had just destroyed her chance of escape.

For a moment Dammartin just stood there by the foot of the slope; the weak silvery moonlight exposing the dark slash of his scar, the lean hard planes sculpting his face, and the rugged squareness of his jaw. Shadow obscured half his face, making it impossible for Josie to read his expression, but there was something in the way he was looking at her, something in his stance, that made her wonder if this was indeed the same man from whom she had run. Her gaze dropped to hide her confusion and her feeling of vulnerability.

'You do not need to take me back,' she said, 'you could say that you did not find me. It is a plausible story.'

He gave a cynical laugh and shook his head. 'What part of this do you not understand, *mademoiselle*? That you would not survive out here alone, or that I do not lose my prisoners?'

The arrogance of his words rankled with her, urging her pride to deny the truth in his answer. 'I would survive very well, if you would let me.'

'With no weapon, no shelter, no means to make fire, no food or water?' he mocked. 'And what of guerrillas and bandits? You think you can take them on single-handed?'

'As a woman travelling alone, I would present no threat to any such men. They would be unlikely to harm me. I *am* British.'

'You think they care about that?' Dammartin raised an eyebrow.

Josie's indignation rose. 'I would have managed well enough.'

'You are a fool if you think so—' his eyes narrowed slightly '—and you would be a bigger fool to try a further escape.'

'You cannot stop me,' she retaliated. 'I swear I will be long gone before you are anywhere close to Ciudad Rodrigo.'

The wolf howl sounded again, and in the moonlight Dammartin transformed once more to a sinister mode. 'No, *mademoiselle*,' he said softly, 'you are much mistaken in that belief.'

All of Josie's fear flooded back at the certainty in his voice.

She looked at him, not knowing what to say, not knowing what to do, aware only that he had won, and that her failure would cost her dearly when he got her back to the camp.

There was the sound of the wind, and of quietness.

'Please,' she said, and hoped that he would not hear the desperation in her voice.

The scree crunched beneath his boots as he came to stand before her. 'I will not leave you out here.'

Her eyes searched the shadow of his face and thought she saw something of the harshness drop away.

'No more questions this night.' He reached out and, taking her arm, pulled her from where she leaned against the slope.

He led her across to the great chestnut horse that stood waiting so patiently, his grip light but unbreakable around her arm, releasing her only long enough to mount and lift her up before him. She was sitting sideways, holding on to the front of the saddle with her left hand, and trying not to hold on to Dammartin with her right

Dammartin looked pointedly at where the hand rested upon her skirts. 'We shall be travelling at speed.'

She gave a nod. 'I know,' she said.

'As you will, *mademoiselle*.'

As they reached the surface of the road, the horse began to canter, and Josie gripped suddenly at Dammartin to stop herself from being thrown from the saddle. By the time the canter became a gallop, Josie was clinging tight to the French Captain's chest, while he secured her in place with an anchoring arm around her waist.

Stars shone like a thousand diamond chips scattered over a black velvet sky. The silver sickle of the moon bathed all in its thin magical light, revealing the road ahead that would lead them back to the French camp.

For Josie there would be no escape.

Dammartin swigged from the hip flask, the brandy burning a route down to his stomach. The fire burned low before them, and most of the men had already retired for the night. He wiped his mouth with the back of his hand and offered the flask to Lamont.

'The men were taking bets on whether you would find her.' Lamont took a gulp of the brandy before returning the flask.

'Did you win?' asked Dammartin.

'Of course,' replied the little Sergeant with a smile, and patted his pocket. 'I know you too well, my friend.'

They sat quietly for a few minutes, the sweet smell of Lamont's pipe mingling pleasantly with that of the brandy, the logs cracking and shifting upon the fire.

'She has courage, the little *mademoiselle*.' It was Lamont who broke the silence.

'She does,' agreed Dammartin, thinking of Josie halfway up that rock face, and the way she had defied him to the end. He glanced towards the tents.

Lamont followed his captain's eyes, before returning

his gaze to the glow of the burning logs. 'What will you do with her?'

'Take her to Ciudad Rodrigo as I am commanded.'

'I mean, this night.'

'What does one do with any prisoner who has attempted to escape?' Dammartin poked at the embers of the fire with a stick.

'She is gently bred, and a woman. You would not...?' Lamont's words petered out in uncertainty.

There was a silence in which Dammartin looked at him. 'What do you think?'

'I think you are too much your father's son.'

Dammartin smiled at his old friend, and fitted the top back on to his hip flask, before slipping it into his pocket. 'But she is too much Mallington's daughter.'

There was the soft breath of the wind while both men stared wordlessly into the fire.

'Why did she run, Pierre? The girl is no fool; she must have realised her chance of survival was slim?'

'She was afraid.' Dammartin's gaze did not shift from the warm orange glow of the dying fire as he remembered Mademoiselle Mallington's face in the moonlight as she stood at the foot of the slope. He had felt the tremor in her body, heard the fear beneath the defiance in her words. *I will never answer your questions, no matter how many times you ask them.* He heard the whisper of them even now. 'Afraid of interrogation.'

Lamont gave a sigh and shook his head. 'There is nothing of any use she can tell us now.'

'I would not be so certain of that.'

'Pierre...' the older man chided.

'I will question her again,' interrupted Dammartin. 'But her only fear need be what answers she will spill.'

'And when we reach Ciudad Rodrigo, what then?'

'Then she is no longer my problem,' said Dammartin.

Lamont sucked at his pipe for a few moments, as if weighing Dammartin's answer. 'It is a long way to Ciudad Rodrigo.'

'Do not worry, Claude.' Dammartin gave Lamont a clap on the back. 'Mademoiselle Mallington will give us no more trouble. I will make certain of that.' He got to his feet. 'Sleep well, my old friend.' And began to make his way across the small distance to where the officers' tents were pitched.

'And you, my captain,' said Lamont softly, as he sat by the fire and watched Dammartin disappear beneath the canvas of his tent.

The girl was sitting at the little table, busy working her hair into a plait when Dammartin entered the tent. She jumped to her feet, her hair abandoned, the ribbon fluttering down to lie forgotten upon the ground sheet. From the corner of his eye he could see a white frilled nightdress spread out over the covers of his bed.

'What are you doing here, Captain Dammartin?' she demanded, her face peaked and shocked.

'Retiring to bed.'

Her eyes widened with indignation and the unmistakable flicker of fear. 'In my tent?'

'The tent is mine.' He walked over to the small table and chair.

Even beneath the lantern light he could see the blush that swept her cheeks. 'Then I should not be here, sir.' Hurrying over to the bed, she slipped her feet into her boots sitting neatly by its side, before grabbing up the nightdress and rolling it swiftly to a ball. 'There has clearly been some kind of misunderstanding. If you would be so kind as to direct me to the women's tent.'

'You are a prisoner, *mademoiselle*, not a camp follower. Besides, the women's tent is within the camp of the infantry, not my dragoons. As a prisoner of the 8th, you stay with me.'

'Then you can show me the tent in which I am to stay the night.' She stood facing him squarely, clutching the nightdress in a crumpled mass like a shield before her, ready to do battle.

'You are already within that tent.' He turned away and began to unbutton his jacket.

'Indeed, I am not, sir!' she exclaimed with force, and he could see the colour in her cheeks darken. 'What manner of treatment is this? You cannot seriously expect that I will spend the night with you!' Her nostrils flared. She stared at him as if she were some great warrior queen.

'You speak of expectations, *mademoiselle*. Do you expect to be left overnight all alone, so that you may try again to escape?'

She gave a shake of her head, and the loose blonde plait hanging down against her breast began to unwind. 'I would try no such thing. The night is too dark, and I have no torch.'

'These things did not stop you this evening.'

'There was still daylight then.'

'Hardly,' he said, and shrugging off his jacket, hung it over the back of the wooden chair by the table.

'I give you my word that I will not try to escape this night.'

'Only this night?' he raised an eyebrow.

'It is this night of which we are speaking.'

'So you are planning another attempt tomorrow.'

'No!'

'Tomorrow night, then?'

'Very well, I give you my word that I will not attempt

another escape.' She looked at him expectantly. 'So now will you arrange for another tent?'

'Your word?' He heard his voice harden as the memories came flooding back unbidden, the grief and revenge bitter within his mouth. He gave an angry, mirthless laugh. 'But how can I trust that when the word of a Mallington is meaningless.'

'How dare you?' she exclaimed, and he could see the fury mounting in her eyes.

He smiled a grim determined smile. 'Most easily, *mademoiselle*, I assure you.'

'I have nothing more to say to you, sir.' She spun on her heel, and began to stride towards the tent flap.

Dammartin's hand shot out and, fixing a firm hold around her upper arm, hoisted her back. She struggled to escape him, but Dammartin just grabbed hold of her other arm and hauled her back to face him. Her arms were slight beneath his hands and he was surprised again at how small and slender she was, even though he had felt her body beneath his upon the rock face only a few hours since. He adjusted his grip so that he would not hurt her and pulled her closer.

She quietened then, looked up at him with blue eyes that were stormy. The scent of lavender surrounded her, and he could not help himself glance at the pale blonde hair that now spilled loose around her shoulders.

'But I have not finished in what I have to say to you, *mademoiselle*.' The nightdress slipped from her fingers, falling to lie between them.

They both glanced down to where the white frills lay in a frothy pool against the black leather of Dammartin's boots.

And when he looked again, her eyes had widened slightly and he saw the fear that flitted through them.

He spoke quietly but with slow, deliberate intent, that she would understand him. 'All the tents upon this camp-site are filled, and even were they not, my men have travelled far this day and I would not drag a single one from their rest to guard against any further escape attempt that you may make. So tonight, I guard you myself. Do not complain of this situation, for you have brought it upon yourself, *mademoiselle*, with your most foolish behaviour.' He lowered his face towards hers until their noses were almost touching, so close that they might have been lovers.

He heard the slight raggedness of her breathing, saw the rapid rise and fall of her breast, and the way that the colour washed from her cheeks as she stared back at him, her eyes wide with alarm.

The silence stretched between them as the soft warmth of her breath whispered against his lips like a kiss. His mouth parted in anticipation, and for one absurd moment he almost kissed her, almost, but then he remembered that she was Mallington's daughter, and just precisely what Lieutenant Colonel Mallington had done, and all of the misery and all of the wrathful injustice was back.

His heart hardened.

When finally he spoke his voice was low and filled with harsh promise. 'Do not seek to escape me again, Mademoiselle Mallington. If you try, your punishment shall be in earnest. Do you understand me?'

She gave a single nod of her head; as Dammartin released his grip, she stumbled back, grabbing hold of the chair back, where his jacket hung, to steady herself.

He turned brusquely away, pulling two blankets and a pillow from the bed and dropping them on to the ground sheet beside the bed. 'Make yourself a bed. We leave early tomorrow and must sleep.'

She just stood there, by the table, looking at him, her face pale and wary.

He did not look at her, just sat down on the bed and removed his boots.

And still she stood there, until at last his gaze again met hers.

'Make up your bed, unless you have a wish to share mine, *mademoiselle*.'

An expression of shock crossed her face and she hurriedly did as she was bid, extinguishing the lantern before climbing beneath the blankets on the groundsheet.

Dammartin did not sleep, and neither did the girl. The sound of her breathing told him that she lay as awake as he, so close to his bed that he might have reached his arm down and touched her. The wind buffeted at the canvas of the tent, but apart from that everything was silent.

He did not know how long he lay listening, aware of her through the darkness, turning one way and then the next as if she could find no comfort on the hardness of the ground. He rolled over, conscious of the relative softness of his own mattress, and felt the first prickle of conscience.

Goddamn it, she was his prisoner, he thought, and he'd be damned if he'd give his bed up for Mallington's daughter. Just as he was thinking this, he heard her soft movements across the tent, and with a reflex honed by years of training, reached out through the darkness to grab at her dress.

He felt her start, heard her gasp loud in the deadness of the night.

'Mademoiselle Mallington,' he said quietly, 'do you disregard my warning so readily?'

'No,' she whispered. 'I seek only my cloak. The night is cold. I am not trying to escape.

Swinging his legs over the side of the bed, he sat up,

guiding her back towards him, turning her in the blackness and tracing his hands lightly around her, like a blindman, until he found her hands. Even through the wool of her dress he could feel that she was chilled. Her fingers were cold beneath his before she pulled away from his touch.

'Go back to your bed, *mademoiselle*,' he said curtly.

'But my cloak…'

'Forget your cloak, you shall not find it in this darkness.'

'But—'

'*Mademoiselle*,' he said more harshly.

He heard the breath catch in her throat as if she would have given him some retort, but she said nothing, only climbed beneath the blankets that he had given her earlier that night.

Dammartin swept his greatcoat from where it lay over his bed, and covered the girl with it.

'Captain Dammartin…' He could hear her surprise.

'Go to sleep,' he said gruffly.

'Thank you,' came the soft reply.

He turned over and pulled the blanket higher, knowing himself for a fool and slipping all the more easily into the comfort of sleep because of it.

Josie awoke to the seep of thin grey daylight through the canvas overhead. Sleep still fuddled her mind and she smiled, burrowing deeper beneath the cosiness of the covers, thinking that her father would tease her for her tardiness. Voices sounded outside, French male, and reality came rushing back in, exploding all of her warm contentment: Telemos, her father's death, Dammartin. Clutching the blankets to her chest she sat up, glancing round apprehensively.

The bed in which Dammartin had slept lay empty; she

was alone in the tent. The breath that Josie had been holding released, relief flowed through her. She got to her feet, her head woolly and thick from her lack of sleep.

How may hours had she lain awake listening to the French Captain's breathing, hearing it slow and become more rhythmic as he found sleep? For how many hours had the thoughts raced through her head? Memories of her father and of Telemos. She had spoken the truth; the night was black and most of the fires would be dead; she had no torch, and she did not doubt that there would be sentries guarding the camp. Her chance of escape had been lost. He would watch her more carefully now.

A shudder ran through her as she remembered how he had held her last night, his face so close to hers that the air she breathed had been warmed by his lungs. His dark penetrating gaze locked on to hers so that she could not look away. For a moment, just one tiny moment, she had thought that he meant to kiss her, before she saw the pain and bitterness in his eyes. And she blushed that she could have thought such a ridiculous notion. Of course he did not want to kiss her, he hated her, just as she hated him. There was no mistaking that. He hated her, yet he would not let her go.

I do not lose prisoners, he had said. And she had the awful realisation that he meant to take her all the way to Ciudad Rodrigo—far away from Torres Vedras, and Lisbon and the British—and in the miles between lay the prospect of interrogation.

Her eye caught the thick grey greatcoat, still lying where he had placed it last night, on top of her blankets. When she looked at the bed again, she saw its single woollen cover. The chill in the air nipped at her, and she knew that the night had been colder. She stared at the bed, not understanding why a man so very menacing, so very dangerous, who loathed her very existence, had given her his covers.

More voices, men walking by outside.

She glanced down at the muddy smears marking her crumpled dress, and her dirty hands and ragged nails—souvenirs of the rock face and her failed escape.

She was British, she reminded herself, and she would not allow the enemy to bring her down in such a way. So she smoothed the worst of her bed-mussed hair, and peeped out of the tent flap. Molyneux lingered not so very far away. He was kind; he spoke English…and he came when she beckoned him. It seemed that the Lieutenant was only too happy to fetch her a basin of water.

'I apologise, mademoiselle, for the coldness of the water, but there is no time to warm it.' He smiled at her, his skin creasing round his eyes, and the wind ruffling the pale brown of his hair.

'Thank you,' she said, and meant it.

Taking the basin from the Lieutenant's hands, she glanced out at the campsite beyond. All around dragoons were busy putting out fires, packing up, dismantling. She recognised Dammartin's sergeant, Lamont, speaking to a group of troopers, but Dammartin himself was nowhere that she could see.

'Thank you,' she said again, and disappeared within the tent flaps.

Dammartin glanced over towards his tent, but there was still no sign of Mademoiselle Mallington. Coffee had been drunk, bread eaten, portmanteaux packed, and the girl slept through it all. At least he had had the foresight to set Molyneux to guarding his tent, lest the girl took the notion into her head to try to slip away again. And truth be told, this would be the best time to do it, when the camp was in chaos, the men's attentions distracted, and a full day of light ahead.

Lamont appeared. 'The men will be ready to leave in twenty minutes. Only the officers' tents remain. Mademoiselle Mallington…' He looked enquiringly at Dammartin.

'Shall be ready to leave with the rest of us,' Dammartin replied.

'You look a little tired this morning, Captain,' said Lamont, his gaze fixed on Dammartin's tent. 'Perhaps something disturbed your sleep?'

Dammartin gave a wry smile and shook his head at his sergeant's teasing, before walking off towards his tent.

'She is in there still?' he said to Molyneux as he passed, indicating his tent.

'Yes, Captain.'

Dammartin closed the last of the distance to his tent.

'But, sir, she…'

Molyneux's words sounded behind him, but it was too late. Dammartin had unfastened the ties and was already through the tent flap…and the sight that met his eyes stilled him where he stood. A basin of water sat upon his table; Mademoiselle Mallington stood by its side, washing, bare to her waist.

Chapter Five

Josie gave a small shriek and, trying to cover herself with one arm, reached for her towel with the other. In her panic she succeeded only in dropping the soap into the basin and knocking the towel off the back of the table. She clutched her arms around herself, acutely aware of her nakedness and the man that stood not four feet away, staring. She saw his gaze move over her, saw the darkening of his eyes as they met hers, yet she stood there gaping like a fool, staring at him in utter shock.

'Captain Dammartin!' she managed to gasp at last, those two words conveying all of her indignation.

He held her gaze for a moment longer, that second seeming to stretch to an eternity. 'Pardon, *mademoiselle*,' and, with a small bow of his head, he was gone as suddenly as he had arrived.

It was over in less than a minute, yet Josie stood there still, staring at the tent flap, before hurrying round to the other side of the table to snatch up the towel. She barely dried herself before pulling up her shift and petticoats from her waist with hands that were shaking. Humiliation set a scald to her cheeks, and a roughness to her fingers as she pulled down the hair pinned up high and loose upon her head to coil it into a tight little pile stabbed into place at the nape of her neck.

She was angry beyond belief, angry and embarrassed. 'How dare he!' she muttered to herself again and again as she stuffed her belongings back into her portmanteau. 'The audacity of the man!'

Her indignation still burned so that when she left the tent, standing outside with her cloak fastened around her, and her hair neat and tidy beneath her best hat and her fresh blue dress, she was intent on snubbing the French Captain, but Dammartin was only a figure at the other end of the camp and it was Lieutenant Molyneux who waited some little distance away.

The wind dropped from her sails.

'Mademoiselle.' Molyneux appeared by her side, his grey eyes soft with concern. 'I am here to escort you this day.'

Dammartin had assigned his lieutenant to guard her, thought Josie, and her anger at Dammartin swelled even more.

'If you will come this way, it is time we were upon our horses.'

'Thank you, Lieutenant,' she said, as if she were not furious and outraged and humiliated, and walked, with her head held high, calmly by his side.

It soon became clear that her supposition regarding Molyneux was correct for, unlike the previous day, the Lieutenant stuck closely by her side. In Molyneux's company the events of that morning ceased to matter so much to Josie. The young Lieutenant had such an easy and charming manner that she felt her ruffled feathers smooth and her anger dispel.

It was true that Molyneux had been in the monastery at Telemos just as much as Dammartin, but as the hours passed in his company she saw that he was like so many young men who had served beneath her father. His eyes were clear and honest and he seemed every bit the gentleman that Dammartin was not.

When the dragoons stopped to rest and eat, Molyneux sent a boy to fetch them bread and cheese, and then sat beside her on a boulder while they ate together.

'You are kind to me, Lieutenant,' she said, thinking of how much Molyneux contrasted with his captain.

'Why should I not be kind? You are a lady, alone, in a difficult situation.'

She raised her gaze to his. 'I am a prisoner.'

Molyneux's lips curved in a small half smile but there was a sadness in his eyes. 'I believe that prisoners should be well treated.'

'I do, too, as did my father.'

He gave no reply, but a strange expression stole upon his face.

'It seems that Captain Dammartin does not share our opinion, sir.'

'The Captain, he has his reasons, *mademoiselle*.' Molyneux glanced away.

'What reason could he possibly have to act as he has done?' she demanded, feeling nettled just at the thought of Dammartin. 'There is nothing that could excuse that man's behaviour.'

Molyneux's eyes returned to hers and she saw something of astonishment and pity in them. 'You truly do not know.'

'Know?' She felt the prickling of suspicion. 'What is it that I should know?'

Molyneux's gaze held hers for a moment longer than it should, then he turned away and got to his feet. 'Come, *mademoiselle*, we should make ready to ride again.'

'Lieutenant—'

'Come,' he said again, and did not meet her eyes.

And when they resumed the journey, Molyneux was quiet, leaving Josie to wonder as to exactly what the Lieutenant had meant.

Dammartin rode at the head of the 8th Dragoons crossing the bleak terrain before them, but it was not the harshness of the Portuguese countryside of which he was thinking, nor the perils of the mission in which they were engaged. Something else entirely filled Dammartin's mind—Josephine Mallington.

A vision of her standing there in his tent that morning, her clothing stripped aside to reveal her naked skin, so smooth and white and inviting that he longed to reach out and touch its silky surface. The slender column of her throat with the gold chain that hung around it, leading his eye down in invitation over a skin so pale and perfect, to the swell of her breasts.

He had seen them, just a glimpse, firm and thrusting and rosy-tipped, before his view was partly obscured. That slim arm crushing hard against them in a bid to hide herself from him, and in truth, serving only to tantalise even more in what it revealed. He could have traced his fingers over the bulging swell of that smooth white flesh, slipping them down behind the barrier of her arm to cup her breasts in his hands. To feel her nipples harden beneath his palm, to taste what he touched, taking her in his mouth, laving those rosy tips with his tongue…

Dammartin caught his train of thought and stopped it

dead. Hell, but she was Mallington's daughter. The one woman who should repulse him above all others, and all he could think of was her naked, and the sight of her soft lips, and the feel of her beneath him as they perched upon that rock face. He was already hard at the thought of her, uncomfortably so. And that knowledge made him damnably angry with Mademoiselle Mallington, and even more so with himself.

Hour after hour of a ride in which he should have been alert, aware, focused on his duty, spent distracted by Mallington's daughter. Well, no more of it, he determined. Dammartin hardened his resolve. He was here to safeguard Foy's journey to Ciudad Rodrigo—and that is what he would do. He could not refuse the order to take Mademoiselle Mallington with him to the Spanish city, and so he would take her there as he must.

And he thought again that Mallington was dead and all of his questions regarding Major Jean Dammartin's death were destined to remain unanswered for ever.

His mind flicked again to Josephine Mallington and the fact that her father had brought her with him into these hills, and her knowledge of the messengers and of Dammartin's own destination—a girl very much in her father's confidence. Had she been there at the Battle of Oporto, just over eighteen months ago? He felt his lip curl at the thought that she might have witnessed his father's murder, and his heart was filled once more with the cold steel of revenge. There would be no more distractions; Dammartin would have his answers.

Lieutenant Molyneux's pensive mood allowed Josie time to think. She spent much time pondering the Lieutenant's strange remarks, but came no nearer to fathoming of what he had been speaking. There was definitely something that she did not know, something to do with Dammartin and the hatred that he nursed.

Her eyes followed ahead to where the French Captain rode, and she thought how she had caught him looking at her several times that day with an expression of such intensity as to almost be hunger. He was not looking at her now.

She remembered his face from this morning when he had strode so boldly into her tent, *his* tent. The hours spent with Molyneux had mellowed Josie's anger and indignation. There had been an initial shock in Dammartin's eyes before they had darkened to a dangerous smoulder. The camp had been disbanding and she had overslept. And it had all happened so quickly that she doubted he could have seen very much at all.

She thought of the long, cold hours of the night when he had given her his greatcoat, and she wondered as to that small kindness. Josie had heard the stories of what French soldiers inflicted upon the towns that they took and the people who went against them. She knew of the interrogations, and the torture…and the rape. That she was an innocent did not stop her from knowing what enemy soldiers did to women. Within the Fifth Battalion of the 60th Regiment of Foot gossip reached the Lieutenant Colonel's daughter just the same as it reached everyone else. Yet for all the dislike in his eyes, Dammartin had not touched her, nor allowed his men to do so. He had not beaten her, he had not starved her when he could so easily have done so. She knew all of these things, yet whenever Dammartin looked at her, she could not prevent the somersaults of apprehension in her stomach, or the sudden hurry of her heart.

They broke for camp in the late afternoon, before the light of day was lost. Fundao—another day's march closer to General Foy fulfilling his mission, another day's march between Josie and the British lines.

Molyneux stood some distance away, talking with Sergeant Lamont, but the Lieutenant was careful to keep Josie within his sight.

Josie sat on her portmanteau, watching while the tents were erected, wondering how fast Molyneux could move if she were to make a run for it. She could not imagine him with the same harsh rugged determination of his captain.

There was something single-minded and ruthless about Dammartin, something driven. And she thought of the deadly earnest of his warning, and knew that even if Molyneux did not catch her, Dammartin most certainly would. Her eyes closed, trying to stifle the intensity of the memory. Dammartin was not a man to make promises lightly.

'Mademoiselle Mallington.'

The sound of his voice behind her made her jump. She rose swiftly to her feet and turned to face him. 'Captain Dammartin.'

He instructed a young trooper to carry her portmanteau to his tent. Everything about him was masculine and powerful. His expression was closed, his dark brows hooding eyes that were as hard as granite and just as cold.

'You will sleep in my tent tonight—alone.'

Alone? She felt the surprise lighten her face and relief leap within her. 'Thank you,' she said, wondering if she really did have the measure of Dammartin. She did not dare to ask him where he would be spending the night.

He continued as if she had not spoken. 'There will be a guard posted outside all of the night, so do not think to try to escape, *mademoiselle*. I trust you remember my warning.'

She gave a wary nod and made to move away towards the tent.

'I am not yet finished,' he said icily.

Josie hesitated, feeling his words rankle, but she turned back and raised her eyes calmly to his. 'You wish to say something further, sir?'

'I wish to ask you some questions.'

It seemed that her chest constricted and her heart rate kicked to a stampede. 'You said there would be no more questions.'

'No more questions last night,' he amended.

She held her head high and looked him directly in the eye. 'Perhaps I did not make myself clear, Captain. You will waste your time with questions—there is nothing more that I can tell you.'

'We will see, *mademoiselle*.'

She breathed deeply, trying to keep her fear in check. He could not mean to interrogate her, not now, not when she was so unprepared. 'I am tired, sir, and wish only to retire.'

'We are all tired,' he said harshly.

She clutched her hands together, her fingers gripping tight.

'You may retire when you have told me of your father.'

'My father?' She stared at him in disbelief, feeling all of her anger and all of her grief come welling back. 'Is it not enough that you killed him? He is dead, for pity's sake! Can you not leave him be even now?'

'It is true that he is dead, *mademoiselle*,' admitted Dammartin, his face colder and harsher than ever she had seen it, 'but not by my hand…unfortunately.'

She was aghast. 'Unfortunately?' she echoed. 'Our countries may be at war, but my father does not deserve such contempt. He was the bravest of soldiers, an honourable man who gave his life for his country.'

'He was a villain,' said Dammartin, and in his eyes was a furious black bitterness.

'How dare you slur his good name!' she cried, her breast heaving with passion, all fear forgotten. All of her anger and hurt and grief welled up to overflow and she hated Dammartin in that moment as she had never hated before. 'You are the very devil, sir!' And, drawing back her hand, she slapped his cruel, arrogant face as hard as she could.

The camp fell silent. Each and every dragoon turned to stare.

No one moved.

No one breathed.

The audacity of Josie's action seemed to slow time itself.

She saw the ruddy print of her hand stain his cheek, saw his scar grow livid, and she could not believe that she had struck him with such violence, with such hatred, she who was his captive at his mercy.

His eyes grew impossibly darker. There was a slight tightening of the muscle in his jaw. His breath was so light as to scarce be a breath at all. The air was heavy with a rage barely sheathed.

She stared in mounting horror, every pore in her body screaming a warning, prickling at her scalp, rippling a shiver down her spine, and she knew that she should run, but beneath the force of that dark penetrating gaze her legs would not move.

'I...' She gasped, knowing she had to say something, but the way that he was looking at her froze the very words in her throat.

Her eyes swept around, seeing the faces of all his men,

and all of the incredulity and anticipation so clear upon them, waiting for the storm to erupt.

Josie began to tremble and slowly, ever so slowly, as if she could move without his noticing, she began to inch away, her toes reaching tentatively to find the solidity of the ground behind her.

When he struck it was so sudden, so fast, that she saw nothing of it. One minute she was standing before him, and the next, she was in his arms, his body hard against hers, his mouth claiming her own with a savagery that made her gasp with shock.

Dammartin's lips were bold and punishing, exploring her own with an intimacy to which he had no right.

Josie fought back, struggling against him, but his arms just tightened around her, locking her in position, so that she could not escape but just endure, like a ship cast adrift while the lightning flashed and the thunder roared, and the waves crashed upon its deck.

He claimed her as if she were his for the taking, his lips plundering and stealing her all, his tongue invading with a force she could not refuse. And all the while the dark stubble of his chin rasped rough against her.

She felt as his hands slid around her back, one tangling within her hair, anchoring her to him, the other pulling her closer still until her breasts were crushed mercilessly against the hard muscle of his chest. This was no kiss, but a possession, an outright punishment.

And then the anger and violence were gone and she felt his mouth gentle against hers, still kissing her but with a tenderness that belied the ravishment. His lips massaged, stroked, tasted, his tongue dancing against hers in invitation. Kissing her, and kissing her until she could no longer think straight; kissing her until she no longer knew night from day.

Josie forgot where she was, and all that had just happened—Telemos and her father and just who this man was. There was only this moment, only this feeling, only this kiss—so slow and thorough and seductive. And just as she gave herself up to the sensation his lips were gone, and it was over as suddenly as it had started.

The men were cheering as Dammartin released her, the idiotic grins splitting their faces hitting her like a dowse of cold water, revealing reality in all its starkness.

Josie stumbled back, the full horror of the situation hitting her hard, knocking the breath from her lungs, buckling her legs, and she would have fallen had not Dammartin moved to support her, catching her weight against him. She looked up into the dark smoulder of his eyes, and just for that moment their gazes held, before she pushed away, and turning, fled towards the safety of his tent.

She lay that night, fully clothed, in Dammartin's tent, on the makeshift bed, alone, but for Josie there was no sleep—there was only the blood-splattered room in Telemos, and the death of her father...and the terrible weight of what she had just done.

Dammartin lay on his bed within the tent shared by Molyneux and Lamont, listening to their snores, awake, as he had been for hours, running the events of that evening through his mind for the hundredth time. The full-blown argument, her slap, and he would have let it go, done nothing, had not his men been watching.

She was a prisoner, a captive, Mallington's daughter and he knew he could not let her action go unpunished. And he wanted so very much to kiss her, to show her that she could not defy him. And hadn't he done just that? But what had started as a punishment had ended as something very different.

It seemed he could feel her against him still, so small and slender and womanly, her lips gaping with the shock of his assault. She had fought him, struggled, tried to escape, and he, like a brute, had shown no mercy. He had taken from her that which she did not know she had to give, and the taste of her innocence was like water to a man parched and dying.

He did not know what had changed, only that something had, and he found that he was kissing her in all honesty, kissing her as if she was his lover, with tenderness and seduction. And the sweetness of her tentative response, the surprise of it, the delight of it…so that he lost himself in that kiss, completely and utterly. It had taken the laughter and jeering of his men to bring him back from it, awakening him from her spell.

She was as shocked as he. He could see it in her face— shocked and ashamed and guilty.

Too late, Mademoiselle Mallington, he thought bitterly, too damned late, for there was no longer any denying what he had known these days past: he wanted her—the daughter of the man who had murdered his father. The knowledge repulsed him. God help him, his father must be turning in his grave. But even that thought did not stop him wanting to lay Josephine Mallington down naked beneath him and plunge his hard aching flesh deep within her. He wanted her with a passion that both excited and appalled.

Dammartin took a deep breath and forced himself to think calmly with the same hard determination that had driven him these past months. He might want her, but it did not mean that he would take her. More than lust would be needed to make Pierre Dammartin disgrace his father's memory. He had been too long without a woman and that simple fact was addling his brain. He would stay away from her, assign all of her care to Molyneux, and finish this journey as quickly as he could. And on that resolution, Dammartin finally found sleep.

In the days that followed, Josie saw little of Dammartin. He was always somewhere in the distance, always occupied. Not once did he look at her. And strangely, despite that she hated him, Dammartin's rejection made Josie more alone and miserable than ever.

But there was Lieutenant Molyneux and he was so open and handsome and so very reasonable. It did not seem to matter to him that she was British and his prisoner. He was respectful when there was nothing of respect anywhere else, and friendly when all around shunned her.

A hill rose by the side of the camp that evening, smaller and less jagged than those through which they had spent the day trekking. Up above, the sky was washed in shades of pink and violet and blue as the sun began to sink behind its summit. Something of its beauty touched a chord in Josie and she felt the scene call out to the pain and grief in her heart.

She turned to Molyneux in appeal. 'Lieutenant, I would dearly like to climb that hill and watch the sunset. I would not wander from the route, which is clear and within your view from this position. I give you my most solemn word that I would not try to escape and that I would return to you here as soon as possible.' Her voice raised in hope as she willed him to agree.

'I am sorry, *mademoiselle*…' his voice was gentle '…but Captain Dammartin…' His words faltered and he started again. 'I would be very happy to accompany you in your walk up the hill, if you would permit me. The sunset does indeed look most beautiful.'

She gave a nod of her head. 'That would be most kind, Lieutenant.'

'Then we should go quickly before we miss it,' he said.

Josie smiled and wrapped her cloak more tightly around her and pulled her hat lower over her ears.

Together they walked up the hill by the camp side. And when the slope grew steeper, it seemed perfectly natural that Lieutenant Molyneux should take her arm in his, helping her to cover the ground with speed.

The summit was flat like a platform specially fashioned by the gods with the sole purpose of viewing the wonder of the heavens. Josie and Molyneux stood in awe at the sight that met their eyes. Before them the sky flamed a brilliance of colours. Red burned deep and fiery before fading to pink that washed pale and peachy. Great streaks of violet bled into the pink as if a watercolour wash had been applied too soon. Like some great canvas the picture was revealed before them in all its magnificence, a greater creation than could have been painted by any mere man. And just in the viewing of it, something of the heavy weight seemed to lift from Josie's heart and for the first time since Telemos she felt some little essence of peace. Such vastness, such magnificence, as to heal, like a balm on her troubled spirit. Words were inadequate to express the beauty of nature.

Josie stood in silent reverence, her hand tucked comfortably within Molyneux's arm, and watched, until the sound of a man's tread interrupted.

Josie dragged her eyes away from the vivid spectacle before her to glance behind.

Captain Dammartin stood not three paces away. His face was harder than ever she had seen it, his scar emphasised by the play of light and shadows. He looked at where Josie's hand was tucked into his lieutenant's arm, and it seemed that there was a narrowing of his eyes.

'Lieutenant Molyneux, return to your duties,' he snapped.

'Yes, sir.' Molyneux released Josie's hand and made his salute. He smiled at her, his hair fluttering in the breeze. His eyes were velvety grey and sincere and creased with the warmth of his smile. In the deep green of his jacket and the white of his pantaloons tinged pink from the sky, he cut a dashing image. 'Please excuse me, *mademoiselle*.'

'Immediately, Lieutenant.' Dammartin's voice was harsh.

The Lieutenant turned and hurried away, leaving Josie and his captain silhouetted against the brilliance of the setting sun.

'I have tolerated your games long enough, Mademoiselle Mallington.' The colours in the sky reflected upon his hair, casting a rich warmth to its darkness. The wind rippled through it making it appear soft and feathery. It stood in stark contrast to the expression in his eyes.

All sense of tranquillity shattered, destroyed in a single sentence by Dammartin.

'Games? I have no idea of what you speak, sir.' Her tone was quite as cold as his.

'Come, *mademoiselle*,' he said. 'Do not play the innocent with me. You have been courting the attention of my lieutenant these days past. He is not a lap-dog to dance upon your every whim. You are a prisoner of the 8th Dragoons. You would do well to remember that.'

Shock caused Josie's jaw to gape. Her eyes grew wide and round. It was the final straw as far as she was concerned. He had kissed her, kissed her with violence and passion and tenderness, and she, to a shame that would never be forgotten, had kissed him back—this man who was her enemy and who looked at her with such stony hostility. And she thought of the blaze in his eyes at the mention of her father's name. He had destroyed everything that she loved, and now he had destroyed the little transient peace. In that moment she knew that she could not trust herself to stay lest she flew at him with all the rage that was in her heart.

'Must you always be so unpleasant?' She turned her face from his, hating him for everything, and made to walk right past him.

'Wait.' He barked it as an order. 'Not so fast, *mademoiselle*. I have not yet finished.'

She cast him a disparaging look. 'Well, sir, I have.' And walked right past him.

A hand shot out, and fastened around her right arm. 'I do not think so, *mademoiselle*.'

She did not fight against him. She had already learned the folly of that. 'What do you mean to do this time?' she said. 'Beat me?'

'I have never struck a woman in my life.'

'Force your kiss upon me again?' she demanded in a voice so cold he would have been proud to own it himself.

Their gazes met and held.

'I do not think that so very much force would be required, *mademoiselle*,' he said quietly.

She felt the heat stain her cheeks at his words, and she wanted to call him for the devil he was, and her palm itched to hit him hard across his arrogant face.

His grip loosened and fell away.

She stepped back and faced him squarely. 'Well, Captain, what is of such importance that you must hold me here to say it?'

'What were you doing up here?'

'Surely that was plain to see?'

His eyes narrowed in disgust and he gave a slight shake of his head as if he could not quite believe her. 'You are brazen in the extreme, Mademoiselle Mallington. Tell me, are all English women so free with their favours?'

Josie felt the sudden warmth flood her cheeks at his implication. 'How dare you?'

'Very easily, given your behaviour.'

'You are the most insolent and despicable of men!'

'We have already established that.'

'Lieutenant Molyneux and I were watching the sunset, nothing more!' Beneath the thick wool of her cloak her breast rose and fell with escalating righteous indignation.

'Huddled together like two lovers,' he said.

'Never!' she cried.

Anger spurred an energy to muscles that had not half an hour since been heavy and spent from the day's ride. All of Josie's fury and frustration came together in that minute and something inside her snapped.

'Why must you despise me so much?' she yelled.

'It is not you whom I despise,' he said quietly.

'But my father,' she finished for him. 'You killed him and you are glad of it.'

'I am.' And all of the brooding menace was there again in his eyes.

'Why? What did my father ever do to you, save defend his life and the lives of his men?'

He looked into the girl's eyes, the same clear blue eyes that had looked out from Lieutenant Colonel Mallington's face as he lay dying, and said quietly. 'Your father was a villain and a scoundrel.'

'No!' The denial was swift and sore.

'You do not know?' For the first time it struck him that perhaps she was ignorant of the truth, that she really thought her father a wondrous hero.

'No,' she said again, more quietly.

All that was raw and bloody and aching deep within

Dammartin urged him to tell her. And it seemed if he could destroy this last falsehood the Lieutenant Colonel had woven, if he could let his daughter know the truth of the man, then perhaps he, Dammartin, would be free. Yet still he hesitated. Indeed, even then, he would not have told her. It was Mademoiselle Mallington herself with her very next words that settled the matter.

'Tell me, Captain Dammartin, for I would know this grudge that you hold against my father.'

The devil sowed temptation, and Pierre Dammartin could no longer resist the harvest. 'You ask, *mademoiselle*, and so I will answer.'

Dammartin's gaze did not falter. He looked directly into Josephine Mallington's eyes, and he told her.

'My father was a prisoner of the famous Lieutenant Colonel Mallington after the Battle of Oporto last year. Mallington gave him his parole, let him think he was being released. He never made it a mile outside the British camp before he was murdered by your father's own hand. So, *mademoiselle*, now you have the answer to your question, and I will warrant that you do not like it.'

She shook her head, incredulity creasing her face. 'You are lying!'

'I swear on my father's memory, that it is the truth. It is not an oath that I take lightly.'

'It cannot be true. It is not possible.'

'I assure you that it is.'

'My father would never do such a thing. He was a man to whom honour was everything.'

'Were you there, *mademoiselle*, at Oporto?' The question he had been so longing to ask of her. 'In May of last year?'

She shook her head. 'My father sent me back to England in April.'

He felt the stab of disappointment. 'Then you really do not know the truth of what your father did.'

'My father was a good and decent man. He would never have killed a paroled officer.'

'You are mistaken, *mademoiselle*.'

'Never!' she cried. 'I tell you, he would not!'

He moved back slowly, seeing the hurt and disbelief well in her face, knowing that he had put it there. He said no more. He did not need to. The pain in her eyes smote him so hard that he caught his breath.

'What do you seek with such lies? To break me? To make me answer your wretched questions?'

And something in her voice made him want to catch back every word and stuff them back deep within him.

She walked past him, her small figure striding across the ragged hilltop in the little light that remained, and as the last of the sky was swallowed up in darkness Pierre Dammartin knew finally that there was no relief to be found in revenge. The pain that had gnawed at him since learning the truth of his father's unworthy death was no better. If anything, it hurt worse than ever, and he knew that he had been wrong to tell her.

He stood alone on the hill in the darkness and listened to the quiet burr of the camp below and the steady beat of a sore and jealous heart.

Chapter Six

Josie avoided both Lieutenant Molyneux and Sergeant Lamont and headed straight for her tent. The smell of dinner filled the air, but Josie was not hungry. Indeed, her stomach tightened against the thought of eating. She sat in the darkness and thought of what Captain Dammartin had said, thought of the absurdity of his accusation and the certainty of his conviction. His words whirled round in her head until she thought it would explode. *He never made it a mile outside the camp before he was murdered by your father's own hand.* She squeezed her eyes shut. Not Papa, not her own dear papa. He would not murder a man in cold blood.

Josie knew full well that her father, as a ruthless commander in Wellington's army, had been responsible for the deaths of many men, but that was on a battlefield, that was war, and there was a world of difference between that and killing a man who had been given his parole.

Josie could think of nothing else. She did not move, just sat as still as a small statue, hunched in her misery within the tent.

A voice sounded from the flap. *'Mademoiselle.'* It was Lieutenant Molyneux.

'Please, sir, I am tired and wish to be left alone.'

'But you have not eaten, *mademoiselle.*'

'I am not hungry.'

'You must eat something.'

'Perhaps later,' she said, wishing that the Lieutenant would go away, and then, feeling ungracious, added, 'but I thank you, sir, for your concern.'

He did not reply, but she knew he had not moved away.

'Mademoiselle,' he said softly, 'has the Captain upset you?'

She paused, unwilling to reveal the extent to which Dammartin had hurt her. Then finally she said, 'No, I am just tired, that is all.'

'He does not mean to be so...' Molyneux searched for the right word in English and failed to find it. 'He is a good man, really. He just never got over the death of his father.'

Something twisted in her stomach at his words. Slowly she moved to the front of the tent, pulling back the flap that she might see Lieutenant Molyneux.

He smiled and held out the mess tin of stew that he had collected for her.

'Thank you.' She took it, but did not eat. 'What happened to Captain Dammartin's father?' she asked, and inside her heart was thumping hard and fast.

The smile fled Molyneux's face. 'Major Dammartin was a prisoner of war,' he said quietly.

She waited for his next words.

He flushed and shifted uncomfortably. 'It was a dishonourable affair.' He cleared his throat and glanced away.

'What happened?' she prompted.

He did not look at her. 'He was killed by his English captors.'

'No,' she said softly.

'Unfortunately, yes, *mademoiselle*. It is a story famous throughout France. Major Dammartin was a very great war hero, you see.'

'Do you know who held him? Which regiment?'

He looked at her then and she could see the pity in his eyes. And she knew.

But Molyneux was much more of a gentleman than Dammartin and he would not say it. 'I cannot recall,' he said. He gave a small smile. 'You should eat your dinner, *mademoiselle*, before it grows cold.'

She raised her eyes and looked across the distance, to the other side of the fire that burned not so very far away from the tents. Dammartin was standing there, talking to Sergeant Lamont. But his face was turned towards her and she felt the force of his gaze meet hers before it moved on to take in Lieutenant Molyneux. She felt herself flush, remembering what Dammartin had said, and knowing what it must look like with her standing by the tent flap, and the Lieutenant so close outside, their conversation conducted in hushed tones.

'Thank you,' she said to Molyneux, and she let the canvas flap fall back down into place.

The morning was as glorious as the previous evening's sunset had predicted. A cloudless blue sky filled with the soft, gentle light of pale sunshine. A landscape over which drifted small pockets of mist that had not yet blown away, and which during the night an ice maiden had kissed so that everything within it glittered with a fine coating of frost.

Josie noticed none of the beauty.

She thought again and again of what the Frenchmen had said, both of them. And the thing that she could not forget was not the terrible words of Dammartin's accusation with his fury and all of his bitterness. No, the most horrible thing of all was Molyneux's kindness. *I cannot recall*, he had said, but he could and he did. She had seen the pity in his eyes, and his silence roared more potent than all of Dammartin's angry words.

She knew now why the French soldiers looked at her as they did, and understood the whispers. Yet Josie clung with every ounce of her being to her father's memory, refusing to believe her gentle papa guilty of such a crime.

Molyneux was ever present during the long hours of the day, attempting to cheer and amuse her when in truth what Josie needed was time alone to think—time away from all of the French, even Molyneux. No sentries, no feeling of being for ever watched, for ever guarded, and definitely no Dammartin, just space to think clearly.

As they struck camp that evening, Josie waited until Dammartin and his men were at their busiest before making her excuse of the need to relieve herself. It was the one place to which neither Molyneux nor his men would accompany her.

Looking up into the Lieutenant's face, she felt a twinge of guilt at her dishonesty, for Molyneux alone in this camp had tried to help her. But her need for some little time alone overcame all such discomfort.

'Come, sit down, take a drink with me.' The Major steered Dammartin back to the table and sat down. He unstoppered the large decanter of brandy and poured out two generous measures. 'Here.' He pressed one of the glasses into Dammartin's hand.

'Thank you, sir.' Dammartin took a sip.

'Snuff?' The Major extracted an exquisitely worked

silver snuffbox from his pocket and, opening the lid, offered it to Dammartin.

Dammartin shook his head. 'Thank you, but, no, sir.'

'Forget the "sir". We are alone now. You are Jean's son, and since my old friend is no longer with us, I look upon you as my own son.' La Roque took an enormous pinch of snuff, placed it on the back of his hand, sniffed it heartily up into his nose and then gave the most enormous sneeze. He lifted his own glass of brandy from the table and lounged back in his chair.

'So tell me, how are you really doing, Pierre? I've been worried about you since Telemos.'

Dammartin took another sip of brandy, and gave a wry smile to the man who had helped him so much since his father's death. 'There's no need. I told you I am fine.'

'Who would have thought that Mallington would have been holed up in that shit-hole of a village? There truly must be a God, Pierre, to have delivered that villain into our hands. I am only sorry that he died before I got to him. At least you had the satisfaction of looking into the bastard's eyes while he died.'

'Yes.' And even La Roque's finest brandy could not mask the bad taste that rose in Dammartin's throat at that memory. 'Yet I found no joy in Mallington's death.'

'Come, come, boy. What is this? At long last your father's murder has been avenged.'

'I know.'

'We both waited a long time for that moment.'

'Indeed we did.' But the sourness in Dammartin's throat did not diminish. He took another sip of brandy.

'Jean can now rest in peace, and you can move on with your life.'

'At last,' said Dammartin, but his voice was grim.

La Roque drained the last of the brandy from his glass and reached again for the decanter. 'Come along, hold your glass out, time for a top-up.'

'I need a clear head for the morning,' protested Dammartin.

'I insist,' said the Major, 'for old times' sake.' He refilled Dammartin's glass. 'Let's drink to your father. The finest friend a man ever did have and a hero for all of France.' La Roque raised his glass. 'Jean Dammartin.'

Dammartin did likewise. 'Jean Dammartin, the best of fathers.'

They drank the brandy and sat in silence for some minutes, Dammartin lost in memories of his father.

And then La Roque asked, 'What of the woman, Mallington's daughter? Her presence cannot be easy for you.'

'Mademoiselle Mallington does not affect me in the slightest,' said Dammartin, and knew that he lied. 'She is a prisoner to be delivered to Ciudad Rodrigo as you instructed, nothing more.'

'That is what I like to hear, Pierre.' La Roque smiled. 'Drink up, boy, drink up.'

Josie sat perched near the edge of the ravine, looking out over the swathe of the rugged Portuguese landscape beyond. The air had grown colder with a dampness that seemed to seep into her very bones. She did not know how long it would be before Molyneux missed her, so she just savoured each and every moment of her solitude.

The fingers of her left hand kneaded gently at her forehead, trying to ease the knotted confusion of the thoughts that lay within. From beyond the trees and bushes behind her through which she had passed came the now-familiar sound of tent pegs being hammered in the distance, and the faint chattering and laughter of the soldiers.

She breathed deeply, allowing some of the tension, which had since Telemos been a part of her, to slip. Within this light the rocks in the ravine looked as brown as the soil that encased them. A bird called from the cool grey sky, gliding open-winged on a current of air, and Josie envied its freedom. The breeze fluttered the ribbons of her bonnet beneath her chin and loosed some strands of hair to brush against her cheeks.

She thought again of Dammartin and of his accusation, and as terrible and ridiculous as it had been, at least she now understood something of the French Captain's darkness. He was a man drowning in bitterness and vengeance…and hurt. And all because of a lie.

Dammartin's father was dead, but not by her papa's hand, not by murder. Papa had been honest and steadfast, a strong man whose integrity was not open to compromise. But Dammartin believed the lie; she had seen the absolute conviction in his eyes. That knowledge explained all of his hatred, but little else.

Why had he taken her from the monastery in Telemos? For she knew now that he had never intended to honour her father's dying wishes. For information? Yet he had known of the messengers, and not from her. And why had he come after her across the Portuguese countryside? What did it matter to him if she lived or died?

She thought of his coaxing her down the rock face, and giving her his cover in the night, of his kiss that had gentled to become… Josie did not want to think of that. So many questions, to which she did not have the answers.

A twig snapped behind her, the noise of a footstep upon the pebbled soil. Josie glanced round to tell Molyneux that she was just coming. But it was not Molyneux that stood there.

* * *

'What do you mean she has not come back?' demanded Dammartin. 'Where the hell is she?'

'She wished to use the latrine,' said a white-faced Molyneux.

'And you let her go alone?'

Molyneux wetted the dryness of his lips. 'I could not expect her to attend to her…needs…in front of me.'

'No? You were instructed not to leave her side.'

Molyneux faced Dammartin with a slight air of defiance. 'She is a lady, Captain.'

'I know damn well what Mademoiselle Mallington is,' snapped Dammartin, peering into the bushes. 'Fetch your musket, Lamont, and a couple of troopers. We have not much time before the light is lost.'

Molyneux saluted and moved away.

'And, Molyneux,' Dammartin called after him. 'You'll be tracking her on foot down towards the ravine.'

A calloused hand clamped over Josie's mouth, a brawny arm fastened tight around her chest and upper arms, hauling her to her feet.

She kicked out, her boot hitting hard against the man's shin.

He grunted and, drawing back his hand, dealt her a blow across the face.

She made to scream, but his hand was already around her throat, squeezing tight, and she was choking and gasping with the need for air. She heard his words, fast and furious Portuguese, as he lifted her clear of the ground by that single hand encircling her neck.

A cracked, grubby finger with its dirt-encrusted fingernail touched against his lips, as he looked meaningfully into her eyes.

She nodded, or at least tried to, knowing that he was demanding her silence. The world was darkening as at last his grip released and she dropped to the ground, limp and gasping for breath.

More voices, talking, and she raised her eyes to see five more shabby, dark-bearded men coming out from among the bushes. They were all lean to the point of being gaunt, their clothes dirty and faded, their faces hard and hostile as they encircled her, like wolves closing in around a kill. Bandits, realised Josie, just as Dammartin had warned.

'Inglês,' she said hoarsely, and raked through her brain for some more Portuguese words that would make them understand. *'Não francês.'*

But the men were talking quietly among themselves, gesturing in the direction of the French camp.

'I am British,' she said, swallowing through the pain of the bruising on her throat. 'British,' she said, and tried to scramble to her feet.

The large man, her attacker, pushed her back down and crouched low to look into her face. 'I like British,' he said, and traced a thick tongue slowly and deliberately over his lips in a crude gesture that even Josie in all her innocence could understand.

'General Lord Wellington will pay well for my return,' she lied. 'W-e-l-l-i-n-g-t-o-n,' she said enunciating slowly so that they must be sure to understand, and 'g-o-l-d, much gold.'

But the bandit just leered and spoke words to the men behind him to make them laugh. He spat and something brown and moist and half chewed landed close to her leg.

Josie's heart was racing and fear flowed icy in her veins at the realisation of her situation. She skittered back, driving her heels against the ground, trying to put some space between her and the bandit, but he grabbed hold of her

ankle and with one wrench, she was flat upon her back
with the man climbing over her. She kicked and punched
and tried to scream, but his mouth was hard upon hers,
the unwashed stench of him filling her nostrils, the weight
of him crushing her down upon the rocky soil so that she
was staked out, unable to move. His hand ranged over her,
rough and greedy and grasping, ripping aside her bodice,
tearing at her petticoats and shift. She bucked beneath
him, trying to throw him off, but he smiled all the more,
and she felt him pressing himself against her, forcing his
brown-stained tongue into her mouth. The foul taste of
him made her gag, but he did not stop, not until she bit
him. He drew back then, his face contorted, his filthy hand
wiping the blood from his lower lip.

'Bitch!' he cursed, and lashed out, slapping her face hard.

The men behind him were saying something, looking
back nervously towards the dragoons' camp.

Josie knew she had only one hope. She prayed that
Dammartin would come, and unleash all of his darkness,
and all of his fury, upon these bandits. *I do not lose prisoners*, he had said. In her mind she called out his name
again and again, as if that mantra would summon the devil
to deal his revenge and save her.

But the bandit's hands were at her skirts, bunching them
up, ripping at them, clawing to reach beneath so that she
could already feel his ragged fingernails raking the soft
skin of her thighs. The others gathered closer to watch,
smiling with lust, and cruelty and anticipation.

Josie's hope weakened and began to wither, and just
as it had almost died, she heard the French war cry, and
knew that Dammartin had come.

Dammartin saw the ruffians gathered round, and he
knew without seeing what they were watching. He sig-

nalled to his men, sending Molyneux and a trooper silently through the undergrowth to cover one side, and Lamont with a second trooper to the other. And even while they moved into place, he was priming his musket ready to fire.

He roared the war cry, the sound of it echoing throughout the hills and down across the ravine.

The bandits reacted with a start, some reaching for their weapons, the others trying to run.

He saw the flash of exploding gunpowder and the shots rang out, deafening in their volume. Three of the bandits were downed, but Dammartin was not focusing on them. He looked beyond to where the man was scrabbling up from a woman's prostrate body, saw him snarl at her as he turned towards Dammartin, his hands raised in the air in submission.

'Surrender! Surrender!' the bandit shouted in garbled French.

Dammartin did not even pause in consideration. His finger squeezed against the trigger, and the man dropped to his knees, a neat, round, red hole in the middle of his forehead, his eyes wide and staring, before he crashed facedown to the ground.

When Dammartin looked again, Josephine Mallington was on her feet, clutching what was left of her bodice against her breasts, and standing over the bandit's body. She was staring down at the gore the dripped from his head, her breast heaving, her eyes flashing with barely suppressed emotion.

'Villain!' she shouted, 'Damnable blackguard!' and delivered a kick to the dead man. 'Rotten evil guttersnipe!' Dropping to her knees, she lashed out, hitting again and again at the body. 'Wretched, wretched brute!'

'*Mademoiselle*,' Dammartin said, and tried to guide her from the corpse, but she just pushed him away.

'No!' she cried. 'Leave me be!' She struck out all the harder.

'Josephine.' Dammartin stayed her flailing arms, pulling her up, turning her in his encircling arms so that her face looked up to his.

And all of her anger seemed to just drop away, and in its place was devastation. Her eyes met his then, wide and haunted. Beneath the smears of dirt, her face was so pale as to be devoid of any colour, save for beginnings of bruises where a fist had struck, and the thin trickle of red blood that bled from the corner of her mouth.

'He was going to…'

'I know.' Dammartin felt his outrage flare at the thought.

'Like a rutting animal…' And her voice was hoarse with distress and disgust. 'Like a great, filthy beast.'

'Josephine—' he tried to calm her '—he is dead.'

'And I am glad of it!' she cried in her poor, broken voice, 'So very glad! Me, a Christian woman, my father's daughter.' Her eyes squeezed shut and he thought that she would weep, but she did not. Her head bowed so that she stood, resting her forehead lightly against his chest. And he could not imagine the strength with which she held back her tears. Within his arms, he felt the rapidity of her breathing and the tremble that ran through her.

'I prayed that you would come,' she said so quietly that he had to strain to catch her words. 'I prayed and prayed.'

Dammartin stroked a gentle hand against her hair, and held her to him. 'You are safe now, *mademoiselle*,' he said, 'safe, I promise.'

He stood for a few moments and the wind blew, and the sky grew darker, and he was overwhelmed with the need to protect her, to make all of her terrible hurt disappear.

And then Molyneux moved, Lamont cleared his throat, and Dammartin forced himself to think straight.

'Mademoiselle Mallington,' he said softly, and stripping off his jacket, wrapped it around her. 'We must return to the camp.'

She focused down at the ground. 'Of course.' There was nothing left of resistance, nothing of the fight she had so often given in the past.

He kept his arm around her waist, supporting her, as she walked by his side.

In silence and with grim expressions upon each of their faces, Dammartin and his men made their way back to their camp.

Dammartin sat her down on the chair at the table within his tent, speaking fast words of command over his shoulder, to Molyneux or Lamont, she supposed, but she did not look to see. She could not, for all that her eyes were open and staring. She was frozen, unable to move from beneath the terrible, heavy emptiness that weighed her down.

There was the trickle of water, a cloth being wrung out over a basin. The water was warm, his touch gentle, as he cleansed away the blood and the dirt, carefully wiping and dabbing and drying her face and hands, while his jacket hung warm and protective around her shoulders.

She looked at him then and there was nothing of bitterness in his eyes, only compassion.

'I told him I was British,' she said, and the words crawled like glass through the rawness of her throat. 'And it made no difference, just as you said.'

'Josephine,' he said softly. 'I should have guarded you better.'

She shook her head. 'I was not escaping.' It seemed

important to make him understand and she did not know why. 'I just wanted some time alone, some place where I might sit and think of all you had said…of my father.'

They sat in silence and the flicker of the lantern danced shadows upon the canvas walls. Outside all was quiet.

She felt the touch of his fingers, as light as a feather, against the bruising at her throat and the tenderness of her mouth.

'He hurt you very badly, *mademoiselle*—for that I am sorry.'

And his gentleness and compassion almost over-whelmed her.

'But you are safe now, I swear it.'

She looked deep into the darkness of his eyes, and saw a man who was resolute and strong and invincible, and she believed what he said.

The smallest of nods. And she sat there, dazed and battered and not knowing anything any more.

And when he unlaced her boots to ease them from her feet, and laid her down upon the bed beneath the blankets, she let him.

'Do not leave me alone,' she heard her lips murmur.

He gave a nod and returned to sit upon the chair. 'I will be here all the night through. You can sleep safe.'

She could hear his breathing, the creak of the chair at his small movements, and every so often she opened her eyes just by the slightest to check that he was still there. Checking and checking until finally the blackness of sleep stole over her.

But sleep brought no refuge, only more horror, so that she could smell the stench of the villain and feel the claw of his hands upon her, and hear again the thunder of Dammartin's musket shot. The wound in the bandit's skull gaped, leaking the dark, rich liquid to drip into an expanding pool. So much blood. Just like in Telemos.

Blood and more blood. Upon the bandit, upon the men of the 60th and her father, upon herself as she hit out at the bandit's dead body. One blow and then another, and as she reached to strike him a third time the bandit sat up with an evil grin. She felt her heart flip over, for in his hand was the musket that had shot her father, all sticky and dark with blood. The barrel raised, the bandit took aim directly at Josie's heart. Death was certain. She cried out, pleading for him to stop.

'Mademoiselle Mallington. Josephine.' Dammartin's voice was close and quiet, his hands on her arms, dragging her from the nightmare. She stared through the darkness, reaching out to find him.

'Captain Dammartin,' she whispered, and on her tongue was the saltiness of tears and in her nose was the congestion of weeping.

'It is a bad dream, nothing more. I am here. All is well.' He stroked a hand against her hair. 'Go back to sleep.'

But when he would have left, she caught at his fingers, unable to bear being alone. 'Stay,' she said.

He stilled in the darkness.

'Please.'

In answer he lay down beside her, and covered them both with the weight of his greatcoat. He was warm even through the blankets that separated them and she could feel the linen of his shirt soft against her cheek and smell the clean, masculine smell of him. With his strong arm draped protectively over her, holding her close, the nightmare receded and Josie knew, at last, that she was safe.

As Dammartin rode the next day his thoughts were all with Josephine Mallington. She had been seconds from being raped. In his mind's eye he could still see the bandit lying over her, and the memory made his blood run cold so that he wanted to smash the butt of his musket into the man's face again and again. Death had come too quickly for the bastard.

He remembered her anger, and her devastation, and the way she had clung to him in the night. *I prayed that you would come*, she had said. Him. Her enemy.

And he thought of Lieutenant Colonel Mallington firing the shot into his father's body, just as he had thought of it every day for over the last eighteen months. She was the murderer's daughter, his flesh and blood. He had every right to hate her, but it was no longer that simple. She had not known of her father's crime, and she did not deserve what had happened to her, not in that room in Telemos, not his contempt, nor the assault by the bandits. Lamont had been right. She was a woman, a woman who had watched her father die, who was alone and afraid and the captive of an enemy army.

But there was still the matter of what Mallington had done, and Dammartin could not forgive or forget. The wound ran too deep for that. If he could have understood the reasons underlying Mallington's crime, perhaps then there might have been some sort of end to it all, a semblance of peace. But Mallington had died taking his answers to the grave, leaving Dammartin with his anger and his bitterness...and his desire for Josephine Mallington.

As Lamont had said, it would be a long way to Ciudad Rodrigo, a long way indeed.

Josie rode silently by Molyneux's side that day. The Lieutenant had been kind and understanding, trying to make the journey as comfortable as he could for her, but

she could see that he did not know what to say to her. Even
Sergeant Lamont had brought her a cup of hot coffee when
they stopped to rest and eat, his gruff expression belying
the small kindness. She could see the way they looked
at her, with pity in their eyes, and Josie hated it. Their
contempt would have been more welcome. She did not
want to be vulnerable and afraid, an object of sympathy,
and she resented the bandit even more that he could have
made her so. And she knew what the bandit would have
done had not Dammartin arrived.

Saved by the one man she had hated. It was under his
command that her father and his men had been killed. He
could be nothing other than her enemy. But Josie thought
of the hole that his bullet had made within the bandit's
head, she thought of how he had taken her in his arms and
held her. He had washed away the dirt and the stench and
the blood, and stayed with her the whole night through,
and lain his length beside her when she had begged him
to stay. She had begged him. And that thought made Josie
cringe with shame, yet last night, in the darkness the fear
had been so very great that there had been no such embarrassment. Last night she had needed him, this man who
hated with such passion.

Your father was a villain and a scoundrel, he had said,
and she thought again of the terrible accusation he had
made. Dammartin believed in it with all his heart. And
she wondered why he should ever have come to think such
a thing. How could he be so misled? There was only one
man who could answer her questions.

Yesterday she would not have considered entering into
a discussion with Dammartin over his accusation, but
much had changed since then, and she knew that, for all
the darkness and danger surrounding him, he would not

hurt her. For all else that Dammartin was and for all else that he had done, he had saved her, and Josie would not forget that.

She rode on in silence, biding her time until evening when she would speak to the French Captain.

Chapter Seven

It had been a long day, long and cold and hard, and the dust of it still clung to Dammartin's boots. Smoke drifted from the newly lit fires and the men busied themselves with cooking pots and rice and beans. The air was filled with the smell of wood smoke and the damp air of impending night.

'We head for Sabugal tomorrow,' he said to Lamont. 'The maps show that the mountains do not grow less and Foy is demanding we speed our current pace.'

'Men will be lost if we push them too hard.'

'More of Massena's men are lost with every day that we delay.' Dammartin rubbed wearily at the dark growth of stubble that peppered his jaw. 'Our army is dying in this damned country for need of reinforcements.'

Lamont's gaze focused over Dammartin's right shoulder before swinging back to meet the Captain's. 'I think perhaps the *mademoiselle* wishes to speak with you. She keeps glancing over here.'

Dammartin's expression remained unchanged. 'I am busy. There remains much to be done this evening.' He had no wish to speak to Mademoiselle Mallington. Matters concerning the girl were already too complicated for his liking.

Lamont sniffed and scratched at his chin. 'After last night, I thought…'

Dammartin forced the images from his mind. 'I would not wish what happened last night upon any woman, but she is still Mallington's daughter, Claude. I cannot allow myself to forget that.'

Lamont said nothing for a few moments, just looked at his captain before giving a nod. 'I will see to our evening meal.' And he walked off.

Dammartin nodded over at Molyneux, and began to move towards his lieutenant. A woman's step sounded behind him and there was the scent of lavender.

'I wondered if I might speak with you, Captain Dammartin.' There was a slightly awkward expression upon Mademoiselle Mallington's face; she seemed almost embarrassed, and he knew that she was remembering last night, just as he was.

He opened his mouth to refuse her, noticing as he did the tendrils of fair hair that had escaped her bonnet to feather around her face and the shadow of the bruise that marked her jaw.

'Concerning my father.'

Mallington. And he knew he would not refuse her after all. 'Very well, *mademoiselle.*'

'Perhaps we could talk somewhere more private.'

He felt the register of surprise, along with a sliver of excitement at the prospect of what it could be that she wished to tell him.

'If that is what you desire.'

He saw Molyneux standing not so far away, the Lieutenant's gaze darting between the girl and Dammartin.

'There is a river down through the woodland.'

She nodded her agreement.

Dammartin headed towards the trees, leaving Molyneux staring after them.

They walked in silence through the woodland, down the slope that ran towards the river, with only the tread of their boots over soil and the snapping of twigs between them, until they left the clearing where the 8th Dragoons were camped some distance behind at the top of the gorge. Slightly to the east they could hear the sounds of the infantry's camp, but it was not close enough to challenge their privacy.

He led her to the edge of a fast-flowing river, to where great boulders of rock clustered along its bank.

'We shall not be overheard here,' he said, and, leaning easily against a giant rock, looked out over the river.

Back up through the trees, from where they had come, he could just about see the carmine-coloured lapels of his men's jackets as they moved about the camp. Had the red lapels not been there, the green of their uniform would have made an effective camouflage even though the woodland was bare and barren. Beyond the great stones the water flowed fast despite the lack of rain. In the fading light it was a deep greeny grey that foamed to white where the water splashed hard over its rocky bed. The noise of it was so loud and gushing as to be almost a roar.

Josie turned from the river to face him, feeling suddenly nervous. 'There is not much time, Captain Dammartin. The daylight shall soon be gone and I would prefer to be back at the camp before it is dark.' She took a deep breath, squared her shoulders and prepared to speak the words she had come here to say.

He did not look round, just stayed where he was. 'You are recovered from last night, *mademoiselle*?'

The question unsettled her, reminding of things best forgotten: bandits and nightmares and the warmth of Dammartin's body sharing her bed. 'Yes, thank you, sir.'

His eyes met hers, and they were a clear honey brown, rich with emotion that she could not name—compassion, affinity, protectiveness. 'I am glad.'

And to Josie there was an intensity about the moment that set the butterflies fluttering in her stomach so that she had to look away.

The water rushed on. Somewhere in the distance was the thumping of axes splitting wood, and through the trees ahead she could see the sun was setting: a vibrant red halo surrounding the dark branches of the trees, as if a fire had touched against them, deep and hot and burning.

Still leaning his elbows on the stone boulder with the rosy pink light softening his face, he appeared to Josie ruggedly handsome. 'What is it, then, that you wish to say?'

She turned her mind from its observations, reminding herself of why she had come here. 'I wished to ask you of this...this accusation that you level at my father.'

He resumed his study of the river scene before him. 'It is no mere accusation, *mademoiselle*, but the truth.' And there was a weariness in his voice.

'That is your belief, but it is not correct, sir.'

'And this is what you wished to tell me?' He stopped leaning against the rock and turned to face her, and she could see that anything of softness had vanished, that he was once again the dark and dangerous French Captain who had stormed the monastery in Telemos.

'I did not come here to argue,' she said quickly.

'Really?' He arched an arrogant eyebrow.

She glanced away, suddenly very aware that they were alone down here. 'Did you witness your father's death?'

There was only the sound of the river in reply.

She thought she saw the flicker of pain in his eyes, so brief that she could not be sure.

The muscle in his jaw clenched. 'I did not.'

'But you were there, with him, at Oporto?'

'Unfortunately, no.'

The smallest of pauses, before she asked gently, 'Then how do you know the manner of his death?'

'Mademoiselle,' he said with the hard cynical breath of a laugh, 'all of France knows what your father did to him!'

She bit back the retort that sprang to her lips. 'Then, there were witnesses…to the crime?'

'Yes, there was a witness,' he said harshly. 'An honourable man who is beyond reproach, if it is his word that you are seeking to discredit.'

His words stung at her. 'What is there of honour in dishonesty?' she replied.

A twig snapped close by, and Josie jumped. Both of them peered in the direction of the trees from whence it had come.

There was only silence and the dying light and stillness.

'It is nothing,' said Dammartin dismissively. 'There is nothing to be gained in this, *mademoiselle*, we should return to the camp. The light begins to fade, and you said yourself that you are in a hurry to be back there.' He made to move.

'No, wait.' She stepped forwards, blocking his path, needing to show him that he was wrong. 'Before he died my father told me that you were an honourable man. He bade me trust you. If your accusation is true, I do not understand why he would say such a thing. When he saw you…when you came into that room in the monastery… when it was all but over, there was nothing of guilt or regret or fear in his eyes. He looked at you with respect. Given what you say, sir, how do you explain that?'

'I cannot, but it does not mean that he was innocent.'

'But will you not at least admit that his was not behaviour in keeping with a man that is guilty?'

'It was not in keeping with what is expected of a man that is guilty,' said Dammartin carefully.

'He was dying, for goodness' sake!' she said, and the pain stabbed in her heart. 'Do you really think that he would have bothered with pretence at such a time? What would have been the point?'

'As you said, Lieutenant Colonel Mallington was dying, and leaving his beloved daughter alone with the son of the man he had murdered. I think he had every reason to behave as he did.'

'You did not know him,' she said quietly, and stared up into his now-shadowed face. 'He was not such a man.'

'You are his daughter. Of course you do not wish to believe the unpleasantness of the truth.'

'No, you are wrong.' But with the denial came the first whisper of doubt in Josie's mind.

'You were not there. You can never really know what happened in Oporto last year, can you, *mademoiselle*?'

She bent her head, pressing the tips of her fingers to the tightness across her forehead. The thought came to her in a flash, and she wondered why she had not realised it before. Her father's journals—a log of all that had happened to Lieutenant Colonel Mallington and his men over the years—recorded by her papa's own hand in book after precious book. She raised her chin, staring at him with renewed confidence, feeling the excitement of her realisation flow through the entirety of her body.

'Oh, but you see, I can, sir,' she exclaimed. 'Every detail of every day.' She smiled her relief.

It seemed that Dammartin's lungs did not breathe, that his heart did not beat. 'And how might that be, *mademoiselle*?' he asked in a deathly quiet voice.

His very stillness alerted her to her mistake. 'I…' She swallowed, and glanced away, searching her mind frantically for a safe answer and finding none. She backed away. 'You were right; we should be returning to camp. It will soon be dark and the trees—'

His hand snaked out and caught gently around her wrist, preventing her escape. 'No, no, *mademoiselle*,' he said softly, 'our discussion, it begins to grow most interesting.' The angles of his face seemed to sharpen and his eyes darken, as he became the hunter once more.

'Captain Dammartin—'

'Every detail of every day,' he said slowly, repeating her words. 'Where might you learn that, I wonder?'

She tried to free her wrist, but Dammartin's hold was unbreakable. The thudding of her heart was so loud that she could no longer hear the river. Her breath was shallow and fast.

Foolish, foolish tongue, she cursed, to almost reveal what had remained hidden for so long. Her words had been too few, she told herself; he could not know, he could not. The journals would be safe.

Dammartin slowly pulled her closer, so that they were standing toe to toe within the twilight. 'From your British newspapers of the time?' His face tilted so that he was staring down at her.

'I meant nothing by my words. You are mistaken…' She tried to step away, but Dammartin secured her other wrist, locking her in place.

His head lowered towards hers so close that she could feel his breath, warm and soft against her face, and see the passion and determination within the darkness of his eyes. 'From your father's friends?' he asked.

She felt the jolt that jumped between them as his mouth brushed against her cheek, light and transient.

'Or perhaps from your father's journals?' he whispered softly into her ear.

The breath froze in Josie's throat. The blood in her veins turned to ice. She could not suppress the shiver. 'This is madness,' she breathed at last. 'My father kept no journal. Take me back to the camp at once.' She pulled her face back from his, staring up at him.

'Where are they, *mademoiselle*?' Darkness had crept to cover the sky, but she could still see him through the dim silver moonlight.

'You are quite, quite mistaken, sir.'

'We can stay here all night and play this game. Or perhaps you prefer to tell me now where the journals are kept, so that we may eat something of our rice and beans.'

There was silence in which neither moved nor spoke.

'At home, in England,' she said at last, knowing that it was not the journals' existence that was the secret to be protected, but their location. She thought of the irony of the journals' true hiding place. 'I will read them when I return to Winchester and then I will know exactly what happened between your father and mine in Oporto.' She stared at him defiantly, knowing that she could not allow one shred of fear to show. 'And I will warrant that it is not the lie that you French have told.'

He looked at her with his dark, penetrating stare, and it seemed to Josie that he could see into her very soul.

For too long their gazes held, as if locked in some kind of strange battle of wills, and if battle it was, then Dammartin was the loser, for it was he who looked away first.

'Let us return to the camp, *mademoiselle*,' he said, and,

taking her hand in his, he began to lead her back towards the woodland.

She let her fingers lie where they were, warm and comfortable within his own, despite knowing that she should be fighting his touch. But the night was dark and their route through the woodland steep and uneven, and her sense of relief and of triumph was greater than anything else.

Hand in hand, without a further word between them, Josie and Dammartin walked through the trees that would lead them back to the camp of the 8th Dragoons.

The campaign portmanteau which contained all of Josie's worldly possessions sat opposite her makeshift bed within Dammartin's tent. It was made of brown leather, battered and scratched from its many miles of travel following her father.

Josie unbuttoned the top of her dress and let the woollen material fall back to expose the chain that hung around her neck. Its golden links glinted within the soft light of the lantern. Her hand disappeared down her dress. From just above her breasts she retrieved what had been threaded to hang upon the chain: a small brass key. Kneeling down upon the groundsheet, she leaned forward towards the portmanteau, neatly turned the key in first one lock and then the other. The fastenings opened easily beneath her fingers. She opened the lid and rested it carefully back.

Inside were piles of neatly folded clothes. They were, in the main, garments that had been purchased with the practicalities of life on campaign in winter in mind. There were two woollen travelling dresses, a sensible pelisse, scarves, a shawl, gloves, a pair of sensible shoes that could be worn instead of her boots, and of course, a large pile of plain white warm underwear, the warmest that she had had.

There were stockings and two nightdresses and ribbons and hairpins. Near the top there was a tiny silver and ivory set that included a comb and brush and hand-held looking glass. But Josie was interested in none of these things.

She moved with deliberate care, removing the items one by one, laying them in tidy bundles across the ground-sheet, until at last the portmanteau was empty, or so it seemed. Then she pressed at the rear left-hand corner of the portmanteau and smoothly lifted away the false floor. Beneath it, spread in neat piles over the entirety of the base of the portmanteau, as if a single uniform layer, were notebooks.

Each book was backed in a soft paper cover of a deep pinky-red coloration; some were faded, others stained. Josie picked one from the closest corner and opened it. The white of the pages was scarcely visible beneath the pale grey pencil script that covered it. She checked the date at the top right-hand side of the page—21st June 1807— closed the book, set it back in its place in the pile, moved on to the next, until she found the book that contained the date for which she was searching.

The false floor was slotted back into position. The bundles of clothes were returned in neat order to the port-manteau, as was every other item that had been removed. The lid was carefully closed, the key turned within the locks and the straps rebuckled. Only then did Josie make herself comfortable upon the wooden chair and sit down at Captain Dammartin's little table to lay the notebook upon its surface. She adjusted the direction of the light within the lantern and, taking a deep breath, began to read her father's journal for the Battle of Oporto.

Josie could barely concentrate on Molyneux's chatter the next day, for thinking of the words that her father had written. Dammartin had been correct in saying that his father had been captured by hers. It was true, too, that the French major had been paroled, but that is where any similarity between the two stories ended. Lieutenant Colonel Mallington's telling of the two men's meeting could not have contrasted more sharply with Dammartin's.

Her papa had written of respect and admiration between two men who happened to be fighting on opposite sides of a war. Those faded grey words conveyed an underlying sense of something bordering on friendship.

Why should there be such a discrepancy between the two accounts? It made no sense. The more she thought about it, the more she became convinced that there was something very strange about such a blatant contradiction. And she longed to question Dammartin more on his story.

Who was the man who claimed to have witnessed the murder? Someone honourable, who was beyond reproach, Dammartin had said.

She glanced ahead to where the French Captain rode, her eyes skimming his broad shoulders, and the sway of the long, black mane of horsehair that hung from his helmet. She wanted to show him the journal entry, to prove to him that he was wrong, to show him that her father was indeed an innocent man, but she could not.

Trust was a fickle thing, and Dammartin was still the enemy. Even had she torn that single page from its binding so that he might have read only that and nothing else, then he would have known that the journals were in her possession and she knew that Dammartin would not stop until he had them from her.

Her teeth worried at her lower lip, and she knew that she dare not approach him again, no matter how many questions still burned unanswered. Last night had been too close for comfort, in more ways than one. The memory of his face so close to hers, of his breath warm against her cheek, of the dark, dangerous look in his eyes…and how very close he had come to discovering that all of her father's journals were here under his very nose.

'Your thoughts are elsewhere this morning, *mademoiselle*.' Molyneux smiled that kind smile of his, making Josie feel guilty at her inattention.

'Forgive me, Lieutenant, I am but a little tired.'

'You did not sleep well?' he enquired with concern.

She gave a small shake of her head. 'Not since Telemos.'

'I am sorry, *mademoiselle*. I did not mean to raise such distressing memories.' His smile was small and wry. 'We should talk of happier times, especially as I, too, am feeling a little sad this day.'

Josie glanced up at him with questioning eyes.

'I confess to you alone, *mademoiselle*, and you must keep a very great secret, that I am missing my wife most dreadfully.'

'I did not know that you are married, sir,' said Josie.

'I do not often speak of Mariette. It makes me too emotional, and that is not good for a lieutenant in the Emperor's army.'

Josie felt her heart soften for the poor lieutenant. 'I think it is most commendable that you miss her.'

'We have been married for three years,' he said, 'and we have two fine sons.' He smiled at that.

'Would it be of help if you were to speak of your family, sir?'

'I think, perhaps, *mademoiselle*, that it might.'

So Molyneux told her of his boys and how he missed them. He told her of Mariette and how he had courted her despite her father's disregard for a mere military man. They laughed over the antics that two-year-old Louis got up to, and then Lieutenant Molyneux grew sad when he spoke of how tiny the baby, Dominique, had been when last he had seen him, and how in the months that had since passed that the baby would have grown beyond all recognition. He was trying to keep his emotion in check, but she could hear the wistful longing in his voice and it tugged at her heartstrings.

Impulsively she reached over and briefly touched her hand to his sleeve. 'You must not be sad, sir. Your family would not wish it so and I am sure that you will see them soon.'

'Yes.' But there was nothing of hope in the word. He gave a sigh and then seemed to pull himself from his reverie. 'Now you understand, *mademoiselle*.' He forced a smile to his face.

She could see the slight sheen of tears in his eyes and knew that he would not want the embarrassment of having her see them. 'Indeed, I do, sir,' she said. 'Perhaps we should speak of other matters.' She smiled. 'The weather has been uncommonly fine of late. Do you think that it will hold?'

He laughed at that and she could see that the sadness had left his eyes. 'You English always speak of the weather. It is a national interest, I think.'

'Yes,' she agreed, 'I think it probably is.'

They rode in companionable silence for a little, and Josie was just thinking how pleasant Lieutenant Molyneux was when a small and rather daring idea popped into her head. 'Would you mind if I were to ask you something of a rather delicate nature, Lieutenant?'

'But of course, you must ask,' he replied.

'It concerns the death of Captain Dammartin's father.'

Molyneux's face betrayed a fleeting surprise. 'What is it that you wish to know, *mademoiselle*?'

'I understand that there is a man who claims to have

witnessed the—' She broke off and quickly revised her words. 'To have witnessed Major Dammartin's death.'

'That is the case.'

'I was wondering if you knew the identity of that man.'

Molyneux's grey eyes met hers. There was the jangle of harnesses, and the steady clop of horses' hooves. 'Why do you ask such a question?'

'I wish to know the name of the man who is responsible for falsely accusing my father of murder.'

'Mademoiselle,' said Molyneux softly.

'My father is innocent, Lieutenant, and he is dead,' she said in justification of her request. 'There is no one else to defend his name.'

Concern and pity welled in Molyneux's eyes, and all she could think of was showing Molyneux that such pity was unjustified, that her father really was innocent. 'Do not think that I am misled because he was my father. He is innocent, sir, and I have the evidence that will prove it.'

Molyneux stared at her.

'Will you tell me the man's name, Lieutenant?'

Molyneux looked away and with a gentle sigh, shook his head.

'You do not trust me?'

'It is not that,' Molyneux said quietly.

'Then what?'

He looked back round at her. 'I fear that you will find only sadness if you follow this path.'

'No,' she said with determination, 'you are quite wrong in that.'

He gave a wry smile, and they continued on in silence.

Dammartin saw the way in which Mademoiselle Mallington looked at Molyneux, saw too the brief touch of fingers against his arm before he turned away again. She was

Mallington's daughter, a prisoner, so what did it matter to Dammartin if she flirted with his lieutenant? he thought. Did he not want to be rid of her in Ciudad Rodrigo as soon as was possible? She was nothing to him, just as he had told La Roque.

But Dammartin was not fooling himself. He wanted her, and though he was adamant that he would not act upon it, nothing that he did seemed to alter that desire.

He longed to cup those pale, perfect breasts, to span his hands around the narrowness of her waist, to slide his fingers over the swell of her hips. And those lips...so ripe for the tasting, and he remembered the kiss, and how it had served only to stoke his hunger for her higher. The feel of her long hair beneath his fingers, the clean lavender scent of her, her very softness...

Last night, in the darkness by the river, with her wrists imprisoned in his, he had come close to kissing her again, to claiming her sweet mouth with his own. His lips had been so close that they tingled to kiss away the pain of her bruises. It had been an enormous effort of willpower not to succumb to temptation.

He thought of the excitement that had stirred in his blood when she had said that she wanted to speak to him of her father. The flair of hope that she would tell him what he so longed to know: the workings of a madman's mind. But Josephine Mallington had wanted only to argue her father's innocence, and he supposed that that was an admirable thing.

She was young, her father's only daughter, and he thought what she had told him of following her father around the world, of the death of her mother. It could not have been easy to learn the truth of her father, that he was not the beloved hero she thought him. No wonder she fought so hard for the old man. Dammartin knew he would have done the very same for his own father.

He wondered what Mallington had written in his journal about Oporto and Jean Dammartin. And he wondered, too, as to Josephine Mallington's reaction when he had asked about the journals. What was she so frightened of revealing if the journals were safely stowed in England? Dammartin thought of his own current campaign journal locked within the drawer of his small campaign desk, and of his journals from previous years stored at the bottom of his portmanteau…and he smiled at Mademoiselle Mallington's audacity.

Chapter Eight

It was after they had stopped for a lunch break that the rain started. It was not like English rain that came on slowly enough to give a person time to hurry to cover, or put an umbrella above their head. This was Portuguese rain and it was as if God had decided to operate a pump stand in the heavens. The rain poured suddenly upon them in a great deluge and that is the way it stayed for the next few hours. Molyneux offered her the great cape that covered over him and his horse, but Josie refused it.

The rain penetrated everywhere and at a speed at which she could never have guessed. She had never seen such a torrential downpour from the heavens in all of her life. Josie's hat was soon a sorry, sodden affair that dripped water down her face. Her gloves were wet and her hands were so cold that she ceased to feel her fingers. She could feel the water trickling between the toes of her stockings within her boots. But she made no complaint, just kept her thoughts focused on the strange mystery surrounding Dammartin's father's death. When her mind was fixed on that, Josie felt infinitely better, for then she could not dwell upon what had happened in Telemos, or the bandit's attack, or her worries over what would become of her.

Water dripped from her nose, ran in rivulets down her cheeks, and blurred her vision, and through it all, Josie thought on the words in her father's journal. The road became muddy and great puddles appeared that slowed the horses' progress. Troopers' shouts sounded from the rear of their column, an animal's scream of pain, and with an exchange of looks, both Dammartin and his lieutenant disappeared to investigate—leaving Josie alone. What she would have given for such a situation only a few days ago, but much had happened since then, and any chance of escape had long gone. They were too far into hostile countryside, too far from the British and too close to bandits. And aside from all of that, she knew now with an absolute certainty that Dammartin would not rest until he had hauled her back.

The French escort struggled on, and the only sound was the slop of hooves against the mud, and the constant lash of rain and wind.

They had not yet reached Sabugal when they pitched the tents, but the men could go no farther even though the rain's intensity had lessened. Josie sheltered beneath some trees and watched the speed and efficiency with which Dammartin's dragoons operated even after a day's march through the worst rainstorm imaginable. The men were cold and wet, and completely disciplined. Josie watched in amazement. She had never felt less disciplined in her life. Her clothes clung to her like a heavy, cold shroud, and there was not one vestige of warmth left in the whole of her body. Her nose was running and even the handkerchiefs from her pocket were sodden. She longed for shelter, for dry clothes, for warmth. Overhead the sky was dark with cloud and the promise of more rain. Night would come early.

Across from her tent there seemed to be some kind of altercation. Two dragoons were talking, gesturing with their hands. Dammartin was frowning and firing questions at the men, with Molyneux seemingly involved. Sergeant Lamont stood looking on from the background. There was much pointing at Josie's tent, then back at the place where the mules were clustered. The men looked over at where Josie stood, and she knew that whatever they were discussing involved her.

The dragoons went about their business, and Dammartin began to walk across the field towards her. His caped greatcoat was so long that it touched to the ground. The grey wool was dark and saturated. The long, black crest of horse hair of his helmet hung sodden and lank. Water dripped from his face, and around his face his hair clung dark and wet. She could hear the squelch of his boots in the mud, and his scar etched dark and deep against the pallor of his cheek.

Dread gathered in her stomach and she knew that something was wrong.

'Captain?'

'Mademoiselle.' His face was grim.

Her stomach clenched tighter. 'What is it? What is wrong?'

'I am afraid that there is a problem. Your portmanteau, it cannot be found.'

She stared at him, hardly fathoming the import of his words. 'But it was attached to the officers' mule train. Two of your troopers took it this morning as normal. I saw them load it myself.'

'It is not there now. I have instructed my men to search again through all of the baggage, but I am not hopeful.'

The realisation of what he was saying hit home. The breath stilled in her throat, her eyes looked up at him wide and round. 'No, it cannot be.'

'I am afraid it is true.'

She bit at her lower lip. 'It has been stolen.'

'We do not yet know if that is the case.'

'Of course it has been stolen,' she cried. 'What other explanation could there be?' And she thought of her father's journals stacked so neatly within their hiding place within the portmanteau...now in French hands.

'Oh, God!' She felt a horrible sick sensation heavy in her stomach.

'Mademoiselle,' he said.

'What am I to do?' she whispered, as if to herself. 'What on earth am I to do?' She clutched a hand to her mouth.

'We shall find you some dry clothing and blankets.'

'No, no!' She shook her head. 'You do not understand!'

'Calm yourself, Mademoiselle Mallington.'

But Josie barely heard him, for all she could think of was that she had lost the one thing that remained of her father, the thing that she had been entrusted to keep safe, lost to the enemy. And she could say not one word of the truth of it to Dammartin.

'Thank God that I—' She broke off. 'Please excuse me, Captain,' she said, and turning, ran to her tent, before she could betray herself any further.

Josie sat for what seemed a long time at the small table within the tent, trying to tell herself that there was every likelihood that the thief would not find the hidden compartment within her portmanteau. The journals might be lost, but that did not necessarily mean that the French had found them. She focused on that one small hope and sat motionless upon the wooden chair, just breathing, until all of her panic had gone.

Only when she was calm did she notice that she was shivering. The rainwater from her sodden cloak had seeped through her dress and underwear to touch damp and cold upon her skin, and Josie knew she must try to dry and warm herself. With a sigh she began to peel off her clothing. First came the woollen hat pulled so unflatteringly on her head, next, her woollen mittens and finally her leather gloves. Her fingers were stiff and slow to move, so she took her time, peeling the saturated leather covers off each finger with patience. Her cloak and pelisse followed, being dropped onto the growing pile of sodden material that was gathering by the tent's flap. Her boots took some time to unlace as her fingers would not bend well and she could scarcely untie the knots in her laces, but she persevered and soon the boots and stockings, too, lay on top of the pile.

She then unfastened the tent flap, knelt by the opening and worked her way methodically through the pile of clothes wringing out each item as dry as she could make it. When she had finished she closed the flap, stripped off her dress, petticoats and shift and hid her nakedness beneath her newly wrung-out cloak. She then repeated the wringing operation with her dress and undergarments. She wrung out her hair, and emptied her boots. Finally she slipped back into her shift and dress, and spread the rest of her clothing out across the floor so that it might have some chance of drying. She had just finished this when a woman's voice sounded outside the tent flap.

'Señorita Mallington?'

'Yes.' Josie moved to open the flap. 'I am Josephine Mallington.'

The woman that stood there was of similar height and build to Josie. But she was as dark as Josie was fair, and her face showed that she was perhaps five years older. Her hair was hidden in the main by the great hood of the plain brown cloak that she wore, but around the edges of her face a riot of dark brown curls clustered. Her eyes were soft and brown and tinged with quite the longest lashes that Josie had ever seen. Her lips were full and luscious, her face barely lined and a warm honey colour within the light of the lantern. Her expression was neither friendly nor hostile, but her eyes flickered over Josie and the interior of the tent, appraising and summing up in a matter of seconds.

'Captain Dammartin, he say you need clothes. I give you mine.'

The two women looked at each other for a minute before Josie gave a nod. 'Please come in.' Josie stepped back. 'It is kind of you to lend me a dress. My portmanteau is missing and my own clothes are rather wet.'

'Wet, yes,' said the woman and flicked a glance over the garments spread the length of the floor.

Josie's eyes followed the woman's. 'I thought perhaps the clothes might dry a little.'

The woman looked at her with the same unruffled expression. 'They no dry in here. Too cold, too wet.'

'You are probably right,' said Josie, 'but it seemed better than leaving them in a pile in the corner.'

Whether the woman understood Josie did not know, for she gave no reply.

'Please sit down, take off your cloak.' Josie pointed a hand towards the table and chairs.

At first she thought the woman would decline, but then she pushed back her hood and sat down on one of the small wooden chairs.

'Gracias.'

Josie looked at the woman. She was beautiful, with

her wet hair pinned up and its escaping curls tumbling down the sides of her face and across the bareness of her shoulders. Her skin was smooth and unblemished. She did not look as if she had spent the day marching or sitting on a donkey for hours in the rain. No, the woman that sat in Josie's tent looked damp but untroubled. Her cloak might be of coarse homespun wool, but everything in her bearing was fiercely, almost violently proud.

'For you.' The woman held out a bundle of red-and-black material.

'Thank you.' Josie took it.

'I am Rosa,' said the woman.

Josie gave a small smile. 'Thank you, Rosa.'

Rosa unfastened the ties of her cloak and pushed the garment back, flicking off droplets of rainwater as she did.

Josie's eyes slid down to the dress that Rosa was wearing. It was of a red-and-black material that flattered the olive hues of her skin, cut in the style of Spanish ladies and worn over a white chemise. But it was not the colour that brought a widening to Josie's eyes—that was readily accomplished by the tight-fitting bodice and extreme décolletage of the white chemise that she wore beneath.

The sleeves were pushed off her shoulders. Unlike the high waistlines that were so fashionable with the ladies of Britain and France, this dress was reminiscent of the style of an earlier time, with its waist set lower and pulled in small and tight before the skirt swept out with a fullness of material. The dress revealed much of Rosa's figure and left little to the imagination.

Oh, my! thought Josie and, finding that she was staring, hastily averted her gaze.

'You wish me to help you dress?'

'No, thank you.' Josie could feel a slight warmth wash her cheeks. 'I can manage.' She hoped that the dress that was folded so neatly in her hands was not a match for the one that Rosa was wearing.

There was a moment of silence before Rosa said, 'You are the English Lieutenant Colonel's daughter.' Her eyes were dark and bold.

Josie prepared herself for a defence. 'Yes.'

'The one who murdered the Captain's father.'

'My father did not murder Major Dammartin.' Josie's hackles rose. She eyed the woman angrily. 'The story is a lie perpetrated by the French.'

Rosa shrugged her beautiful bare shoulders in an insolent gesture.

'Thank you, Rosa,' said Josie icily, 'I shall return your clothes as soon as my own are dry.' She got to her feet, signalling to the woman that their conversation was at an end.

'No return,' said Rosa. 'Captain Dammartin, he give me money. You keep clothes.'

'Captain Dammartin paid you?'

Rosa nodded, and her lips curved to a seductive smile. 'Yes, he pay me money. He is very kind.'

A horrible suggestion made itself known to Josie. She blushed at the thought of just what kind of relationship Captain Dammartin might have with this woman. 'You are not a prisoner of the French, are you?'

'A prisoner?' Rosa seemed almost to be laughing at her. 'No, *mademoiselle*, I am not a prisoner… Nothing is simple in love and war,' said Rosa, pulling the hood back up over her head. '*Adios*, Señorita Mallington,' she said, and left the tent.

Dammartin sat his helmet in the corner of the tent and raked a hand through his hair, pushing the sodden strands back from his eyes. The tent was empty. He stood there, relishing the few minutes of solitude. He was tired and cold. His bones were aching and he was hungry. Nothing different from any man that served beneath him. That was not what was bothering Dammartin. He rubbed damp fingers over the rough growth of stubble that had appeared on his face with the progress of the day, and released a sigh. Uneasiness sat in his gut. He sighed again and rubbed harder at the stubble. A noise from the tent flap alerted him. Sergeant Lamont entered.

'Captain.' The small man nodded. 'Rosa has taken the clothes to Mademoiselle Mallington.'

'Good. Thank you, Lamont. You gave Rosa the money?'

'Yes. I told her she should not accept it, sir, but she wants to save.'

'For your future together?'

Lamont laughed. 'She will not stay with an old man like me. Soon she will be off.'

'No, my friend,' said Dammartin. 'I do not think so. You saved her from an ordeal abhorrent to any woman. She will not forget.'

'I demand nothing from her.'

'And that is why she stays. Following the drum is not easy for any woman. There must be something here that makes her wish to stay,' Dammartin said teasingly.

Lamont shrugged as if he did not know, but Dammartin knew better.

'The *mademoiselle*'s portmanteau, it has not appeared?'

'All the baggage, including the women's, has been searched, every tent. It is not to be found.'

'It could not have fallen,' said Lamont.

The two men looked at one another.

'And,' said Lamont, 'a portmanteau is not so easy to steal from the officers' mule train during a day's march.'

'You do not ask the question as to why anyone would want to steal an Englishwoman's portmanteau?' said Dammartin.

'It was not the women. Rosa knows everything that goes on with them. They do not like the *mademoiselle*, but they would not dare to steal from the officers' train. They did not take it.'

'No, the women are not behind this, Claude. Even had they wanted the portmanteau, they could not have lifted the damn thing.'

'There is another possibility, sir.'

Dammartin waited for what the Sergeant would say.

'Mallington is a much hated man and there is no one in this company that does not know she is his daughter. The rain has poured from the skies. She is cold. She is wet. And now she has no dry clothes to change into? Perhaps they play a petty trick to make the *mademoiselle* suffer.'

'Perhaps,' said Dammartin, but in his heart he did not believe that to be the case. If he guessed right, Lieutenant Colonel Mallington's journals lay behind the theft. 'Ask around the men, informally. A portmanteau cannot just disappear. Someone must have seen something.'

'Yes, sir.' said Lamont. 'The food is almost ready. Do you want me to take a tray to Mademoiselle Mallington?'

'I will do that myself. I wish to speak to her.'

Lamont looked at his captain and there was just the suggestion of a smile upon his lips.

'Do not give me that look, Lamont. If I wanted female company of the sort you are thinking, then I would find it in the baggage train. I am not likely to forget who Mademoiselle Mallington's father was.' But even as he said it Dammartin knew that it was not true. He had never used a woman from the baggage train, and as for the other, he had already come too close to forgetting about Mademoiselle Mallington's father.

Lamont laughed and walked off, leaving Dammartin to see to Josephine Mallington.

Josie had just finished lacing the bodice of the dress.

'Excusez-moi, mademoiselle.' The voice from the other side of the tent flap was unmistakably that of Captain Dammartin.

She looked down at just how much that the neckline of Rosa's chemise revealed, and winced. 'A moment, please.' She glanced around the tent in panic, scanning for something with which she could preserve her modesty. There was nothing save the wet clothes spread across the floor or the covers of the makeshift bed. She nipped over to her makeshift bed, whipped off the top blanket and hastily pulled it around her shoulders.

'Mademoiselle Mallington?' he said again and, without waiting further, let himself in through the tent flap.

'Captain Dammartin.' She spun to face him, ensuring that the blanket was firmly in place.

He was no longer wearing his greatcoat, but just his green jacket with its decorated brass buttons. His head was bare, and his dark hair had been slicked back from his face. 'Your dinner.'

Her eyes dropped from his face, lower, to the tray that he held between his hands and the mess tin and half-skin of wine and tumbler upon it.

He sat the tray upon the table.

'Thank you, Captain,' she said, and darted him a glance, suspicious that he had brought the food himself.

He gestured to the table.

She sat down on one of the chairs.

Dammartin sat down in the other.

Josie's heart began to beat a warning tattoo. 'You have news of my portmanteau?' she said slowly.

'Unfortunately, no.'

She waited.

He unstoppered the wine skin and filled the pewter tumbler that sat by its side, clearly intent on staying. 'Eat…' he gestured to the mess tin '…before it grows cold.'

Josie gave a nod and, lifting the spoon, began to eat the watery stew.

She saw his gaze sweep down over the blanket around her shoulders to the full red-and-black skirt covering her legs. 'Rosa brought you the dress, then.'

Another nod.

Dammartin's scar stood prominent and dark against the pallor of his skin. His eyes were dark, but showed nothing of either his intent or his mood. A strange tension sat around him, a stillness almost, as if he were poised, as if he were waiting, and her stomach fluttered with anticipation. She wondered why he was here and what this undercurrent was that flowed between them.

She focused her gaze upon her dinner as her spoon scraped against her tin, the noise seeming too loud in the silence that filled the tent. 'I will return the clothes as soon as I can.'

'There is no need,' he said. 'Rosa has been recompensed for her loss.'

'So I have been told.' Josie looked up at him then, and in her ear whispered the beautiful dark-haired woman's words seemingly taunting her naïvety. For the first time she saw him not as the French Captain who had stormed the monastery at Telemos, nor an officer of Bonaparte's man, not even as her enemy—but just as a man.

She realised that she knew scarcely anything of Dammartin, other than the story of his father. Whether he was married. Whether he had children. Whether he took the beautiful Rosa to his bed at night. Josie did not know why she found the thought of him with the Spanish woman so discomforting. It should not have mattered one iota to her, but, as she sat there in Rosa's dress, she knew that it did matter, very much. She did not want to think of Rosa.

She took a swig of wine. 'Are you married, Captain Dammartin?'

Surprise registered in his eyes. He hesitated before answering. 'I am not married, *mademoiselle*.'

Her heart beat a little faster. She fortified herself with some more wine. 'Rosa is not a prisoner of the French.'

A single dark eyebrow raised at that. 'No, she is no prisoner.' And he looked at her with that too-perceptive gaze.

Silence, and the tension within the tent seemed to tighten a notch.

Josie regretted her impulsiveness. He was the enemy. She was his prisoner. What did it matter what he did? Why was he even here in the tent with her?

'Rosa is Sergeant Lamont's woman,' said Dammartin.

Another silence. Awkward. Tense.

'I just thought…' Josie sipped at the wine and started again. 'I am surprised, that is all, given that she is Spanish.'

'Lamont saved her from being raped and flogged by a group of Spanish guerrillas near her village.'

Josie felt her stomach tighten with shock and the memory of her own experience at the bandit's hands. She pushed the thought away, forced herself to concentrate on Rosa. 'Why would her own people do that to her?'

'They thought she was fraternising with the enemy.'

'And was she…fraternising?'

'She was innocent of the charges, but passions run high

when it comes to our army in Spain. She would have been killed had she returned to her village.'

'So she has travelled with your army ever since.'

'She follows Lamont, and only Lamont,' he said.

'Because he saved her.' And the breath was shaky in her throat as she looked into his eyes.

'Yes.'

They stared at one another, knowing that the subject had come much closer to something that touched them both.

It was Josie that looked away.

'Thank you for bringing me the dinner,' she said, moving the empty mess tin upon the tray. She stood up, hoping that Dammartin would take the hint and leave.

Dammartin lifted the wine skin and refilled the tumbler.

'It has been a long day, sir. I am tired and—'

'Sit down, *mademoiselle*,' he said quietly.

Despite the flair of alarm in Mademoiselle Mallington's eyes, Dammartin knew he could defer his questions no longer. She had eaten, they were both tired...and he had to know for sure.

'You were most distressed by the loss of your portmanteau.'

'I was,' she admitted, but he could hear the note of caution in her voice.

'Clothes can be replaced.' His eyes dropped to the thick, grey blanket draped around her shoulders, knowing that it hid the low-cut Spanish dress beneath.

A slight nod as her gaze wandered over the empty mess tin, the cup and the tray.

'I find myself wondering over your reaction to your missing baggage.' He watched her very carefully.

'I do not understand what you mean, sir.' Still she did not look at him, but her fingers began to toy with the spoon.

'You were distraught, panicked, afraid.'

She forced a dismissive smile. 'I was cold and wet, and I had just learned that all of my possessions had been stolen. What reaction did you expect, Captain?'

'For how long have you followed your father, Mademoiselle Mallington?'

'Most of my life.' He could see her trying to fathom his line of questioning.

'How many years have you, *mademoiselle*?'

'I am two and twenty years old,' she replied. Her fingers played against the spoon's handle.

So young, Dammartin thought. Too damned young to be caught up in this situation. He thought again of Lieutenant Colonel Mallington's utter selfishness. 'Then you know well the rigours of campaign life?'

'Yes, but...' she frowned '...I do not understand what this has to do with my missing portmanteau.'

'I ask myself why Mademoiselle Mallington, who has shown such bravery, such resilience, should be so very upset by a few missing clothes.'

She sat very still.

'And the thought comes to me that perhaps the lady has within her portmanteau something more precious than clothes.'

The colour drained from her cheeks.

'Something that she wishes very much not to fall into French hands.'

Her grip tightened around the spoon.

'Might that be the case, *mademoiselle*?'

Her gaze stayed on the spoon, and he saw how white her knuckles shone.

He let the silence stretch, increasing the tension that was already wound taut between them.

'I begin to think of what is most precious to Mademoiselle Mallington.'

Her breath held.

'And I find the answer is her father.'

There was the slightest widening of her eyes.

He leaned forward, bringing his face closer to hers. 'Lieutenant Colonel Mallington's journals were within your portmanteau.'

The spoon dropped with a clatter. Her gaze swung to his, showing all of her shock and her hurt and her anger. 'It was you!' she whispered, and then she was on her feet, the chair falling over behind her. 'You stole my portmanteau!'

'Mademoiselle Mallington.' He rose.

But she backed away, increasing the space between them, staring at him with outrage blatant upon her face. 'And now that you cannot find what you seek, you come back to me to discover…' She touched her knuckles to her mouth, as if to stopper the words and her breath came in loud ragged gasps.

He moved towards her.

But she trod back farther, shaking her head, warning him away. 'Not once did I think that it might have been you.'

He stepped closer. *'Mademoiselle.'*

'Leave me alone,' she said, and her face was powder white.

His arms closed around her, pulling her against him.

She tried to push him away, but he just held her closer, aware of the tremble through her body.

'Listen to me.'

'No.' She shook her head and pushed harder at his chest. 'Leave me!'

'Josephine.' He gazed down into her eyes, needing to reach her, needing to make her understand. 'I did not steal your portmanteau. What need had I to do such a thing? Had I wanted to search it, do you not think that I would have come in here and done just that?'

Josie looked up into Dammartin's eyes, and his words permeated the mist that had clouded her brain. The air she had been holding tight and still within her lungs escaped in a single fast breath.

He was right. Dammartin would have emptied her whole portmanteau before her very eyes without the slightest compunction.

'I…' She shook her head, unwilling to betray her father further by admitting the existence of the journals. Dammartin was still French. He was still her enemy. 'You are mistaken, Captain, there were no journals within my portmanteau.'

'Perhaps,' he said, but she knew that he was not convinced.

'I would just like to have my possessions returned to me, that is all.'

He looked deep into her eyes. 'A portmanteau is not so easy to hide on the war trail. If it is here, then it shall be found. I will discover who is behind this, *mademoiselle*.'

He *was* French. He *was* her enemy. But in that moment she believed what he said. And now that the panic had gone she became aware that she was still standing in the French Captain's arms, and that he was staring down at her with an intensity that made her shiver.

'You are cold,' he said quietly.

'No,' she whispered, conscious that she was trembling. She should have pulled herself free, for the grip of his hands had gentled. But Josie just stood there.

His hand moved up and she felt the stroke of his thumb

brush against her mouth and her lips burned where he touched.

There was only the sound of their breath between them.

'*Mademoiselle,*' he whispered, and not once did the intensity of his gaze falter. His eyes had darkened to a smoulder that held her so completely that she could not look away. It seemed as if she were transfixed by him, unable to move, unaware of anything save him, and the strange tension that seemed to bind them together.

Her eyes flickered over the harsh, lean angles of his face, over the straightness of his nose, over the dark line of his scar, down to his lips. And she was acutely conscious of the hardness of his chest and hip and, against her, the long length of his legs. The breath wavered in her throat, and she was sure that he would hear its loud raggedness.

'Josephine,' he said, and she could hear the hoarse strain within his voice. 'God help me, but you tempt me to lose my very soul.'

His hand moved round to cradle her head. His face lowered towards hers, and she knew that he was going to kiss her. Slowly Josie tilted her face up in response, and the blanket slipped from her shoulders to fall upon the groundsheet.

A noise sounded from outside: a noisy tread over the grass, a man clearing his throat.

They froze.

'Captain Dammartin,' a man's voice said.

The spell was broken.

The truth of Josie's situation hit her. One of Dammartin's hands was threaded within her hair, the other rested against the small of her back. Her blanket lay upon the floor, showing Rosa's dress and just how much it revealed. Their bodies seemed to cling to together.

Dammartin released her and moved towards the tent

flap, opening it by the smallest crack so that whoever stood there would not have a view of Josie.

There was the soft, fast lilt of French voices. They spoke so low she had to strain to hear them. She did not catch every word, but she heard enough of them to know why Sergeant Lamont had seen fit to interrupt his captain. The lantern within the tent created the perfect lighting for a shadow show. The Captain's actions and those of Mademoiselle Mallington were clear to see for anyone outside the tent…and their actions were not going unnoticed by the men. Josie's face scalded with heat.

If Dammartin was embarrassed, there was no sign of it upon his face as he let the tent-flap drop and faced her.

'Pardon, *mademoiselle*…I must go.'

She bit at her lip, uncertain of what to say, knowing what they had been on the brink of doing.

He gave her one last look before he turned and was gone.

Chapter Nine

In view of Lamont's words, Josie extinguished the lantern before undressing for bed. She kept on only Rosa's shift and laid the blankets on to the bed once more before climbing within.

She lay there in the darkness, and the silence. Her heart was beating with a strong, steady thud, and her body tingled with awareness of what would have happened had not Lamont interrupted. Dammartin would have kissed her and she would have kissed him back. She was sure of it. Not a kiss that had started as a punishment, not a kiss to humiliate her before his men, but a real kiss between a man and a woman.

Her fingers touched to her mouth, exploring gently just as Dammartin had done. She knew that she had wanted him to kiss her—Captain Pierre Dammartin, the man responsible for her father's death, her enemy. It was a sobering realisation, and one that brought a wave of guilt and shame. Lord help her, what would her father have said? She was supposed to be fighting the enemy, not fraternising with him. And she remembered what Dammartin had said of Rosa and the terrible consequences of the accusations against her.

She groaned and whispered into the darkness, 'Papa, forgive me.' She lay there for a long while, contemplating what she had come so close to doing, and the madness of it and the badness of it.

Josie had been around soldiers and the army for most of her life. There had been many officers who had been friendly towards her, there had been some who had taken her hand, but not one had ever tried to kiss her. Men did not see Josie in that light. Not even during that awful year in England when she had been dangled before every young man in the hope of catching her a husband. Josie, who could ride a horse faster than most men and shoot a rifle with accuracy, and make good of the hardship of the campaign trail, had floundered and stumbled beneath the ridicule. The men had thought her gaucherie something to be laughed at; the women had been more spiteful.

Dammartin was different: he did not laugh at her; he did not make her feel foolish or inept. Indeed, he made her feel alive and tingling and excited; he made her want to press her lips to his and feel his strong arms surround her. With him she forgot all else—the journals and her papa and the bandits and Telemos. There was only the French Captain and the prospect of his kiss…and the realisation both shocked and appalled her.

Her eyes peered though the darkness as if she could see through two layers of canvas, into the neighbouring tent, which housed Lamont and Molyneux and…Dammartin. A tingle ran down Josie's spine just at his name. She closed her eyes and prayed for the strength to resist her own wanton nature.

But Dammartin was not in the nearby tent. Only Molyneux sat in there. Dammartin and Lamont stood across the field beneath a copse of trees that, while being distant from the tents, showed a clear view of them. Lamont was smoking his long clay pipe, drawing the tobacco in the pipe head to glow like a small orange spot in the darkness. The sweet scent of tobacco smoke surrounded them. Occasional droplets still dripped from the tree's bare branches, remnants of the day's downpour.

Lamont sucked at his pipe and seemed content to stare up at the dark grey cloud that covered the night sky above them.

There were no stars. The brightness of the moon was masked by the dense cover. The night was dark and gloomy.

Lamont sniffed. 'You want her, the English *mademoiselle.*'

Dammartin stared over at his tent which now lay in darkness. 'She is the daughter of my father's murderer; she bears the family name that I have for so long lived to hate. She is British, my very enemy, the one woman of all that should repel me.' His mouth curved in a crooked smile filled with irony. 'And none of it is enough to stop me.' He glanced round at his sergeant. 'That is a problem indeed, Claude.'

'Some problems are easily solved.'

'Not this one.'

Lamont said nothing.

'Where Mademoiselle Mallington is concerned, it seems that I can no longer trust in my own resolve. Had it not been for your interruption...'

'I am sorry to have spoiled things, but I thought that you would wish to—'

'You did right.' Dammartin cut him off. 'I am grateful that you stopped me.'

'Are you really?' Lamont turned his gaze upon his captain.

Dammartin looked right back at him. 'Do you think I want to insult the memory of my father?'

'I know what his murder did to you, Pierre.'

Dammartin turned his gaze back to the tent.

'What of the girl? From what I saw tonight, she is not averse to your interest.'

Dammartin thought of the softness in Josephine Mallington's eyes, of the parting of her sweet lips as her face tilted up to his, of the way she had stood within his arms, so trusting. 'It makes no difference. It is all of it still wrong.'

'There has been something between the two of you from the very beginning, a spark, an attraction, call it what you will. You cannot fight such a powerful desire, for it will always win in the end. If you truly do not wish to have bedded her before we have reached our destination, then there is only one thing you may do: send her into another's care—Emmern, La Roque or one of the infantry officers, it does not matter who, just as long as she is no longer here with you. Otherwise...' He shrugged. 'It is your choice.'

Dammartin rubbed at the stubble on his chin. 'I am sure that she still holds information regarding Mallington that may be of use. If I let her go, then I lose my last hope of understanding why Mallington killed my father.' He looked at his sergeant. 'And there is another matter to consider, Claude.' He thought of the journals. 'The loss of Mademoiselle Mallington's portmanteau is perhaps not as straightforward as it seems. I suspect she had her father's journals hidden within some kind of secret compartment within the portmanteau.'

'I understand now why the *mademoiselle* was so upset to hear the portmanteau was gone. So how did the thief know of the journals?'

'I do not know. Mademoiselle Mallington is not foolish enough to speak of them to anyone here. There was a mention made of the journals when I walked with her the other evening, but we were some distance from the camp and we were alone. I suppose that there might have been an eavesdropper.'

Lamont looked grim. 'Were that the case, it would have to have been one of our own men.' He sucked harder on the pipe. 'I do not like it.'

'I am not enamoured of the idea myself.'

Lamont's small, beady eyes glittered in the darkness. 'There is something uneasy in the air, Pierre.'

'I sense it too.'

They sat in silence. Pipe smoke drifted up and disappeared into the night sky. 'What will you do with Mademoiselle Mallington?' asked Lamont.

The two men looked across the field to Josie's tent.

'I do not know, my old friend, I really do not know.'

The next morning was grey, but without rain. For all its absence the ground was still sodden.

Josie awoke feeling surprisingly calm. Last night, with Dammartin, had been an aberration, a temporary madness that would not happen again. She had been drenched through and exhausted. She had suffered the loss of all her possessions and her father's precious journals. And Dammartin had guessed the truth of the journals. It was little wonder she had been rendered...susceptible... to strange fancies. But morning was here and Josie was strong again, strong enough to face the French captain.

'Mademoiselle Mallington?'

She jumped, her heart suddenly racing, for the voice that called her name came from immediately outside her tent.

'It is I, Lamont.'

She scrabbled from beneath the blankets, wrapping one around her shoulders.

'*Mademoiselle,*' he said again, and she recognised the Sergeant's accented tones.

'Sergeant Lamont,' she said quickly, trying to forestall his entry. 'I am coming.'

But Lamont was not like Dammartin; he merely stood by the door and waited.

'The Captain, he sends me with food for you.' He passed a mug and mess tin into her hands.

The heat rose in her cheeks. 'Thank you, sir.'

Swirls of steam rose from the mug. The smell of the coffee and warmed bread spread with honey caused her stomach to growl. 'I do not understand...'

The little Sergeant looked at her knowingly.

Her cheeks grew hotter as she remembered just what Lamont and all the rest of Dammartin's men had witnessed last night.

'The fires, they are put out,' Lamont said by way of explanation. 'We leave soon. Captain Dammartin has sent me to collect your bedding and wet clothing to be transported. I will wait here until it is ready, *mademoiselle.*'

She gave a nod and disappeared back inside the tent to hurriedly dress herself in Rosa's dress and woollen stockings before returning with her own clothing, neatly folded and still damp, on top of the blankets and pillow.

Lamont said nothing, just took the pile from her and walked back across the field, leaving her standing there in the stark morning light in the revealing Spanish dress and her hair flowing long and loose around her shoulders.

She watched him go, her focus shifting to look beyond him across the field. There, in her line of vision, was Captain Dammartin talking to a trooper. He was dressed just as he had been last night in full uniform, the green jacket neatly brushed, its carmine collar clean and bright, the long curved sabre hanging down by his left leg. He was without his helmet, his hair being ruffled by the breeze; his stance was relaxed and easy. As her gaze rested upon him, he looked up and for a moment their eyes met across the field.

Josie, her cheeks burning hotter than ever, retreated quickly into the tent. With shaky hands, she drank the coffee and ate the bread and eventually her heart slowed enough to allow her to fix some semblance of order to her hair. The trudge of boots sounded outside, troopers' voices—Dammartin's men come to dismantle the tent. Grabbing her damp woollen cloak and her small leather satchel, she squared her shoulders and walked out to face the day.

In the light of Lamont's words the previous evening, Dammartin was taking great care to stay well away from Josephine Mallington, but although he had sent his sergeant to collect her clothing, as he would have him deliver it again this evening, it was his own portmanteau into which Dammartin packed the clothes.

There has been something between the two of you from the very beginning, a spark, an attraction, call it what you will. You cannot fight such a powerful desire, for it will always win in the end. The words haunted him. But Dammartin would fight it and, contrary to Lamont's warning, he would win…he had to, for the sake of all that he believed in, for the sake of his father.

The luxury of Major La Roque's tent made Dammartin's look like something fit for a peasant. Normally the Major preferred to take over some local's house when he camped. Tonight, in the middle of the mountains with no buildings as far as the eye could see, he had had no choice but to sleep under canvas the same as the rest of his officers and men. Canvas is where the similarity ended.

Firstly, the Major's tent was enormous, with partitions that separated it into two rooms. Secondly, it was decorated with fine rugs and a few items of furniture. Within the impromptu dining room where the Major was hosting dinner there was also a long dining table on which a white tablecloth, matching napkins, china plates, bowls and crystal glasses had been set. Along the longitudinal midline of the table were three silver-branched candelabras, in which beeswax candles burned extravagantly. Decanters of red and white wine sat on a small tray, their cut-crystal bodies sparkling in the glow of the candles. The brandy would not be brought out until later. There were ten guests for dinner, all of them commissioned officers.

Each man's jacket was spotless, the blue of France's liberty or the green of her dragoons and chasseurs, the uniforms decorated with cording and frogging, sashes and epaulettes. Spirits were good, and the Major was in generous mood as usual. The dinner, served by the Major's staff, made the men's mess taste like pig swill, and not for the first time Dammartin wondered that a meal of such superior taste and quality could be prepared in a field kitchen with provisions that had been carried by mules for days across country.

They spoke of their mission and that soon they would reach Ciudad Rodrigo. They spoke of Bonaparte and of Paris. They spoke of the whores that followed the army. They ate. They drank. They smoked cigars. They took snuff. The waxing moon was high in the sky when the Major drew a close to the evening, each man deep in his cups, and each one happier for having spent the evening in Major La Roque's company.

Dammartin let the others leave first, waiting until they had all gone before he spoke. 'I wondered if I might talk to you, sir...in an informal capacity.'

'Of course, of course, Pierre.' La Roque clasped a friendly arm across the young captain's shoulders. 'Come, boy, sit down. Let us have a drink together, mmm?' He poured some brandy into two glasses and handed one to his godson. 'So, how are things with the 8th Dragoons?'

'They are well.'

'The presence of your prisoner is not causing any problems?'

'None,' replied Dammartin, wondering if the Major had come to hear of last night.

'Good, good. I am glad to hear it. I had thought that the fact she is Mallington's daughter might affect your sensibilities.'

A vision of Josephine Mallington in that revealing dress with her fair hair all tumbling down across her shoulders and her lips parted and moist, ready for his kiss, swam into his head. 'Nothing I cannot deal with,' he said with a great deal more confidence than he felt.

With a leisurely, lazy action La Roque swirled the brandy around his glass. 'Does she know what Mallington did?'

'She refuses to believe it.'

'I suppose that is to be expected.'

'Mademoiselle Mallington's portmanteau was recently stolen.'

La Roque swigged his brandy. 'I am not surprised that her presence has roused dislike among the men. Everyone knows who her father was.'

'I do not think that it is that simple. It is this of which I wished to speak to you.'

La Roque raised his brows in surprise.

'I believe that she may have had hidden some of her father's campaign journals within the baggage. I cannot be certain.' Dammartin thought of Josephine Mallington's reaction in his tent last night. 'But I am convinced that it is so; I think that the portmanteau was stolen for the journals.'

'But why would *she* be carrying her father's journals?'

Dammartin shrugged. 'Because they would not be looked for in the baggage of his daughter?'

'Pierre, you are too much focused on Mallington. You grow obsessed over him. You do not even know that these journals were in the portmanteau. It is more likely that one of your troopers took the portmanteau as a prank because she is Mallington's daughter. I am only surprised that it has taken so long for something like this to happen. She is, after all, a most hated woman.' La Roque sighed, and leaning forward, placed a hand on Dammartin's shoulder. 'Pierre, Mallington is dead. You must put this behind you and move on, for the sake of your father.'

'Perhaps you are right.' Dammartin sighed and turned his gaze to the brandy glass. The meniscus did not move. The pungent aroma drifted up to fill his nostrils amid the fading smells of cigar smoke and food and low-burning candles.

'Maybe it would be better to send Mademoiselle Mallington to travel in my company. At least then she would not be around to stir up such painful memories,' said La Roque.

Dammartin thought of Lamont's advice and for a moment he was tempted to accept his godfather's offer, but that would mean an admission of Josephine Mallington's power over him, and Dammartin was not about to admit any such thing. 'Thank you, but no. I can handle Mademoiselle Mallington.'

The Major drained the rest of his brandy and the glass hit the table with a clumsy thump. He rose from his seat. 'If you change your mind, you need only say the word. You know I only want to make things easier for you.' He swayed rather unsteadily on his feet and kissed Dammartin's cheeks. 'Goodnight, Pierre.'

'Goodnight, sir.' Dammartin made his way out into the freshness of the cool night air.

La Roque stood by the tent flap and watched him go, raising a hand to bid him good-night. He stood there a long time after Dammartin had disappeared from sight, still looking as if he could follow the Captain's trail through the blackness of night. The smile slipped from his face, and his gaze was hard and thoughtful.

Josie woke with a start, her heart beating too fast within her chest, her throat tight with emotion. She lay very still and let the image of the room in the monastery at Telemos slowly fade. She forced her breathing to slow from the ragged pant, wiped the tears from her cheeks and blew her nose.

The night was unnaturally quiet. It seemed that the silence hissed within her ears.

She pulled the blanket higher so that it tucked beneath her chin.

The moon was bright outside, casting a hint of light through the thick canvas of the tent to lift something of the pitch from the black. She forced her eyes to stay open, would not let them shut until the last of the nightmare had left her. But it seemed that nothing would stop the thoughts in her head. Even with her eyes staring up at the canvas above her head, she could see the bullets that annihilated the door within the monastery, wood splintering as if it were feeble with rot. Without mercy the nightmare pulled her once more into its clutches. Her eyes closed.

The stench of powder and blood surrounded her. The line of six men crouched across the room, her father on her left side, the bare wall on her right. It was almost as if she could feel the weight of the rifle pulling at her arms, and the terrible slowness of its loading. Her fingers did not move fast enough, snatching at bullets, fumbling with powder, and she could feel the terrible frustration at her own dull speed. The noise all around was deafening and she knew that the attack would not fail. But it was not the French who were firing through the door, it was the bandits.

Smith took a bullet in the thigh and kept on shooting. Cleeves fell without so much as a whisper, a round red hole in the white of his forehead. The men's muskets were firing twice as fast as Josie's. She heard her father's shout, *We will not surrender!* But as she looked through the disintegrating wood of the door she saw the face of the bandit laughing.

Josie sat bolt upright, suddenly, quickly awake. The blankets fell back, and, grabbing one up, she ran to the mouth of the tent, unfastening the flap with shaking fingers to stumble out into the brightness of the night.

The fat moon hung shining and high in the sky and stars were scattered as tiny jewelled pinpricks. The air was so icy as to make her gasp as she stood there, outside her tent, not moving, looking up at the sky, glad of the harshness of the cold, feeling the cleansing purge of the chilled night air enter her lungs. Out here, in the open, the drowsy drug of sleep had no power. She was awake in the here and now, and the nightmare seemed far away. So she stood with the blanket wrapped around her and let the peace enfold her.

She had no idea of what time it was, but she knew by

the empty state of the camp and the burned-down fires that it was late. The men were all in their tents asleep. Everywhere was silent.

She had only been there some few minutes when she heard the footsteps come across the grass from the direction of the horses. She turned towards her tent, then instinctively glanced back at the presence she sensed.

Dammartin was standing at the other side of what remained of the fire, the flicker of tiny flames lighting his face from below, making him appear dangerous.

A shiver swept across her stomach. She gave a small nod of her head to acknowledge his presence and turned her face back to the tent. Her fingers closed around the flap, drawing back the heavy canvas.

His feet moved. 'Mademoiselle Mallington.' His voice was as soft as a caress, and when she looked round again, he was standing right behind her.

She let the canvas slip through her fingers and turned to face him. 'Captain Dammartin,' she whispered.

He looked devastatingly handsome.

Warning bells began to ring in her head. She took a step back and felt the brush of the tent against her shift. The chill of the ground rose up through the soles of her bare feet.

'You could not sleep?' he said quietly.

'No.' A little shake of her head, and the long tresses of her hair fluttered pale and loose in the moonlight. He was looking at her with that same intense expression as last night within the tent, before Lamont's interruption. And for all that she knew that she should not, Josie could not help herself from looking right back.

They stared at one another in the silence of the surrounding night, without words. A tension that was taut between them holding them there, that neither seemed able to break.

He stepped closer, so that there was nothing to separate his long cavalry boots from the hem of her shift.

Nervousness fluttered through Josie. She glanced away, breaking the gaze that seemed to lock them together, knowing that she should not be standing here in the middle of the night talking to this man who was her captor, this very man responsible for the deaths of her father and his men. She had to go now, walk away while she still could.

'I should go.' She lowered her gaze to the polished black sheen of his boots, and made to move.

'No.'

She felt the warmth of his hand catch gently at her fingers, and glanced back up.

The moon touched a silver frosting to his hair, and revealed each and every plane that sculpted his face.

Josie stood where she was, captured by the magic of the moonlight and the man.

The fingers of one hand entwined with hers, anchoring her to the spot, while the other hand caressed her cheek, sliding down to her chin. Slowly, with a touch that seemed too light, too gentle to be from the tall, strong man that stood before her, he tilted her face up to his.

'Mademoiselle Mallington,' he said softly. 'Josephine.' And his eyes were filled with a depth of emotion she had not seen before and such promise.

She knew that he would kiss her, and, Lord help her, but she wanted him to, so very much.

His mouth lowered towards hers.

She stood on tiptoe and reached her face up, her lips parting in expectation.

He took her with such gentle possession as to wipe everything else from her mind, and it seemed to Josie as if she had waited all her life for this moment, this wonderful, amazing sensation that was so much more than just a kiss.

His arms stretched around her, holding her to him, his palms warm and enticing against her back, stroking her, caressing her. She ran her hands up the wool of his coat, feeling the strength of the muscle across his back. And amid the warmth of him, the smell of him, the brandied taste of him, was the feeling that this was meant to be, that she had met her destiny, and nothing had ever felt so right.

She did not remember that he was the enemy. She forgot all about her father and the terrible events of Telemos and the bandits. She lost herself in his kiss and for Josie, in that moment, there was nothing else.

He kissed her gently, undemanding, revelling in the sweetness of her. She tasted of innocence, of all that was goodness and light, and her purity cleansed the darkness from Dammartin's soul.

For so long he had thought of nothing other than wreaking vengeance upon the man who had murdered his father. And now that man's daughter was in his arms, and there was in her something so incorruptible and pure that she filled his very mind and there was no room for thoughts of his father or hers, no room for any other thoughts at all.

He wanted her, all of her, every last bit of her, all of her warmth, all of her softness, all of her comfort. She was like a fine down pillow on which a man might lay his head and never wish to rise. He wanted her and his body ached with the need.

She met his mouth with encouragement, but in it he knew her innocence. The small, soft movements of her hands against his back and the press of her body against his warmed his blood to a fire so that it seemed that he was not in the barren winter plains of Iberia but somewhere else altogether. Dammartin had never known a feeling like it, and he wanted it never to stop.

His hand slid beneath the blanket, feeling the curves of her woman's body through the thin linen of her borrowed shift, knowing that only it separated him from her nakedness. He cupped her buttocks, pressing her closer to his hardness as his tongue entwined with hers in such erotic play to leave him breathless with desire.

'Josephine,' he whispered, and gentled the kiss against her lips so that he might look down into her eyes. He stroked the silk of her hair, stroked the softness of her cheek, felt the raggedness of her breath against his fingers.

'Captain Dammartin,' she said, and he heard his need mirrored in her breathy words.

'Pierre,' he said, 'my name is Pierre.'

'Pierre,' she whispered as his mouth closed again on hers.

He wanted her, wanted her more than life itself.

A noise sounded. He glanced towards the tent that he shared with his lieutenant and sergeant—movement, the sleepy clambering of a man with a need in the night.

He reacted in an instant, pushing her within the flap of her tent and moving quickly round to the other side of the fire to retrace the steps he had taken not so very long ago, pretending that he had only just returned.

Molyneux appeared at the mouth of the tent, his hair ruffled, his expression sleepy. 'Captain?' He yawned.

'I hope you have not stolen my bloody blankets again,' said Dammartin.

'Not this time,' said Molyneux, and, crawling from the tent, pulled his boots on and made his way across the field to the latrines.

Dammartin said nothing, just entered the tent, and stripped off his clothes as best he could in the dark. As he lay down in his bed, he could still taste her sweetness on his lips. And he knew that this battle with his desire for Josephine Mallington was going to be a great deal more difficult than anticipated.

Josie lay flat on her back in her tent, the blankets loose around her. For once she was not cold. Her whole body tingled with warmth, and her lips felt hot and swollen where Captain Dammartin had kissed her. She touched a finger gently to their surface, as if she could not believe what had just passed between herself and the French Captain. And in truth she did not. Yet even as she lay there with her heart still thudding and her blood still rushing, her eyes slipped to the canvas wall on her left-hand side through which was the tent in which Dammartin slept, so close that she could have called his name in a soft voice and he would have heard her.

A strange kind of vibrancy flowed through her and it seemed to Josie that she had never felt more alive. She forgot all that had gone before, all of the bandit's attack, all of the anxiety of the 60th's sacrifice, all of the horror of Telemos. For the first time since that terrible day, Josie felt glad to be alive. She would not sleep, she told herself. Her body hummed with wakefulness and something that was almost joy. She closed her eyes, and sleep surrounded her like a warm woollen cloak. Josie sank into it without even knowing that she did so. She was cosy and cosseted within its dark comfort, and her sleep was untroubled.

'You say that he kissed her?' Major La Roque narrowed his eyes and peered at the man before him.

'Yes, sir, and with a great deal of passion.'

'And there have been no other incidents of this nature?'

'No, sir, apart from those of which you already know:

when he kissed her in punishment for her slapping him, and in his tent the other evening he had her in his arms. Had not Lamont interrupted them, I believe that he would have kissed her then.'

'And the night they left the campsite together, you are sure there was nothing then?'

'Nothing other than talk.'

'And what talk! The journals will prove most useful. You have done well so far. Your loyalty will not go unrewarded.'

Lieutenant Molyneux smiled and took the proffered glass of brandy from Major La Roque's hand. 'Thank you, sir.'

'So, there is something between Captain Dammartin and Mallington's daughter. What do you think of that?'

Molyneux sipped the brandy from the glass that he had been given and looked cagily at his superior officer. 'I confess I find it most surprising, sir, given the history of their fathers.'

'It is a damnable abomination, that's what it is.' La Roque poured the rest of the brandy down his throat and set the glass down hard upon the table. 'What is she like, this Mademoiselle Mallington? Is she pretty? Does she have a figure to drive a man's senses from his head?'

Molyneux cleared his throat, unsure of how much to reveal.

'Come, come, Molyneux, do not be shy. Tell me, do you find her distasteful?'

The Lieutenant swallowed hard. 'No, she is...a most attractive woman.'

'Good.'

Molyneux glanced up quickly, the surprise clear across his face.

'Captain Dammartin does not know what he is doing. The shock of meeting Mallington has affected him. But he will disgrace himself if we let him continue as he is. This Mallington woman will turn him into a laughingstock. The next thing we know, he will be crawling between her legs. What would the Emperor say to that? Jean Dammartin's son ploughing Mallington's daughter!'

Molyneux kept quiet.

'Jean would turn in his grave,' said La Roque. 'Dammartin was my friend. I saw what that bastard Mallington did to him. And I've still got the scars of what he did to me.'

Molyneux nodded, placatingly.

'It is up to us to protect Captain Dammartin.'

'Yes, sir. Perhaps you could forbid him from seeing her, move her into the care of another company.'

'You have much to learn of human nature, Molyneux. If I take her from him, all I shall succeed in doing is to make him want her all the more. No, we must be a little more clever than that…'

Molyneux took another sip of brandy.

'I have another little job for you, Lieutenant.'

'Sir?'

The Major smiled. 'It might not be all that bad if you try to forget who she is, and you did say that you found her attractive.'

Molyneux looked across at La Roque.

'I have heard that you have quite a reputation with the women, Lieutenant, so I am sure that what I ask will not be beyond you. We must all do what we can for the good of our country, must we not, Lieutenant?'

'We must, sir.'

'Good, for here is what I want you to do…'

Josie awoke the next morning in a panic, her eyes springing open immediately.

She could hear the milling about of soldiers. Footsteps,

chatter, clank of mess tins, the smoky aroma of coffee and of burnt wood. Daylight shone bright through the paleness of the canvas.

There was only one thought in her head and that was the French Captain's kiss. Dammartin had kissed her and she had kissed him back with just as much vigour, and with every bit as much wanting. She gave a groan and buried her face against the pillow.

She had kissed him! He was French and her captor. He was the captain of the force that had destroyed her father and his men. He was the man that believed her father guilty of a heinous crime. Josie clutched a hand to her forehead. *Fraternising with the enemy*—the phrase seemed to taunt her.

What was this madness that seemed now to overcome her in Dammartin's presence? Nothing could excuse it. Her behaviour was worse than reprehensible. She was a disgrace to the British, a disgrace to her father and the men of the 60th that had died. And yet if Dammartin strode into her tent this very moment and took her in his arms, she could not trust her foolish, selfish, traitorous heart that she would not kiss him again.

She got to her feet, pulled on her borrowed clothes and began to fold up her bedding.

'Pardon, Mademoiselle Mallington.'

The voice from the tent flap made her jump and she thought for a moment that it was Dammartin. Her heart began to race and the blanket that she had been folding slipped from her fingers. She turned to face him.

But it was not Dammartin that stood there.

'Lieutenant Molyneux.' She was caught unawares, her thoughts still lingering with Dammartin. 'Is there any news of my portmanteau?' she asked, smoothing back her hair with a flustered hand and wondering why the Lieutenant was here. Only Dammartin strode straight into the tent.

'Unfortunately not, *mademoiselle*. It is not easy to lose all of one's possessions.'

'No, but Rosa has been kind enough to lend me some clothing.' Josie suddenly remembered that she was, at this very minute, wearing the red-and-black dress, and without the protection of her cloak. She darted a rather horrified glance at the Lieutenant, but he was looking at the bedding she had been folding and his expression was kindly. Molyneux was too much the gentleman to stare at what the dress revealed.

'The Captain has sent me to collect your possessions to be transported this morning, *mademoiselle*.'

'Of course, Lieutenant. I am afraid that my clothes are still damp.'

'There has been little chance for them to dry.'

She sat the clothing on top of the blankets and pillow and passed the pile to Molyneux.

'At least it does not rain this morning.' He smiled. 'You see, you are making me like the English with all this talk of the weather,' he teased.

Molyneux's kind lightheartedness dispelled her tension. She felt herself smile in response as she opened the tent flap for him to leave. Across the field, Dammartin was talking to Lamont. The smile fled her face. Her heart began to race as her eyes met his. The expression on his face was hard and angry. All of the darkness was back, and she wondered that he could be the same man who had kissed her with such passion and tenderness last night. And as she looked, he coldly turned his gaze from hers.

Dammartin, together with half his men, watched Molyneux leave Mademoiselle Mallington's tent, the Lieutenant's arms piled high with her clothing and bedding. He saw, as did the men, the way she held the tent flap open for him, and smiled so sweetly. His eyes noted how very well the fully exposed red-and-black dress showed off her figure. The men's tongues were practically hanging out over the sight of her as she stood so boldly in the entrance of the tent.

The tent flap had barely closed before Molyneux managed to drop half her clothing upon the wetness of the ground; when he had gathered it back up again, Mademoiselle Mallington's shift was clearly displayed on the top, while one of her stockings dangled precariously from the side.

'Captain,' said Molyneux, when he reached him. 'Mademoiselle Mallington asked me to carry this.'

'Then carry it,' said Dammartin coolly.

From among the troopers someone laughed.

'See to your horses,' he snapped at them, and the men exchanged glances as they moved to follow his command.

It was late afternoon when they had set up their camp for the night near Hoyos. The light had gone by the time the meal was ready, paltry as it was—a thin stew of onions with the odd lump of meat. Supplies were running low and the foraging parties had come back with little. Having finished the dregs of the insubstantial meal, Dammartin was sitting at his desk within the shared tent, writing his report. The men would go hungry again tonight. He had just dipped his pen into the ink when Lamont appeared.

'Sir.'

Dammartin glanced up at him, and, seeing the expression on his sergeant's face, laid the pen down within its holder. 'What is it, Claude?' he asked quietly.

Lamont's voice lowered. 'Lieutenant Molyenux is within your tent with Mademoiselle Mallington.'

'They are alone together?'

Lamont nodded.

Dammartin quirked an eyebrow. 'It is up to Mademoiselle Mallington how she conducts herself.'

'There is something that you should see, sir.'

Dammartin stilled. Lamont would not have come to fetch him if it were not necessary. He gave a grim nod and followed the older man outside.

He could hear the men's appreciative murmurs as they stared. His gaze followed round to what their attention was so riveted upon. His tent was light and illuminated, the canvas the perfect screen on which the silhouettes of those within were projected. Josephine and Molyneux were standing close. They were talking, and Josephine had taken Molyneux's hand up between hers. Her head was bent as if she would kiss his hand. It was a most intimate gesture and one that roused a fury in Dammartin.

He had thought her an innocent. He had thought that the attraction that had exploded between them was unique and special. The shadow show playing out on Mademoiselle Mallington's tent showed him that he had been wrong. His lip snarled in disgust at his own weakness. She was Mallington's daughter, in truth.

He became aware of his men's attention, that they were watching to see what he would do. And his pride burned sore. He wanted to go in there and pulverise Molyneux's perfect handsome face. He wanted to call Josephine Mallington the whore that she was.

'Captain.' Lamont's voice was low, his hand touched lightly against Dammartin's arm to stay him.

'The men are expecting a show, Claude. It would be a pity to disappoint them.'

'Pierre,' Lamont whispered with urgency. 'Think how you do this.'

'Do not worry,' said Dammartin, and his mouth curved to a hard cynical smile. 'I shall not give them quite the show they are expecting.' And with that he walked towards his tent.

Chapter Ten

Josie was adjusting Molyneux's hand within her own directly beneath the bright hanging light of the lantern to peer closer at his palm.

'I feel so foolish to bother you with such a trivial complaint,' said the Lieutenant sheepishly.

'I am afraid that I still cannot see it properly, sir.'

'The light, it is poor and I fear I have driven the wretched thing deeper when I tried to pull it out. I would not ask, but I fear the infection will grow.' He looked up at her, anxiety clear in his velvet grey eyes. 'It is my sabre hand.'

'Do not worry, I will fetch the splinter out for you.' She smiled wryly.

'Perhaps you think me less than a man to worry over such a small thing, but I watched my good friend die because of a dirty splinter of wood. He thought it nothing, and left it where it was. Two months later, he was dead from a poisoning of the blood.'

Josie's heart softened at his words. 'I am sorry that you lost your friend.' Her eyes met his briefly in compassion before she turned her focus to his hand once more. The small sewing needle between her fingers glinted in the light. 'Now hold still and I will soon have the splinter out.'

He smiled at her.

She bent her head and concentrated on a delicate probing of the Lieutenant's hand with the needle. It was strange to notice that, as she held on to Molyneux's hand, his touch elicited none of the same reactions that she had experienced with Dammartin. Had it been Dammartin's hand held so gently between her own…

'Mademoiselle Mallington and Lieutenant Molyneux.' There was no mistaking the steel beneath the quiet control of the voice.

Josie gave a gasp and jumped, inadvertently pricking Molyneux with the needle.

Dammartin stood within the tent. The line of his jaw was hard and uncompromising, and his eyes filled with a deadly darkness.

Molyneux paled and drew his hand swiftly from Josie's grasp.

'Captain Dammartin,' she said, her heart suddenly racing. 'You startled me.'

'So I see, *mademoiselle*.' His voice was harsh.

Outside the murmur of voices had gone; the camp was in total silence.

'Lieutenant Molyneux has a splinter in his hand. I am in the process of removing it. If you do not mind, I shall have it out shortly.'

'Please, go ahead. Do not allow my presence to stop you,' said Dammartin. 'I am content to wait.'

Josie ignored his sarcastic tone. She reached for Molyneux's hand, conscious of Dammartin's scrutiny.

'It is no matter, *mademoiselle*.' Molyneux stepped away, looking awkwardly at Dammartin. *'Capitaine,'* he said, and, with a salute, hurriedly left.

Josie was alone with Dammartin.

She stood unmoving beneath the lantern light, the small needle flashing silver in her hand. She could sense his tension. It was latent, coiled, ready to spring, the calm before the storm. She did not know what had happened to make him so angry, yet she had the unassailable notion that it was related to Molyneux and her removing the splinter. Very carefully, she set the needle down upon the tabletop.

'Is there something wrong, sir?' She forced her voice to stay calm and low.

He walked towards her and stopped where Molyneux had stood.

Josie's heart was thudding so hard it seemed to echo within the silence that surrounded them.

He glanced at the table to where the needle lay. 'You were removing a splinter?'

'Yes. What else did you think that I was doing?'

Every angle of his face sharpened. His eyes narrowed ever so slightly. The scar was livid against his cheek. Everything about him was dark and predatory and dangerous. 'What else indeed might a woman standing so close to a man and holding his hand within her own be doing? Every dragoon in this company has been asking himself that question this evening. The lantern, it lights your silhouettes so well.'

She flushed scarlet at his implication. 'I have done nothing improper.' Even as she said it, the realisation of just how her actions might have been misconstrued was dawning on her. But beneath Dammartin's cold, arrogant stare she was not about to admit any such thing. 'And if the lantern has shown my actions so clearly to all, then every man here should know that.'

His eyes were on her, hard and disbelieving, razing all of her defences. She made to move, but as she did so he reached up above their heads and quickly extinguished the lantern. The darkness was sudden and complete.

Josie gasped, and froze where she was. 'What are you doing?'

'I do not mean to continue the night's entertainment for the men.'

The thick blackness that surrounded them hid him from her, but every inch of her body tingled with awareness of his proximity.

'This is madness. You cannot mean to continue a conversation in the dark.'

'I do not mean to continue a conversation at all, *mademoiselle*.'

The skin at the nape of Josie's neck prickled. The drum of warning beat through her veins. She licked her lips nervously, and whispered, 'Then you should leave.'

She heard him move closer.

'But I am not yet finished with you, *mademoiselle*,' he said quietly.

A shiver rippled through her, and she felt her nipples harden as if a rush of cold air had blown through her. 'If you will not go, then I will,' she replied and, thrusting out her arms before her, she began to step hesitantly through the darkness towards where there was some light at the entrance of the tent.

There was the tread of his boots, and the sensation of movement. As the panic began to rise, she quickened her steps and reached out towards the tent flap.

His arm fastened around her waist and Josie knew that there would be no running away from this.

'No,' she whispered, but whether it was to Dammartin or herself, she did not know.

He came up behind her, pulling her closer until her back was snug against him, her buttocks at his groin. She felt his palm splay over her abdomen, holding her in place, while his other hand closed over her breast.

While his hands imprisoned her, she felt the moist touch of his mouth on the skin at the side of her neck, where her pulse throbbed so violently. The touch became a kiss, a slow tantalising kiss that grew hungrier and hungrier until his lips were sucking her and his tongue was lapping her as if he would draw the very lifeblood from her veins. And as his kiss possessed her, his hand slid lower down her belly, stroking and teasing it went, creeping ever closer to that most secret of her woman's places. His fingers roved over one breast as if the cotton of Rosa's chemise were not there, feeling her, claiming her, circling her taut and straining nipple.

She gasped aloud, amazed both at his audacity and the sensations flowing within her. Somewhere on the outer recesses of her mind a faint voice whispered that this was wrong, that she should stop, but Josie barely heard it. She was quivering beneath his touch, trembling with the need for it never to cease. And when his fingers loosed her buttons, and freed the pins from her hair, she barely noticed, just turned to him and let him take her, kissing his lips, breathing his breath.

He pulled the bodice of her dress and chemise down, his hands cupping her breasts though the linen of her shift, stroking them, petting them, rolling her hardened nipples between his fingers as his mouth moved against hers. And just when she thought the pleasure could not be any greater, he dropped to his knees, pulling her down with him, to lay her beneath him. She heard his breath as ragged as hers, felt the urgency that strained throughout the entirety of his body as his mouth traced lower to close hot and wet over her breast, devouring her through the thin material.

The sensation was so overwhelming, so ecstatic that she was endlessly gasping. There was the sound of linen tearing, and her shift separated them no more. He suckled her bare breasts, first one and then the other, his mouth ranging over their mounds until it fastened upon her nipples, to suck and lick and tease. Josie groaned and arched beneath him, threading her fingers through his hair, pressing him to her that he might never stop. And still it was not enough, still she wanted more of him.

'Oh, Pierre!' she moaned, feeling him nudge her legs open while his mouth stayed busy against her breast.

Then he seemed to catch himself, to stop. She felt his face come up to hers, his breath hot against her mouth.

'No,' he whispered in disbelief. He was panting hard and she could feel the slight tremor that ran through him.

Through the darkness she sensed his face move back to stare at her. 'God help me.' His voice was low and gritty and filled with agony.

Gentle fingers stroked her cheek as he collapsed down to lay by her side, holding her gently against him as his lips dropped small, isolated kisses to her forehead.

'God help us both, Josephine Mallington,' he said softly into her hair, and Josie lay in his arms, knowing that his prayer was futile.

Her tight, sensitised nipples still moist with his saliva and her unsated desire were the evidence. She craved his kiss. She needed his touch. Josie had stepped beyond redemption. Pierre Dammartin was no longer her enemy, but her temptation, and it made a mockery of the sacrifice in Telemos, of her father's death and those of the men of the 60th; it made a mockery of everything in which Josie believed.

Dammartin's men saw him leave the English *mademoiselle*'s tent. They saw, too, the harshness of his face and they wondered what had happened within those canvas walls. Would the Captain be prepared to share the woman with his lieutenant? From his face it did not seem so. The men began to take bets on the outcome.

The first thing that Dammartin saw on leaving Josephine Mallington was Molyneux sitting over at the farthest side of the fire. The two men's gaze met and held for a few seconds until the Lieutenant looked away.

Dammartin strolled to stand by the fire directly opposite to where Molyneux sat near to Lamont.

Lamont quietly slipped away to stand by some troopers.

Molyneux got to his feet, looking nervously across at Dammartin. He cleared his throat. 'She offered to remove a splinter from my hand, sir.'

Dammartin said nothing.

'She was most insistent. I did not wish to be rude. She fetched the needle and before I knew it...' His voice trailed off.

Still Dammartin said nothing, just looked at Molyneux as if he would tear the Lieutenant's head from his body.

'I did not realise that she...that you...' Molyneux cleared his throat again.

Dammartin paused long enough to make Molyneux squirm. 'What are you still doing within my line of vision, Lieutenant?'

A moment's hesitation and then Molyneux saluted and walked quickly away.

Dammartin stood there alone for a few moments, staring into the flames of the fire, then he turned and headed towards the stables, and not long after, the sound of his horse was heard galloping away into the night.

Josie had slept little, but she was up and ready early, sitting on the chair by Dammartin's table within his tent. Her stomach was churning, and she both dreaded and desired to see Dammartin again. What had occurred between them last night had shocked her. She had not known herself capable of such...such wantonness. She thought again of his mouth, hot and hard against her breast. Her nipples tightened at the memory and her cheeks flushed warm. Beyond redemption indeed.

For all of her determination, for all that he was and had done, when he was near, when he touched her, when he as much as looked at her, she could not help herself from wanting his kiss. She was within his power, and yet last night there had been the sensation that it was he who was within hers. Dammartin did not want this any more than she did. There had been anguish and torment in his voice. *God help me*, he had said, *God help us both*.

This craving that linked them together was beyond both their controls, and it frightened her to think where it would lead, so Josie did not allow herself to think. One day at a time, she told herself, one hour, one minute, one second. She could not hide for ever. With her cloak wrapped around her, she stepped out to face the aftermath of the night.

Lieutenant Molyneux was sitting outside altering some tack for his horse. He nodded good morning, but did not speak.

Dammartin was over speaking to a small group of dragoons. He gave no sign of having seen her.

Josie stood there.

Molyneux kept his head bent, concentrating on his task in hand. Men arrived and began to remove the furniture and baggage, first from the officers' tent and then from her own. They cast looks of overt interest towards her and their lieutenant, but what they said was a low murmur and could not be heard. She walked over and waited by her horse. All around her men worked to deconstruct their camp, to ready themselves and their mounts. No one spoke to her. She waited alone, the men leaving a wide space around her.

Josie adjusted the strap of the leather satchel that still hung around her. It did not need to be adjusted, but she felt so uncomfortable, just standing there, that it made her feel better to pretend to be doing something. The satchel was adjusted and lay against her hip. And still Josie waited.

At last Molyneux came to set up his mount. She caught his eye, but he just murmured, '*Mademoiselle,*' and looked away.

A little seed of dread sprouted in her stomach. For all of the discomfort of facing the men of the 8th this morning, of facing Molyneux, she knew something far worse was coming. She could feel it in her bones. She turned her face to the little horse, and taking off her gloves, began to stroke its smooth neck. Her fingers rubbed at the soft muzzle.

'Fleur,' she whispered softly, and was glad when the mare blew softly against her fingers and licked at her hand. She did not look again at Molyneux or the men around her, but kept her focus fixed solely on the little horse. Something brushed against her shoulder, warm breath blew against her, and something moist nuzzled against her neck. Josie gave a yelp of surprise.

'Dante!' She turned to find Dammartin's great war-horse at her shoulder. He stood tall, perhaps seventeen hands high, his chestnut coat glossy in the sunlight, quite dwarfing Josie and the little mare by her side. The horse was trained for battle: long, muscular legs to carry his rider with speed in the charge towards the lines of British infantry, strong hooves that would rear and smash a man's skull, and a mouth taught to bite hard and mean.

Dante had heard the drums beating for war many times, he was not afraid of the roar of cannons or the screams of men. He knew what he was to do. He was a killer every bit as much as the man that sat upon his back. But not this morning.

The saddle and stirrups had not yet been fitted to his back. He wore the thickly sewn sheepskins that Dammartin covered him with through the cold of the night. His eyes were dark and soft and soulful and he was determined that Josie would feed him the nuts that his master normally brought. But Josie had nothing to give him. He nosed at her stomach, inadvertently pushing her back against Fleur. Then he nibbled at the tie to her cloak and knocked the hat from her head

'Dante!' Dammartin's voice sounded close by, and then the big chestnut horse was being pulled away from Josie.

'Captain Dammartin.'

'Mademoiselle Mallington. Did he hurt you?' He kept his face impassive.

She looked very small and slender this morning, and his heart had skipped a beat when he saw her pressed between the two horses. One move and Dante would have her crushed. Dammartin had made his way swiftly over. And now Dante was at his back and Josephine Mallington before him, her eyes a vivid blue within the pale oval of her face. Some of her pins had been loosened and a few long strands of hair had escaped to hang down the side of her face, their pale trail stark against the bodice of her own high-necked, dark blue dress, and he thought of the red-and-black Spanish dress that he had stripped from her breasts last night. He saw the colour rise in her cheeks. Desire tightened his gut.

'No. He is just looking for his treat.'

They looked at each other in the bright light of morning,

before Dammartin stooped to retrieve her hat from where Dante had knocked it to the ground. He handed it to her.

'Thank you.' Their fingers brushed, gloveless, bare, and he felt her jump before he drew his hand away. Her blush deepened.

He told himself again that what he was doing today was for the best. This thing between them had been released in earnest and would never be recaptured. It would not be hidden or suppressed. It would not be ignored or broken. Its strength was far beyond anything of willpower. It was a living, growing thing, spiralling out of control…and it would destroy them both if he let it.

She fixed the hat back on her head and fitted the gloves on to her hands. She no longer looked at him, but the scald still marked her cheeks.

He would tell her now. He had to, for they would come for her soon. 'Josephine,' he said softly. 'What happened last night, what has been growing between us…this attraction…' He groped for the best words to convey his meaning. 'It cannot be allowed to exist, for the sake of our fathers, for the sake of our honour. And so, because of this, there has been a change of plan.'

She glanced up at him and he could see the question in her eyes.

He forced himself to continue. 'From today you no longer ride with the 8th. You shall be in the care of the 47th Regiment of Line and Major La Roque.' He held her gaze. 'You asked me once of witnesses to my father's murder. Major La Roque was my father's closest friend. It was he who was with him at Oporto when my father died.' And he wondered if he was telling her this as some kind of reparation to make up for the fact that he was sending her away.

'Thank you for telling me.'

He gave a small nod of acknowledgement.

Silence and awkwardness stood between them.

'It is for the best that you must go,' he said.

'Yes.'

Dammartin's hands itched to pull her into his arms. His fingers gripped together behind his back. There was nothing more he could say.

'When do I leave?'

Dammartin was struck anew by her courage and her dignity.

The sound of horses' hooves sounded in the distance.

They both glanced towards the road. They both knew who was coming.

'Now,' he said.

Two infantry officers of La Roque's first company came into the field and dismounted. They were being directed to where Dammartin stood with Josie.

She saw them coming.

'You may take Fleur.' Another salve for the wound.

'Thank you.' She was watching the officers in their blue coats and black shakos cross the field towards her. When they had almost reached her, she turned to him and said, 'Did you take my portmanteau?'

'No, Josephine, I did not.'

Then the officers of the 47th were there saluting him. He moved to help her climb up on to Fleur, but she stepped quickly and pulled herself up without the need for his hand.

'Goodbye, Captain Dammartin.' She looked at him for one last time and what he saw in her face stilled the breath in his throat and made him want to pull her back down from the horse and send La Roque's men away empty-handed.

'Goodbye, Mademoiselle Mallington.'

She twitched her heels and the small grey moved off, flanked by the two larger mounts of the officers. Her back was ramrod straight as they moved slowly across the field, breaking into a trot when they came close to the road. Dammartin stood and watched until Josephine Mallington disappeared from sight.

Josie followed the officers down the road at the side of the camp to where the infantrymen had pitched their tents. She could see another small party of officers ahead on horseback, and took a deep breath, steeling herself for what was to come.

She knew La Roque before he even spoke. His jacket was of the Emperor's blue with white facings and gilt buttons. On his left shoulder he wore a full epaulet and on his right, a contre-epaulet without the fringes; both were gilt and a fine contrast to the red collar and cuffs upon his jacket. Around his neck, fitting snug beneath his collar, sat his metal badge of office—a gilt gorget—and at his left hip hung his sword with its golden tassels around the hilt. The pure white of his breeches and the shine on his riding boots struck Josie as strange, given that they had spent the past days riding through such hostile terrain. On his head he wore a black bicorne hat as befitted his rank, complete with a white pompom and a small circular tricolour in the centre and tassels of gold at either corner.

He was not as old as she had expected. His hair was dark slashed with silver, his face full from too much good living. Across his top lip sat a large moustache. He would have been what was termed a handsome man in his youth, and the semblance of it could still be seen in him. She met the gaze of those pale silver-grey eyes, and knew that this was the man who had lied about her father and something twisted in her stomach.

He smiled and his teeth were white and even.

When he spoke, his voice held the heavy accent of his country. 'We meet at last, Mademoiselle Mallington.'

'Major La Roque,' she said, but she did not return his smile.

'You come into my care now.'

She said nothing.

'The *47e Régiment d'Infanterie de Ligne* shall convey you in safety. We do not harm our prisoners.'

The unspoken accusation hung between them. She knew that he was baiting her.

She gave no reply.

'Do you know that I met your father once?'

'So I have heard,' she said.

He arched a silver brow. 'Perhaps Lieutenant Colonel Mallington spoke of me?'

'He did not.'

'Or of Major Jean Dammartin, the man that he murdered.'

She bit back the response that she would have given him, taking her time to fashion some civility into it. 'My father was no murderer.'

The Major looked round at the officers surrounding them, smiling as if she had just cracked a joke. 'Her loyalty is admirable.'

'My father did not kill Jean Dammartin.'

'I saw him with my own eyes, *mademoiselle*. Perhaps you do not know that I was with him when he died, or that your father tried to kill me too.'

'I know that is the story that is told.'

She could almost hear the sudden intake of breath from the surrounding group of officers.

But La Roque just smiled. 'What can you be implying, Mademoiselle Mallington?'

'I am implying nothing,' she said. 'But I know that my father did not kill Major Dammartin.'

La Roque shook his head sorrowfully. 'Poor child. How difficult it is to face the truth.'

Josie bit back what she would have said.

'I trust Captain Dammartin treated you well?'

'He did, thank you.'

'He is very like his father, you know—a fine man and a good soldier for France. Such a shame that your father murdered his in the most dishonourable of ways. How he must hate you, *mademoiselle*.'

Once there had been hatred between her and Dammartin, but not any more. Josie lowered her face to hide the truth.

La Roque leaned forward in his saddle and said quietly, 'It is little wonder he makes a whore of you.' He sat back and smiled again. 'You will be escorted today by Lieutenant Donadieu. Such a pleasure to welcome you to our company, *mademoiselle*.' The Major turned his horse around and, together with his officers, made his way slowly up the side of the thick column of infantry.

One man stayed behind, a young man with fairish hair and a soft pink complexion—Lieutenant Donadieu—a man-boy, hardly old enough to be out of his school gown. But Josie barely noticed him. She was watching the retreating figure of Major La Roque, and hearing again the cruelty of his words.

'Mademoiselle Mallington.'

She turned her eyes slowly to Lieutenant Donadieu.

He was looking at her with undisguised disgust.

She met his gaze and held it defiantly, daring him to say the words that his face so clearly expressed.

Donadieu averted his eyes and led off.

Josie had no choice but to follow.

The sky above was blue and clear. The sunlight was bright and white. Birdsong sounded over the noise of horses' hooves. But to all of these things Josie was both blind and deaf. The column of French infantry moved forward.

In the day that followed Josie came to realise what being a prisoner of the 47th Regiment of the Line meant, and, try as she might to remain unaffected, she found herself growing more and more miserable. None of the officers or men spoke to her. They looked at her plenty, their expressions ranging from curiosity to pity to blatant dislike. Lieutenant Donadieu was not like Lieutenant Molyneux. He rode close to her, but that was all. He did not bring her anything to eat or drink. He did not make conversation or strive to turn her mind away from the misery of the march to lighter things.

Donadieu was at her side. Four officers and Major La Roque rode ahead. Four hundred men formed the column of the 47th. Before them rode one-hundred-and-twenty cavalrymen, and Captain Dammartin. Over five hundred men. And amidst them all Josie was alone.

La Roque rested the men halfway through the day's march. As with Dammartin's dragoons, there was no time to cook a meal; instead, bread and hard biscuits were distributed. The men ate and drank the water from their canteens, sitting spread on the ground in uneven clusters, some resting, some even sleeping.

Donadieu left her in the middle of a group of his fusiliers, a clear space of ground separating her from the infantrymen in their imperial-blue coats with their distinctive white facings and cross-belts, and matching dirty white pantaloons. Like La Roque, their collar and cuffs were red. Most of them had taken off their shakos as they lounged,

leaving their hats lying on the ground beside their knap-
sacks and rolled greatcoats. They watched her with interest. She could hear their conversations quite clearly, for
they did not think that she could understand, and they did
not care. Some called her the murderer's daughter, some
speculated as to why Dammartin had kept her for a week
before sending her to La Roque. Most of the comments
were so crudely obscene as to send an angry blush to her
cheeks.

She sat alone, and pretended that she could hear none of
them. Yet still she listened and she learned that the French
thought La Roque a hero and that they anticipated that
they would reach Ciudad Rodrigo late the next day. Only
twenty-four hours. She had endured much more. She could
endure this.

Chapter Eleven

That night Lieutenant Donadieu delivered her to the large tent that was erected for the women of the baggage train. The women, who were for the main part French, remained distant. They knew who she was judging from the ferocity of their comments, yet not one woman said anything to her face; they just looked at her with cold eyes and sullen mouths. These were the women who were wives to the ordinary soldiers and non-commissioned officers. These, too, were the women who were whores to whatever man would pay for their services.

She knew some of the women's faces from having seen them come into the 8th's camp, and she knew Rosa, the only woman who displayed any vestige of friendliness towards her. It was Rosa who gave her a mess tin and spoon, and Rosa that made sure that Josie had food and water that evening. And for that Josie could only be glad.

The two women ate their stew.

'Will you stay travelling with the French?' Josie chewed at a small, fatty lump of meat.

Rosa lifted a suspicious face. 'Why do you ask?'

'I just wondered.' Josie thought of what Dammartin had told her of Rosa's history.

Rosa seemed to accept Josie's answer. 'Where Claude goes, then I go too.'

'And after the war?'

She shrugged. 'Still then I follow him. There is nothing in Spain any more for me, there is only Claude.'

'Do you love him?'

'Yes.' Rosa smiled at that. 'Do you love, *señorita*?'

'I loved my parents and my brother.'

'And Captain Dammartin,' Rosa said, and her dark beautiful eyes seemed too knowing to Josie. 'Do you love him?'

'No!' she exclaimed. 'Of course not. He is my enemy. It is because of him that my father and all of his men are dead.' But as she said it, there was the small, insistent thought in her head that her words were not true. Dammartin had given them more than enough chance to surrender. He had wanted Lieutenant Colonel Mallington taken alive. It was her father himself who had signed all their death warrants—so that the information might reach Wellington.

Rosa's eyebrows raised by the smallest degree. 'That is no difference if you love him. I see his eyes on you, and I see, too, your eyes on him, *señorita*.'

Heat scalded Josie's cheeks scarlet. 'I do not love him!' She did not understand this thing between her and Pierre Dammartin, but it was not love, it could not possibly be love.

'You say no too many times, too loudly. Who do you try to convince, *señorita*, me, or you?'

Josie's eyes widened. 'You are mistaken, Señora Rosa,' she said coolly.

The hint of a smile touched to Rosa's lips, but she said nothing more.

They sat in silence for a few minutes, Josie feeling angry and embarrassed, Rosa seemingly contented. It was Rosa who recommenced the conversation.

'What will they do with you at Ciudad Rodrigo?'

'Send me back to Santarém, to General Massena,' said Josie, relieved at the change of subject from Dammartin. 'He will exchange me for a French prisoner of war held by the British—I hope.'

'And then?'

And then? It was the question that Josie had not yet dared to ask herself. What would happen? 'I suppose I will be sent back to England.'

'To your mother?'

'My mother is dead.'

'I am sorry.'

'She died four years ago.' Josie scraped her spoon at some invisible contents of the mess tin. 'My brother was in the cavalry. He was killed two years ago. There is no one waiting for me at home.'

'You have an aunt, an uncle, cousins?'

'No one.'

'Then where will you go?'

Josie set the mess tin and spoon down, and did not look at Rosa. 'My father's friend and his wife were kind enough to let me stay with them last year. They might be willing to help me arrange a position of some sort—a ladies' companion, perhaps.' But she held little hope and much dread.

She had no skills that would be of use in genteel life in England. She was useless to the point of being inept at any formal social occasion. She could not sing or play music, or paint or embroider. Her voice had been commented upon as being dull and her conversation even duller. Before the ladies of the *ton* Josie's mind was sure to go blank. She knew not one thing that would be of any interest to such women. It would be that dreadful year all over again, being forced into a society into which she did not fit. The prospect of such a future seemed unbearable. Josie looked up suddenly at Rosa, unaware that all her fears showed in her eyes.

Rosa touched a hand to Josie's arm in a token of comfort. 'You and I, we are the same. Without father or husband, without home.'

Josie averted her gaze.

But Rosa continued just the same. 'But we are strong. We survive. Claude, he save my life. Captain Dammartin, he save yours. There is nothing in Spain for me, there is only Claude. For you it is England and another man.'

'Rosa, no—'

'We are sisters.'

Josie left her words unspoken.

The two women looked at one another, a bond of friendship forming.

'Thank you, Rosa, your kindness means much to me.'

Later that evening Rosa left the women's tent to go to Lamont. Josie stayed alone, sitting cross-legged on the blanket bed, trying to repair her torn shift. One stitch sewn and she remembered Dammartin's hands ripping the shift from her body. A second stitch and the image flashed in her head of his mouth upon her breast. She felt the breath catch in her throat, felt the flush rise in her cheeks and the press of her nipples against her underclothes. No. She shook her head as if by so doing she could deny the thoughts and pretend they did not exist.

Dammartin had been right to send her away, for, Lord

help her, she could not stop this fire that burned in her for him. She wanted his kiss, his touch, his taste upon her tongue. It was like some kind of madness that robbed her of all rational thought so that not the memory of her father, nor the war, nor all that had happened, could quench her desire.

Dammartin had acted for duty and for honour in sending her away. La Roque had been wrong; it was not Dammartin that had made her a whore, but Josie herself. She swallowed down that hard realisation, and felt the misting of her eyes. She blinked the tears away, scorning her own weakness and set the shift and its memories aside.

One hand reached and extinguished the lantern before she rose silently to stand by the tent's entrance.

The night sky above was a deep, dark velvet. Stars glittered small and bright. The moon had grown larger so that it was a fat three-quarters full. The air around her was cold and filled with the dampness that always came with night. Her breath smoked in small puffs of condensation. And as she stood there, under the great vastness of the sky, and the settling silence, Josie thought of her father and of Dammartin's, and of the lies that had been told of them…and of La Roque, a man that Dammartin had said was his father's close friend.

La Roque had woven a web of lies to destroy Lieutenant Colonel Mallington's reputation across all of France, that much was clear, but the question was why. The only person who could answer that question was La Roque himself. She glanced over to where the two infantrymen lounged that had been set to guard her, knowing that, whatever she said, they would not let her leave the tent.

A group of three women, wearing dresses so low cut as to appear positively indecent, pushed past her. Josie stepped aside to let them pass, pulling her cloak tightly around her and watching them go. No one stopped their progress. They moved forwards unaccosted, their laughter and teasing voices loud across the field. An idea slipped into Josie's mind.

She turned and, back inside the tent, found the clothes that Rosa had given her. And then from within the leather satchel she had carried with her so closely she removed the thin precious book she had guarded for so long. Within the darkness she changed into the Spanish dress, hiding the book in the safest of places and unlacing the top of the chemise like she had seen the other women doing. Instead of her cloak she wrapped a shawl around her shoulders. Quickly she pulled the pins from her hair, mussing it with her fingers to lie long and wanton. She hesitated by the tent's doorway, darting a nervous glance across at the guards.

One deep breath and she hesitated no more. Josie walked out into the night, feeling the breeze chill the tops of her breasts and the wind stir through her hair. She held her head up and walked out with the same sway of the hips mimicked from the women, and the same air that she knew exactly where she was going.

She had almost made it across the field when the fusilier stopped her.

He stared at her suspiciously. *'Madame?'*

Josie's heart was thudding fit to leap out of her chest. She forced herself to smile at the man. *'Monsieur,'* she said in as sultry a tone as she could manage and let the shawl that she held wrapped tightly around her fall open. The light of the man's flambeau danced across the bareness of her skin that Rosa's dress revealed. 'I am afraid that I already have an appointment for this night. Perhaps tomorrow…' Her French was flawless and without the trace of an English accent.

The man no longer looked at her face. He addressed
the rest of his comments to the neckline of the dress at
the place where her breasts rose and fell. 'I am Antoine
Nerin and I would be very pleased to accommodate you
tomorrow, *madame.*'

He was still staring.

Josie suppressed the urge to wrap the shawl as a shield
around her.

'You will come?'

'Naturally,' she said, and gave what she hoped sounded
like a trill of laughter. Then she turned to go and jumped
as she felt the man's hand stroke across her bottom.

'Until tomorrow.'

She nodded.

And finally she was on her way and pulling the shawl
tight around her.

It was not difficult to locate Major La Roque's tent. It
was large and set slightly apart from the others. She saw
him standing by the opened flap, looking out, watching, as
if he were waiting for someone, and then he moved back
inside and she saw him no more.

A fusilier looked at her suspiciously. She let the shawl
gape and looked away.

He saw the nature of her business and approached no
farther, allowing her to continue on her way towards the
Major's tent.

There was a campfire to the right with a group of blue-
coated men sitting around it. She saw to her consternation
that one of them was Donadieu, so she skirted away, going
round the other way to come at La Roque's tent from
behind. She began to walk towards the tent flap.

A flambeau mounted on a stand burned near the front.
On the inside of the tent a lantern illuminated the figure
of La Roque lounging in a chair at his table.

Footsteps sounded and she saw the figure of Lieuten-

ant Molyneux approaching. She ducked down out of sight
and waited for him to pass. But Molyneux did not pass;
instead, he reported to the Major's tent. Josie crept back
behind the tent, wondering why Dammartin had sent his
lieutenant to La Roque at this time of night. She crouched
low as if she were lacing her boot.

La Roque's French words sounded clear from within.
'Brandy?'

'Thank you, sir.'

There was the sound of glass chinking against glass,
and the fall of liquid. 'You have done well, Molyneux.
What have you to report tonight? Has he made any mention of the girl?'

'No sir. Not a one.'

'Then it seems that our plan has worked. You must have
convinced him most thoroughly of her perfidious nature.'

'Indeed sir, Mademoiselle Mallington was most easily
manipulated.'

Josie felt her blood turn to ice. Shock kicked her hard
so that she held her breath, poised and waiting for what
was to come.

'Did you manage to search her person for the missing
journal?

'Unfortunately the Captain arrived before I could progress to that stage. I must confess I was rather disap-
pointed.'

La Roque laughed. 'Why so, Molyneux? If you want
the girl, you may have her.'

Josie bit hard at her lip, disbelieving the words that she
was hearing.

'But she is a lieutenant colonel's daughter and, as such,
will be returned to the British. If she makes allegations…'

'You worry too much, Molyneux.' She heard the smile
in La Roque's voice. 'The British do not even know that
Mademoiselle Mallington is still alive. They will believe

her killed with her father. You may do what you like with her and no one will mind in the slightest.'

Josie's stomach constricted to a small, hard ball.

'Captain Dammartin will mind,' said Molyneux. 'He was looking at me last night as if he would kill me.'

'Leave Captain Dammartin to me,' said La Roque. 'You concentrate on the journal. It cannot be mere coincidence that Mallington's journal for Oporto is the only one missing. The girl must have it. Take her tonight. Seduce her. Strip her. Search between her damn legs if you have to. I want that journal. You did well to find me the others, but it is this one that we need—for Pierre's sake.'

Josie's eyes widened. Her mouth gaped open.

'I will try my utmost, sir.'

'I like a man that can be trusted. You'll go far in this army, Lieutenant Molyneux, far indeed, if I have anything to do with it.'

She knew then the true extent of Molyneux's treachery.

They started to speak of various women of the baggage train, but Josie had heard enough. She felt sick to the bottom of her stomach, sick and angry and disgusted. Molyneux was La Roque's spy. The shock of what he had done and what he planned to do made her stomach heave and her legs shake. Josie swallowed hard and breathed deeply before rising and moving swiftly from her crouched position by La Roque's tent.

She did not retrace her steps back to the women's tent. Instead, Josie hurried through the campsite towards Bonaparte's 8th Dragoons, and the man that commanded them—Captain Pierre Dammartin.

Dammartin and Lamont were sitting by what was left of the fire.

'So, the problem of Mademoiselle Mallington is no more.'

Dammartin rubbed at the stubbled growth of his jawline and gave no reply. What could he say—that even now he could not stop thinking about her, that he wanted her, that a part of him regretted sending her to La Roque?

'Then, what happened in the tent with Molyneux made up your mind?' Lamont puffed at his pipe.

'No,' said Dammartin, 'it was what happened afterwards.' He thought of her beneath him, of his mouth suckling upon her perfect breasts, of the raggedness of her breathing and her low seductive moan of heated desire.

Lamont wisely said nothing.

'You saw her with Molyneux. The whole bloody camp saw her. And even that did not make a difference. I would have had her, taken her right there, had I not come to my senses in time.' Dammartin shook his head. 'I think I have been too long without a woman, my friend, that I am so willing take Molyneux's leavings.'

A cloud of tobacco smoke released from Lamont's mouth, filling the air with its sweet aroma. 'I could not help but overhear about the splinter.'

Dammartin smiled cynically. 'Ah, yes, the splinter.'

'The girl's interest is in you, Pierre, not Molyneux. God only knows why, given who she is and what happened in Telemos...and the fact that you have hardly been gentle with her.' He sniffed and gave a philosophical shrug. 'But then, I suppose, there is nothing of reason in the affairs of the heart...or of the breeches.'

Dammartin stared sullenly into the dying flames. 'What game is our lieutenant playing at, I wonder?'

'Who can know? But at least now she is with La Roque it will be an end to the matter.'

Dammartin said nothing.

'Goodnight, Captain,' said Lamont, and, getting to his feet, made his way to his tent.

'Goodnight, Sergeant,' came the reply.

Dammartin sat for only a few moments more, before he, too, retired for the night, leaving the dragoon camp deserted.

The night was quietening down as Josie made her way through the line of camps. She did not know when Molyneux would leave and she had no wish for him to discover her on the road. Three times men made advances to her. Three times she told them she already had an appointment. One of the men clasped his arm around her waist and pulled her close to him, his foul breath hot against her neck. 'Let me persuade you otherwise, *madame*,' he had said, and pulled a handful of coins from his pocket.

Josie pushed him away, but he would not release her. She held the panic that threatened to break loose in check. 'I tell you, I have an arrangement with an officer. Now release me, sir, or you will have him to answer to.'

'Let her go, Thomass,' his friends said. 'We don't want any trouble. This bloody forced march is bad enough without being pulled up over a whore.'

The man, Thomass, sneered, but eventually he threw her away, and spat noisily after her.

Josie quelled the urge to run. She walked away, pulling the shawl tight around her, refusing to look back. But her heart was thrumming fast and the blood was pounding in her ears, and she could not rid herself of the notion that Thomass was following her.

Eventually she came to the dragoons' camp and the tents that belonged to their officers. A fire burned low in the foreground, but the tents themselves were in darkness, and for one fearful minute she wondered if they would be empty and that her journey would have been in vain.

This camp was quiet. The two identical tents sat before her and she realised that she did not know which was Captain Dammartin's and which was that of his officers. She dare not make the mistake, especially if Molyneux had returned.

Looking around her, she found a small stone upon the ground. She stooped and caught it up, then, taking careful aim, she threw the stone at the tent pitched farthest to the right-hand side. There was a soft thud as the stone found its target against the canvas.

She waited, but there was nothing. Another stone. Another hit.

This time a man appeared at the tent flap. He was garbed in an unfastened shirt, breeches and hastily donned boots. Even in the low light from the fire that stood between Josie's hiding place and the tents, she could see quite clearly that it was Pierre Dammartin.

He looked out into the night, peering across to the bushes where Josie crouched. She heard him treading about by the tent until he eventually went back inside. A quick glance around and then she rose and silently crossed the ground that separated them.

Dammartin did not climb back into bed upon his return to his tent. Instead, he slid his sabre quietly from its scabbard. Awareness tingled and he could not rest. The sound had most likely been one of his men fooling about, but Dammartin's instinct told him otherwise, and through the years Dammartin had learned to listen to his instinct. On the war trail it was often the only thing that kept a man alive. So he stood there and listened to the silence of the night, and eventually he heard the soft pad of footsteps

cross the soil to his tent. He stuffed his pillow beneath
the blanket on the bed so that it would vaguely resemble
the bulk of a figure. Then his fingers closed around the
sabre's hilt. The weight balanced in his hand and he moved
forwards noiselessly to stand at the side of the tent flap.
Whoever was stealing into his tent would find Dammartin,
but not quite as they expected.

His mouth was hard, his eyes narrowed. He wondered
as to the identity of the intruder, knowing that it had to
be someone from within Foy's escort. Maybe Molyneux
in retaliation for what had happened between them over
Josephine Mallington.

Someone was untying the fastenings of the tent flap. His
body tensed. The canvas that made the tent's door drew
back and the figure stepped inside into the black within that
was slightly darker than the black without. Too small and
slight for Molyneux. Silently, the intruder moved towards
the bed.

Through the darkness Josie could just make out the
mound of Dammartin's figure within the bed. She stepped
forwards and felt a sudden press against her back. An
involuntary gasp escaped her, and she did not need to look
round to know the touch of a blade.

'Turn around slowly,' he said in French. His voice was
quiet and low, but she knew that it was Dammartin. Relief
swamped her. She released the breath that she had been
holding.

'Captain Dammartin…Pierre.' She spoke as quietly as he.

The pressure dropped from her back. The sabre blade
hissed as it was plunged back into its scabbard. 'Josephine?' There could be no mistaking his shock. 'What
the hell—?'

'Thank God!' She turned and slipped into his arms. 'I had to come, I had to warn you…'

Releasing her, he caught up a lantern, intent on lighting it.

'No.' She stayed his hand. 'No one must see me here. It is not safe.'

'The men are abed. There is no one to see.'

'There is Lieutenant Molyneux,' she whispered, knowing that even as she spoke Molyneux was probably looking for her in the women's tent.

'He also has retired,' he said coldly.

'Believe me, Molyneux is abroad this night.'

'Josephine, what are you—?'

'No, you must listen to me. There is not much time. Molyneux will soon realise that I am gone and La Roque will be alerted.'

'Mademoiselle Mallington,' he said more sternly.

'Captain Dammartin,' she countered, catching at his hands through the darkness. 'Please just listen.'

Dammartin felt the urgent press of her fingers against his and knew that what had been achieved by sending Josephine Mallington to his godfather had just been undone. She had come to him and he knew by the coursing of his blood and the strength of his desire that he could fight no more this night.

'Very well.' The scent of her teased beneath his nose. He wrapped his arms around her waist, pulling her closer.

'No,' she pushed him away, and he could hear the slight breathlessness in her voice. 'I must tell you…'

'Then speak.'

'I went in search of Major La Roque's tent. I intended to go in, to talk to him, to ask him why he had lied about my father…and yours.'

'Josephine—' he started to chide, but she cut him off.

'But Lieutenant Molyneux arrived before I could.'

Dammartin's eyes narrowed. Molyneux.

'I heard them talking through the canvas.'

'Molyneux and La Roque?'

'Yes.' Her breaths were fast and shallow, her anxiety barely suppressed. 'Molyneux is spying for him.' He felt her fingers touch gently to his wrist. 'He is spying on you, Pierre.'

He let her words drop between them, feeling a spurt of anger at what she sought to do. Quite deliberately he moved from her touch, smiling a sardonic smile through the darkness. 'You must try harder, *mademoiselle*, to think of something more convincing. The story of the splinter and your flirtation with Molyneux was a much better effort.'

'What are you speaking of?' The pitch of her voice rose with incredulity.

'Do you think that you can so easily cause trouble between us?'

'It is the truth, I swear!' she gasped. 'La Roque used Molyneux to make you send me away. And Molyneux is the Major's spy. It was they that stole my portmanteau... and my father's journals.'

'You admit, then, that the journals were in the portmanteau?'

'Yes,' she said simply, no longer pretending any denial. 'They were hidden beneath a false floor. La Roque has them now.'

'Does he indeed?' he asked quietly.

A pause.

Dammartin rubbed his fingers against the roughness of his chin as he remembered La Roque's dismissive attitude to Dammartin's own suspicions regarding the journals and the portmanteau. She had to be lying. She was Mallington's daughter, an English prisoner, his enemy. La Roque was his senior officer, his godfather, a man who had been like an uncle to him since childhood. And then it dawned on him what he had been missing.

'*Vous parlez français, n'est pas?*' he shot at her.

'*Oui,*' she said, then reverted to English. 'It was the one advantage that I had. I could not let you know of it.'

'Then your story of following your father around the world, without schooling or governesses, was a lie too.'

'It was the truth,' she said.

There was a silence. Still, Dammartin did not believe what she was saying, and yet… He raked a hand through his hair.

'How did you get here? There are sentries posted at all the camps. Did no one stop you?'

Josie thought of the men that had done precisely that. She thought of Thomass and the cruelty of his grip and the anger in his face. There was no need to tell Dammartin of such things. 'I am in disguise. They did not see an English prisoner.'

He grabbed hold of her wrist and dragged her to the tent flap, opening it so that he could look on her in the moonlight.

'No!' She tried to resist.

'I see no disguise, *mademoiselle.*'

'*Vraiment?*' she whispered furiously. '*Regardez-moi de près, monsieur.*'

Dammartin's gaze drifted to her hair that was flowing long and wanton over her shoulders, then down lower to the thin shawl. The skin of Josie's throat was exposed. He could see it, pale and smooth through the light of the moon. Anger flashed in her eyes as she yanked open the shawl that was wrapped around her. The low-cut bodice and unlaced chemise presented a very full view. Her breasts swelled pale and smooth and inviting. Dammartin remembered too well how they had felt, how they had tasted. He swallowed as his gaze skimmed down over the red-and-black dress that fitted so neatly to her figure. Its skirt was overlapping his left leg.

'Am I not *une femme française*?'

'Your accent...' He stared at her, understanding now why the sentries had believed her so readily.

She stared right back before the anger seemed to wash from her and she glanced away, a distant look in her eyes. 'My mother was French,' she said quietly.

Dammartin felt the shock like a kick in the gut. He stared all the harder, feeling that the foundations of his beliefs of Mallington and the woman before him had just been shaken. He let the tent flap fall back into place.

'You risked much to come here, *mademoiselle*. Why?'

She did not move, just stood where she was, so still that he did not think that she would answer. 'To warn you,' she said.

He felt his heart beat a little faster.

'To let you know what manner of man this La Roque is. He is spying on you, Captain. That is hardly conducive with a man whose word as a witness is above reproach.'

He understood now, and he smiled that he could have believed anything else. His voice hardened. 'You are lying about La Roque in an effort to persuade me of Mallington's innocence.'

'My father was innocent, he *is* innocent. I have no need to lie about La Roque.'

'You have every need,' he said curtly.

She sighed. 'I did not come here for this.'

'Then what *did* you come here for, Mademoiselle Mallington?'

Silence.

'For this?' He reached for her, hauling her into his arms, pressing her body to his.

'Or this?' He slid a hand round to capture one breast, his fingers raking beneath the unlaced chemise.

'Or perhaps this, *mademoiselle*?' His mouth closed harshly over hers, kissing her with the hunger that had gnawed at him all the long day through.

She fought him, but he did not release her, just deepened the kiss, until she softened against him, and yielded the fight. But unlike before, she did not return his kiss.

He ceased his onslaught and rested his forehead against hers. 'I am sorry, Josephine.' The tightness of his grip loosened. One hand slid up to cradle her face as he felt the brush of her eyelashes against his. 'You did not deserve that.' Her breath was warm against his mouth. He skimmed a caress down the length of her back.

'I came because La Roque has told Molyneux he may have me…tonight. I…I thought that you would help me.'

He stilled. He drew his face back slightly as if he could see into her eyes through the darkness.

A minute passed, and then another, in which there was only the hush of their breaths, the beat of their hearts.

When he spoke his tone was grim. 'Stay here,' he said. 'I will be back soon.'

'No.' She gripped at him. 'You cannot go to La Roque. He will be enraged. It is too dangerous.'

'Your concern touches me,' he said, 'but it is unwarranted.' He smiled and dropped a kiss to her cheek. 'Try to get some sleep. You will find the bed most comfortable.' He pulled his jacket on and was gone.

Major La Roque pressed the full glass of brandy into Dammartin's hand. 'Mademoiselle Mallington seeks to turn us against each other. Such a scheming little vixen for one so young, but then we must remember who sired her. Mallington's poison runs in her veins. She hates us French just as her father did before her.'

'Her mother was French.' Dammartin tasted the brandy and set the brandy glass on the table before him.

'Mallington's wife?' La Roque stiffened before relaxing back into his chair. 'The girl told you that?'

Dammartin gave a nod.

'It is probably another lie spun to garner your sympathy.'

Dammartin thought of the Josephine's fluency in French. 'I do not think so, Frederic.'

'Pierre, Pierre…' La Roque sighed. 'The girl is dangerous. She watches you kill Mallington and his men. Then you tell her the truth of her beloved precious father, that he is a murdering bastard. There is no honour in the killing of a paroled officer; even Mademoiselle Mallington must know that. So she hates you, and she sets about finding a way to destroy you…with seduction and lies.'

La Roque's words made sense. Dammartin knew that Josephine Mallington had every reason to hate him. But there had been nothing of hatred in her kiss, or the response of her body to his.

'Are you saying that Molyneux did not report to you this evening?'

La Roque set his glass down on the table and looked at Dammartin. 'I will tell you the truth, Pierre. You are my godson; I care for you, and your mother and your brother very dearly. You know that. When I heard something of this Mademoiselle Mallington, the way she was with you, I began to worry. And so I asked Molyneux to keep an eye on her, to let me know what she was up to. That is all, Pierre, I swear, nothing more.'

'You might have told me of your concerns rather than have my first lieutenant spy upon me.'

La Roque shook his head. 'There was nothing of spying in it. I was concerned for you. She is the spawn of that monster and you…' he sighed with heavy sadness '…you are still affected by your father's death. Had I tried to warn you of her, you would have resented me for it, so I thought I would just keep a gentle eye on things myself.'

'Frederic…'

'Perhaps I was wrong to do so, but I am proved right about the girl. With her slyness she has caught you like a worm upon a hook. You want her, even knowing who she is.'

Dammartin said nothing, just downed a mouthful of brandy, focusing on the heat burning its way down into his chest.

'I am right, am I not? You want Mallington's daughter in your bed.'

Again Dammartin ignored the assertion spoken with its disgust. 'What of her portmanteau?' he said instead. 'What of the journals?'

'I told you before. I know nothing of her damn portmanteau, and as for Mallington's journals, we have only her word that they even exist. Do you think I would have that demon's journals in my possession and say nothing of it to you? Do you not think that I want to know just as much as you why Mallington did what he did that day? If we had his journals, we might have the answer to the questions that we both have asked for so long.' La Roque rose from his seat and walked round to stand before Dammartin. 'I have known you since you were a boy,' he said. 'I have watched you grow to a man. You, Marie and Kristoffe are in my heart, along with the love I bore your father. Do you believe the word of a murderer's daughter over mine, Pierre?'

Dammartin shook his head. 'Forgive me, Frederic.'

La Roque reached a hand across and touched to Dammartin's shoulder. 'I understand how hard this has been for you.'

'She said that you would give her to Molyneux.'

'The girl is playing you, Pierre. She is here because you asked me to take her. Molyneux has nothing to do with it.'

Dammartin thought of the way that Josephine had clung to him, her relief at finding him spontaneous and overflowing. He thought of her standing so quietly before him. *I thought that you would help me*, she had said, and he had seen the unspoken fear in her eyes. Such an adept liar, such persuasive acting. Logic and all that Dammartin had believed in told him that La Roque was right, yet a stain of unease marred his soul.

'I envy her her loyalty to her father. Had I but an ounce of it, I would not be in this damnable mess.'

'Pierre.' La Roque's hand gripped at Dammartin's shoulder. 'I know how hard you have fought against this… this appetite she has whetted within you. But maybe you are using the wrong tactics; maybe it would be better if you just took her and be done with it. Use her. Ride her like the whore that she is. Eat until you are sated, and perhaps then the hunger shall be no more.'

'Perhaps you are right,' said Dammartin. He knew that no matter what La Roque said, no matter whether Josephine Mallington had lied or not, once he was alone with her, all of it was inconsequential. He was like some animal, wanting her, needing her so much that he could no longer think straight…so much that he thought not of his father or of his duty or even of honour, but only of Josephine Mallington.

He had thought that sending her to La Roque would be an end to it, but it had only been an accelerant. Now she was in his tent, and before the night was out she would be in his bed.

Chapter Twelve

Josie heard the footsteps and saw the movement of the tent flap. Her heart began to pound as she wondered if it really were Dammartin returning. If something had happened to him, if it were Molyneux that had come in his stead… Her hands clenched by her sides. She rose swiftly to her feet, turning from the little table to face the tent flap, waiting, poised, ready.

'Captain Dammartin…' she breathed her relief '…it is you. I thought…' She gave a little smile and let the words fall unsaid.

'You thought what, *mademoiselle*?' he asked, and she could see that his eyes were dangerously dark and that something had changed since he had left. And she knew then that La Roque had destroyed any belief that Dammartin might have had in her.

The smile flitted from her face. 'It does not matter,' she said, and wrapped her shawl more tightly around her.

He lit the lantern and closed all of its shutters save for one. 'La Roque denies your accusations. He says that you are trying to cause trouble between us.'

'Of course he does,' she exclaimed. 'You did not think he would admit the truth, did you? Molyneux was *there*. I know what I heard.'

'Molyneux *was* there, but it is not how you think.' She saw the shadow of something flicker in his eyes.

'I have told you the truth, Captain Dammartin. It is Major La Roque who is lying.'

'It is your word, *mademoiselle*, against his. You are the daughter of the man who murdered my father. La Roque is a hero to all of France. He is a senior officer in the Emperor's army, a friend to my family; he is my godfather. Were you in my position, who would you believe?'

'La Roque is your godfather?' she said, and gave a mirthless laugh. 'Then I never had a chance of your belief.' She looked at him. 'Are you sending me back to him?'

His eyes held hers. 'No.'

The silence hissed between them.

'And what of Molyneux?'

'Molyneux is of no consequence.'

'You would keep me here, and yet you believe not a single word that I have said, not of La Roque or of Molyneux or my father. Why?' In that single questioning word there was disappointment and dread...and anticipation. She fixed her eyes on him, hoping that she was wrong.

'We both know why, Josephine,' he said, and began to unfasten his jacket.

She swallowed hard, feeling the sudden skitter of her heart. She shook her head as if to deny it, but she recognised too well the smoulder in his eyes and the familiar heat that ignited in response low in her belly.

'No,' she said, and shook her head again. 'I will not let you kiss me.'

He walked the few steps towards her, not stopping until

the skirt of her dress was brushing the toes of his riding
boots.

She felt his warmth across the small distance that separated them, and smelled the scent of him.

He raised a hand and traced a finger lightly against her
cheek.

Josie bit at her lower lip and resisted the sensation.
'Would you force me against my will?'

'No.' His voice was as gentle as his caress.

'Do not kiss me,' she pleaded, not trusting herself to
resist him if he did. 'Please do not.'

The dim flickering light shadowed his face, and softened
his eyes. He stared at her for a moment longer, and then
he turned away and moved to sit down in the same chair
in which Josie had been seated upon his arrival. He sighed
and raked a hand through his hair.

'What am I then to do with you, Josephine Mallington?'

She sat down in the other chair, to his left, resting her
hands gently upon the table's smooth wooden surface.

There was only the quietness of the night.

'I wish there was some way I could make you believe
the truth,' she said quietly.

'We will never agree on what is the truth.' His hand slid
over hers, even though he did not look at her, but faced
straight ahead, watching the tiny light of the lantern.

They sat there, not moving, not speaking, with only the
warmth of his hand resting on hers.

'I will ask you just one question, and then no more.
Were your father's journals within your portmanteau?'

'Yes.'

'Then I can never know what was in your father's mind
in Oporto. The one chance that I had is lost.'

Josie knew then a way that she could convince Dammartin of the truth. The cost was high, traitorous even;

once she would have died rather than pay it, but things had changed since then, much more than she ever could have known.

He was still looking in front of him, staring at the canvas, and it seemed that there was a despair about him. Her eyes traced the outline of the scar running down his cheek, the harsh lean planes of his face, the sweep of the dark lashes, the straightness of his nose, the hardness of his lips. A man that seemed invincible, and yet he hurt as she did. He had lost a father, like her.

'It is not lost,' she said softly. And her hand rotated beneath his so that their palms touched together and their fingers entwined. 'There is something I have not told you, Captain Dammartin.'

Slowly he turned his face to her.

'My father's journal for Oporto was not amongst the others in my portmanteau.'

She saw the hope leap in his eyes.

'It was the night that we walked together by the river. I took it out to read and did not replace it.'

His gaze clung to hers like a man drowning clings to life. 'You have this journal?'

'Yes. It is the reason La Roque was sending Molyneux to me tonight. He wanted the journal.'

'Josephine,' he whispered, 'do not lie to me of this above all things.'

'It is the truth. I have read my father's words from Oporto and there is nothing of murder in them. He writes of admiration and respect for your father, of their issuing invitations to visit each other's homes after the war. His are not the words of a man who would kill that same officer when he was paroled.'

His thumb stroked against hers. 'How am I to believe you, that man's daughter?'

She looked deep into his eyes and she saw the darkness of his pain and anguish, and the hope that her words had lit.

'Show me the journal, Josephine,' he said quietly. 'Let me read the words with my own eyes.'

'You will tell La Roque. He will take it like he took the others.'

'No, I promise.' He moved, his hands slipping up to cup her face. 'Please, Josephine. I will beg if that is what you want.'

Seconds seemed to stretch to minutes, and minutes to hours, in which they sat there like that—until at last Josie nodded.

She moved away, turned her back to him and began to unlace her dress.

Dammartin watched across the small distance between them while Josephine loosened her dress. For a moment he thought she had misunderstood, that what she would offer him was something quite different from the journal, but something that he wanted just the same. He felt himself harden at the thought, but then he realised that she was not stripping off the clothes, but seeking beneath and within, and he knew that she had not lied about the journal.

He waited, unable to take his eyes from her, anticipation spiralling within, until at last she fixed her clothing back in place and turned towards him.

She brought the notebook to the table and laid it down before him like some precious offering.

His eyes slid down to the small, battered book with its deep red covers all blotched and warped.

She sat down in the empty chair. 'The rain soaked through the leather of my satchel to reach its pages, but the writing is still legible.'

He stared at it, knowing that this was it, at last—

Mallington's voice from the past; Mallington's thoughts on Jean Dammartin.

His heart was beating fast now, and he could feel the prickle of sweat upon his palms. It was feeling that came before battle. That time of tense stillness, when fear churned in every man's gut, and his nostrils filled with it and his fingers grew numb with it, that time when one could scent his own death and the urge to run to safety was strong. The worst time, when men could do nothing but endure until with relief the order came to charge, or to fire, or to move, and the waiting was over. It was the same now.

'Read it,' she said.

He took a deep breath and with infinite care opened the book's covers, feeling them still warm with the heat from her body. Within, the pages were stained a pinky red where the dye had seeped from the covers. But it was as Josephine had said, the pencilled flowing script with its small, neat letters and its words crammed close together was still clear enough. Mallington had filled the page one way, and then turned it upside down and continued his writing in the spaces between his original lines.

His skin tingled as his fingers touched the paper. He turned the delicate pages, one by one, until he came at last to the date he was looking for: May 1809.

His heart was racing, his blood pumping hard. He held his focus on the date and breathed before allowing it to slip along the line and read the words that Lieutenant Colonel Mallington's hand had written.

He read the entries for the days from 12th May 1809 onwards, from the time that Wellington had routed the French from Oporto. His eyes raced over the words, pausing over the pertinent ones: *Dammartin...a most worthy adversary...confess to liking the fellow heartily...regret that fate has seen fit to place us each on opposing sides of this war...La Roque is scarcely to be noticed beside Dammartin...the two officers will be paroled...I bid adieu to Major Dammartin...agreed that should we survive this war then when peace is instilled we should become friends... invited me to his villa in Evran...I made a reciprocal invitation that he should come to Winchester...I returned their swords and provided them with weapons with which they might defend themselves against attack...it is the first time I pray that an enemy's journey shall be safe...having witnessed Dammartin's and his men's bravery and met the man himself...I can do nothing else as a gentleman.*

Dammartin closed the journal and sat back in his chair. There was a curious numbness within. All that he had believed these past months, all that he had done, were contrary to what was written in these few fragile pages. Mallington wrote of respect and honour and admiration. Josephine had been right: they did not sound to be the words of a murderer.

Upon the table her fingers wrapped gently around his. 'I am sorry,' she said gently.

'Why should you be sorry?' He tried to smile, but the curve of his lips was bitter. 'You have achieved what you wanted.'

'No.' She bit at her lip and looked at the flame's flicker within the lantern. 'I never wanted any of this.'

He lifted her hand, still entwined with his, and touched it to his mouth before placing it back down upon the table. 'Fate has played a cruel game with us.'

Her eyes met his. 'What are we to do?'

He shook his head, feeling empty and set adrift from all that was real. 'I do not know, Josephine. I honestly do not know.'

There was such a note of despondency and despair in

his voice that it seemed to Josie that a hand had reached into her chest and squeezed upon her heart.

She reached to touch his arm, patting a comfort.

And when he looked round at her, she could see the teardrop that ran down his ravaged cheek.

'Oh, Pierre,' she whispered, and went to him, wrapping her arms around him, cradled his head against her breast. She rocked him gently, soothing him, dropping small kisses to his hair. And with every breath she felt his pain, so raw and bleeding, as he wept silently into her heart. She held him for what seemed like hours, until the tight tension had gone from his body, and anguish had left, leaving in its place an empty quietness.

All was silent.

He rested against her, his arms around her waist, his cheek against her heart. Her fingers were threaded through his hair, massaging a slow rhythm. He raised his face and looked up into her eyes, and she knew in that moment that nothing would ever be the same again.

Gently she cupped a hand against his scarred cheek and moved her mouth to his. She kissed him with all that was in her heart, seeking to take away his pain, to heal the wound he had been dealt. And as she kissed him, she felt his lips awaken beneath hers, and he was kissing her back, his mouth sliding against hers.

He pulled her on to his knee, kissing her harder, with the same urgency that was rising within Josie. Their tongues danced together, teasing and moist. He kissed her and licked her and sucked her, while his hands worked at her dress's laces until her breasts were free beneath his fingers.

She knew what he would do, and she wanted it, wanted to feel his tantalising caress, wanted to feel his mouth roving over her breasts.

Her nipples were heavy and sensitive as he rolled them

between his fingers, plucking at them to make her pant with a desire that could no longer be suppressed. And when he licked at those hardened, rosy peaks, she closed her eyes and almost drowned in the ecstasy of it, arching her back, driving herself deeper into him.

He carried her to his bed, laid her down within the blankets. Stripping off his boots and his jacket, he discarded his shirt, until only his breeches remained. Beneath the low lantern light his naked skin was honey-gold, his body lean and hard with muscle. She reached up and trailed her fingers down the taut plane of his stomach, feeling the twitch of his muscles beneath her touch. His eyes closed momentarily and he groaned before his hand closed over hers and he lifted it to his mouth.

'Josephine,' he pleaded, and his voice was low and guttural as if in pain.

'Not Josephine,' she said, 'but Josie.'

'Josie.' Her name was like a caress from his lips.

He kissed the tip of her smallest finger before taking it into his mouth and sucking gently upon it.

The heat in Josie's thighs burned hotter.

He did the same to her ring finger and the finger next to it.

She dragged the air noisily into her lungs.

By the time he had reached her forefinger, her eyes were closed and she wanted to beg him to do whatever it was that her body was crying out for.

And then came her thumb.

'Pierre!' She arched upon the bed, thrusting her nipples into the air so that he would take them again. But he did not. He lowered himself over her and kissed her mouth. He kissed her face, her hair, her neck. He kissed every inch of each pale breast, teasing round their rosy summits, but his tongue stopping agonisingly short of taking them. 'Pierre!' she cried again, and tried to guide his mouth to suckle.

He raised his face to look into hers, the intensity of his gaze searing her. 'Josie,' he said, and seemed to stare into her very soul. *'Mon amie.'* He lowered his mouth and kissed her, deeply, passionately, giving all as she had done. She revelled in it, and felt his hand move beneath her skirts, his fingers sliding against the bare skin of her thighs, creeping ever up towards her most secret of places.

His face drew back and he looked into her eyes as he touched her.

Josie gasped loud.

'Sweet Josie,' he murmured and, holding her gaze with his, he began to caress her, sliding against her moist heat, slowly at first, then a little faster, building to a rhythm. She arched her neck, panting, feeling the blush of heat spreading throughout the entirety of her body. And still, he gazed into her eyes and she into his, as he stroked her in her most intimate of places. There was nothing of shame, nothing of embarrassment, only the most pressing of needs, escalating, urging his fingers to move faster, to never cease their magic.

'Pierre!'

He threaded the fingers of his left hand through the fingers of her right, pressing her hand into the softness of the pillow above her head. And all the while his other fingers worked busily.

Through the pleasure was a desperation, a need so utterly overwhelming that she could not help herself reaching for it. She needed him, needed him more than life itself. And the urgency was so great and the pleasure so strong that she could not help herself panting faster and faster as she strained towards it. Her eyes shuttered with the intensity of it. She felt his mouth close over her nipple, sucking at it, laving it, and at this final touch that she had so craved the world seemed to explode in a myriad of pleasure. She cried out loud as a thousand sunbeams danced throughout her body and a wave of total bliss rippled out from the warm pulsating centre between her legs.

Dammartin's hand was no longer moving, his fingers cupped her still, warm and gentle as they lay there.

She opened her eyes to find that he was watching her.

He smiled. 'My sweet girl.' Then he lay down by her side, curving his body around hers so that she could feel the strong steady beat of his heart against her back, and he held her.

And Josie knew that she had given herself to him completely, holding nothing back. She was his. She did not think of what the future would bring, only of here and now, of Pierre Dammartin...and how she loved him.

'She is not to be found because she is with Dammartin. There has been a change of plan.' La Roque swilled the brandy around the glass. 'He knows that you have been watching the girl for me.'

Molyneux's eyes bulged. 'He will kill me!'

'He will not. Captain Dammartin understands that you were acting under my orders and that it was for his own good.'

'He is a hard man, sir, a cold-hearted, ruthless killer who—'

La Roque raised his eyes from the brandy glass. 'He is my godson, Lieutenant.'

Molyneux stared down at the ground. 'I apologise, Major.' There was a pause before he looked back up. 'Then Mademoiselle Mallington is to stay with the Captain?'

'For now.' La Roque smiled and pulled at his moustache. 'Do not worry, Molyneux. Dammartin will soon tire of shagging her. And when he does, you must be ready to act. The journal must be found…and the girl, Lieutenant, will be yours.'

'What if Dammartin finds the journal first? Do I still get her?'

'Dammartin knows nothing of the missing journal, and he is the last person that Mademoiselle Mallington will reveal it to. You, on the other hand, Molyneux, must be a little more persuasive. Do whatever it takes to get me that journal. Make the most of her in Ciudad Rodrigo, for we will leave her to General Gardanne's men when we return to Santarém. Then maybe Mallington's influence will be destroyed and my godson can resume his life once more.' La Roque filled Molyneux's glass with brandy. 'To Ciudad Rodrigo and all that awaits.'

The glasses chinked, and the two men drank in silence.

Dammartin sat by the rekindled fire and watched the beginnings of the new day dawn as over in the east the darkness of the night sky began to pale. The tin mug was warm between his hands, the steam from the coffee within rising up as wisps of smoke to drift into what was left of the night.

He needed time to think, even though he had lain awake most of the night hours doing just that. Could the man who had written such words of Jean Dammartin within his journal then have killed him? It was not impossible, he supposed, but the Mallington that the journal conjured was the same Mallington that had given his daughter into Dammartin's keeping as he lay dying within a cold monastery room. The scene from Telemos was etched upon Dammartin's mind. He had replayed it a hundred times in his head, studying each of Mallington's words, his every nuance. *He was a most worthy opponent*, Mallington had said. *I do not need to ask that you treat her honourably. I already know that, as Jean Dammartin's son, you will do nothing other.*

More than eighteen months of hatred, eighteen months of planning a revenge…against a man who it now seemed was not guilty. It had to be Mallington. La Roque had witnessed the murder, La Roque had seen his father die by Mallington's hand. Could his godfather have been mistaken? Could he be lying as Josie had said? Lying about his father, lying about the journals, and about Molyneux? Major Frederic La Roque—a man that he had known all of his life, a man that had kissed his father's cheek, and dangled his brother upon his knee, who had laughed with his mother, who had eaten at his parents' table and slept beneath their roof. The thought was anathema.

Maybe Mallington had not pulled the trigger, but there had to be some reasonable explanation as to why La Roque had thought it was so. Or maybe Mallington had truly been insane and killed the man he had written so warmly of, avoiding a record of the crime to spare his daughter the truth. Maybe Mallington really was guilty after all.

He heard the soft tread behind him and did not need to look round to know that she stood there.

'Pierre?' she whispered.

She was standing with a blanket wrapped around her, the crumpled red-and-black skirt visible below. Her eyes were wide and cautious, as if she doubted what she would find in him this morning. An image of her beneath him flashed in his mind, her face flushed with passion as his fingers slid within her secret silken folds. And he thought how he had entered his tent last night so intent upon taking her to satisfy only himself, and how differently the night had unravelled. He had wanted to pleasure her, to show what heady delights there could be. He had needed to give to her as she had given to him, just to give, not to take. That his own passion, his own desperate need, had gone unslaked did not matter.

There was such selflessness within her as to wrap around him like a quilt of the warmest softest down. No one, save his father, had ever seen beyond the armour that he wore in this life, until last night. Josie had witnessed the full extent of his weakness, looked upon his despair, vulnerable and raw, and she had gathered up the shattered pieces of his soul and fitted them back together—the daughter of the man he had so hated.

He was ashamed of his weakness, and that she had witnessed it. But his shame was all the greater for knowing how harshly he had treated her for a crime that he was no longer sure that Mallington had committed. Last night had been of despair and guilt and gratitude. None of it was Josephine Mallington's fault.

He held out his arm to her in an encompassing gesture, and she came to him, sitting down beside him, as he snuggled her in close by his side.

'You could not sleep,' she said.

He shook his head gave a wry smile. 'Coffee?' He offered her his mug.

She accepted the cup from his fingers.

'You said that your mother was French.'

She nodded and sipped at the coffee. 'My parents met when *Maman* came to England in 1784, the year after the last war had ended. She was very young and very pretty.'

'Like you,' he said.

She smiled. 'Her parents did not wish the marriage, for my father was English and a military man. He was also older than her—sixteen years, to be precise. But she loved him, and he loved her, and so she defied her parents to marry him.'

He looked into her eyes, noticing the way that they seemed to light up when she spoke of her parents. 'Then your father was a lucky man.'

She smiled again and passed the coffee back to him. 'My mother followed him all around the world with the army and I never once remember hearing her complain of it. First they were in North America, but I remember little of that. Then my father was sent to the West Indies—to Jamaica. That is were my mother died. Yellow fever, the doctor said. There was nothing that could be done for her.'

His arm tightened around her to pull her closer as they sat side by side before the small, weak flames of the fire.

'You stayed alone with your father.'

'And Edward, my brother. Papa was eventually recalled to England before being sent to Ireland. Edward joined the 20th Light Dragoons and was posted to Portugal. I accompanied my father when he was sent here too.'

'Where is your brother now?'

'He died at the Battle of Vimiero; he was three and twenty years old.'

'I am sorry, Josie. You have suffered too much loss.'

'We both have,' she said, and lifted the back of his hand from her waist to briefly touch against her lips. 'May I ask you of your father?'

He nodded, even though he had no wish to reveal any more of his pain.

Her question was worse than he could have anticipated. 'How exactly did he die?'

Something of the old bitterness welled up as it ever did when he thought of what Mallington was supposed to have done. 'Are you sure that you wish to hear this?'

'I think that I must hear it.'

'Very well.' He took a breath and told her. 'My father and Major La Roque were captured by Lieutenant Colo-

nel Mallington at Oporto. They were his prisoners before
being released with their parole. Not a mile after they left
his camp he came after them, alone. And when he found
them he came in close, levelled a musket and fired. The
bullet killed my father instantly. Mallington reloaded and
shot again. La Roque had no choice but to ride for his life.
Mallington's bullet skimmed his arm. He was still bleeding
when he reached the French lines; he was lucky to survive.
So now you know the full extent of it.'

He had expected shock, denial, even distress from Josie,
but not the wide-eyed revelation that he saw there.

She turned to him, gripped at his arm. 'The man that
La Roque saw could not have been my father.'

'Josie,' he said quietly, 'the journal does not touch upon
what happened after La Roque and my father left.'

'No, you do not understand,' she said urgently, and he
could sense an underlying fervour within her. 'My father
was injured at Vimiero, a sword blade across the fingers.
He healed well enough to grip the hilt of a sword, but he
could not pull back the hammer of a flintlock or release
the trigger to fire a bullet. You see, if Major Dammartin
was shot, it could not have been by my father's hand; that
would have been a physical impossibility.'

An image flashed in his head of the little room in the
monastery at Telemos, of the dead bodies of men with their
rifles by their sides, of the one woman that faced them
still, her rifle aimed at his her heart. He thought of the
grey-haired old man and the sword that had fallen from
his hand. What use was a sword against a barrage of bullets? Even his daughter had used a rifle, but Mallington
himself had not.

And it all began to make sense. 'Then La Roque was
mistaken in thinking that the officer was Mallington.'

'Perhaps the man had a look of my father about him.'

'A similar uniform, one of his officers, maybe.'

'No.' Josie shook her head. 'Whoever the villain was, he was not a rifleman. You said he used a musket. The Fifth of the 60th Foot are a rifle battalion. They are issued with rifles, not muskets. And as rifles are so much more accurate over distance, the killer would not have had to approach your father so closely had he used one.'

Dammartin nodded, knowing that everything she said made sense. There was a silence in which he let the thoughts settle. He did not know whether to be sad or glad. He did not know for sure whether she had proved to him at last Mallington's innocence. But the cold, heavy sensation sat upon him that he had persecuted an innocent man and all because La Roque had made a mistake.

'I am never going to know the true identity of the man who murdered my father, am I?'

She slid her hand around his waist, and dropped a small kiss to the side of his arm closest to her face.

They sat in silence, together, and watched as day drew back the dark curtain of night.

Somewhere in the distance a crow cawed. There were stirrings from the tents.

He drained the last of the coffee. 'Come, we should make ready.'

They got to their feet.

'Last night…' she said.

He touched a gentle finger to her lips to stay her words and, taking her hand in his, they walked back to the tent.

In the pale morning light she could see the crumple of his bed, that she had so recently vacated, and across from it the smooth surface of the table, empty save for the burned-out lantern.

'The journal…' She glanced round at him, feeling the sudden flurry of her heart. 'Pierre!'

'It is safe.'

'Where?'

'It is better that the journal stays with me, Josie.'

Her heart skipped a beat. 'You said that you would not take it from me; you promised.'

He took hold of her hand again and pulled her gently to him. 'I said that I would not tell Major La Roque.'

Her stomach seemed to drop to the soles of her feet. 'It is not yours to keep.' She stared at him. 'I let you read it in good faith.'

'Josie.' His thumb soothed a caress against her palm. 'I promise it is safe.'

'I trusted you,' she said, and the ground upon which she had built that trust seemed to tilt.

She saw the slight flinch at her words, there and then gone so quickly. His eyes were dark and unreadable as they met hers.

'You are a British prisoner in a French camp. Already your portmanteau has been stolen. I will ensure both your and the journal's safety until you can be returned to Lisbon.' She saw the flicker of his muscles as he clenched his jaw. 'It is the least I can do for your father.'

Their eyes held.

And in her heart was gladness that at last Dammartin believed in her father's innocence, and a terrible sadness, an ache almost. Papa was dead and Jean Dammartin's murderer would never be found…and soon Josie would be back with the British.

She nodded a small acknowledgement and looked away.

Nothing could change what had happened.

The war and the ghosts of their fathers stood between them.

Chapter Thirteen

The day's march was long, and Dammartin kept Josie by his side for every hour of it. There was no let up in the pace as Foy pushed the men relentlessly on, knowing that they were so close to their destination. Dammartin felt fatigue heavy in his muscles, and the gnaw of hunger in his belly. He glanced again at Josie, knowing that if he felt this bad, then she must be feeling it a hundred times worse. The grey blanket enveloped her as she sat looking straight ahead. He studied her profile.

The shadows beneath her eyes were dark against the pallor of her skin. Although she sat her saddle well, he could see the slight droop in her shoulders, and the weariness about her.

It was ten days since Telemos, ten days since he had watched Mallington die and taken Josie as his prisoner. He remembered her standing there, in that blood-splattered room in the monastery with the rifle in her hand, standing before her father, guarding Mallington against him and his men. One woman against them all. Defiant. Fearless. It was a sight he would never forget. So small, so slender, and yet so strong. He had both hated her and respected her. Only ten days later and it was not hate that he felt for the woman riding by his side.

He remembered the feel of her body pressed against his, her softness, her strength, the beat of her heart beneath his cheek. And the thought of her warmed him against the damp cold of the day, and prevented the chill wind's cut.

Above the sky stretched to an unending white-grey, but Dammartin did not notice. Ahead lay Ciudad Rodrigo.

A massive medieval wall enclosed the city. They marched through the fortified gateway, the horses' hooves clopping loud against the cobblestones that lined the streets. Josie looked up through the twilight to see an ancient castle nestling on the hill just above the town. She was so tired that she was almost slumped in Fleur's saddle, her fingers too numb to know if the reins were still within them. The little mare followed Dante and Dammartin.

She was aware of lights and of buildings, the hum of voices and soldiers dressed in Bonaparte's blue everywhere. The 8th did not stop until they reached the stables. Josie just sat there, knowing that this was the end of the journey. General Foy would go on to Paris, but of Dammartin's fate and her own, she did not know.

'Josie.'

She heard his voice, soft with concern, felt his hands helping her down. And then he took his baggage and placed a supportive arm around her waist, not caring that his men saw. Together they walked out of the stables to face what awaited them in Ciudad Rodrigo.

The room in which Dammartin had been quartered was small but clean and tidy. He could only be thankful that he and Josie had the room to themselves and did not have to share. With five thousand Frenchmen in the town, he knew that he was lucky indeed.

His portmanteau lay abandoned on the floor. Josie sat perched at the edge of the bed.

'What will happen now?' She was glad that her voice sounded calm.

'General Foy will go on with a smaller fresh escort, to Salamanca and Valladolid. We rest here and await our orders to return to Santarém along with Ciudad Rodrigo's garrison and that of Almeida.'

'And what of me?'

'You stay with me until I can return you to Wellington at Lisbon.'

She breathed her relief.

He dropped a kiss to the top of her head. 'Get some sleep, Josie. I must speak with Major La Roque, but I will be back soon. Lock the door behind me and keep it locked. There are too many Frenchmen about this night in search of a beautiful woman.' He pressed his lips to hers in a hard passionate kiss that was over too quickly. 'And I intend to keep you all to myself.'

'Come, come, Pierre, this is not like you. You have let the woman get under your skin, and now she is tormenting you with her lies.' Major La Roque dismissed his servant and refilled both his and Dammartin's glasses of wine before resuming his attack on the pile of chicken that lay on his plate.

Dammartin rubbed unthinkingly at the edge of his jaw. 'But think about it; if Mallington's hand injury meant that he could not fire a musket—'

'Are you doubting my word?' La Roque stopped eating.

'Of course I am not. But I am suggesting that you might

have been mistaken in the identity of the man that fired the shot. The shooter may have looked like Mallington—'

'The shooter damn well was Mallington. He was twenty yards away. I saw the bastard clearly with my own two eyes. Were it anyone else making such an accusation, I would place my sword at their throat.'

Dammartin raked a hand through his hair, his fingers leaving a ruffle of dark fingers in their wake. 'Frederic—'

'You wound me, Pierre, deeply.' La Roque pushed his plate away.

'Forgive me. It was never my intention.'

'I dread to think what your mother would say.'

Dammartin sighed. 'I meant no insult. It is not you that I doubt, but who you think that you saw pulling that trigger. I do not believe that it was Mallington.'

'What can have brought about such a madness in your mind?' La Roque's face paled. His eyes glittered as he stared at Dammartin, intent on his godson's answer.

Dammartin thought of Mallington's journal; he thought, too, of his promise to Josie. 'There is nothing in particular. I have been questioning Mademoiselle Mallington, and her answers have made me think.'

'What has the little bitch been saying?'

'She spoke in defence of her father's character.'

La Roque flushed. 'She is a liar, Pierre, a conniving, manipulative little liar, and the sooner you see it the better. You would do well to remember who she is, and who I am too.'

Dammartin looked into La Roque's now-ruddy face as his godfather made an effort to call back the anger of his words.

'I am sorry, Pierre, but I cannot forget what I saw Mallington do to your father, and I cannot forget that I was forced to ride away and leave him there dead. My feelings run high on the matter; they always will. When I look at Mademoiselle Mallington and see how she has turned your mind from the truth, I am enraged and, at the same time, beyond despair.' La Roque clenched his teeth and blinked away the moisture from his eyes.

'Frederic, Frederic...' Dammartin rose and pouring a large glass of brandy passed it to La Roque.

La Roque sniffed. 'I thought if you bedded her it would destroy her influence over you.' He took a generous swig of brandy.

'I am not influenced by Mademoiselle Mallington.'

'But I am afraid, Pierre, that you are, and it breaks my heart to see what Mallington's daughter has done to you.'

Dammartin took his farewells of his godfather and made his way back to Josie. He heard the echo of La Roque's words, and of his own.

La Roque was convinced that Mallington had fired the bullet that killed Jean Dammartin, and he had been there, witnessed the whole thing. Did what Mallington had written in his journal really change that? Could Dammartin even trust what Josie had said of her father's inability to fire a gun?

He had told La Roque that he was not influenced by Josie, when in truth it was she that filled his mind, his every walking hour. He craved her. He needed her. She influenced him beyond measure, whether he willed it or not. And the realisation of the extent of her control over him made Dammartin uneasy. Far from clarifying matters this night, he seemed only to have made things worse.

Josie was lying half dozing when she finally heard the tap at the door. She slipped from beneath the covers of the bed, shivering as the chill of the night touched her body through the thin linen of her shift.

'Pierre?' Only when she heard his reply did she turn the key within the lock to let him enter.

He smelled of damp night air and brandy, and the wool of his sleeve was cold beneath her fingers. The night was clear and moonlight flooded through the small window to bathe him in its strange silver light and its magic.

Outside the cathedral clock sounded eleven chimes.

She knew immediately that his meeting with La Roque had not gone well. His expression seemed strained, his face harshly handsome, his scar sinister.

'You are cold,' she said, brushing her fingers against his, the words so trivial beside everything that she really wanted to say.

'And tired.' He rubbed at the stubble of his chin. 'We should sleep.'

She retreated to the bed, snuggling beneath the covers over at the side closest to the window, lying there, watching him while he stripped off his clothing.

The contrast of moonlight and shadows played upon his body, revealing the taut rippled muscles of his abdomen, his chest, his shoulders and arms. She felt his weight tip the bed as he sat down upon its edge to ease off his boots and his stockings. His hands moved to free the fall on his breeches and he rose to his feet once more. Josie looked away, feeling her heart beating too fast, and the sudden flash of excitement within her belly. Her mouth was dry; she wetted her lips. She heard the soft thud of his breeches hitting the floor and then the mattress tilted once more as he climbed in beside her. She lay still, anticipating his touch, the feel of his hands upon her. But Dammartin made no move.

He lay there on his back, saying nothing, eyes open and staring up at the ceiling, waves of tension emanating from him.

Apprehension gripped at her and she knew that something was wrong.

The silence strained between them, hissing and loud, until she could bear it no more.

'How was your meeting with Major La Roque?'

She heard him swallow. 'There is nothing to speak of,' he said in a quiet voice devoid of emotion. 'The hour is late, go to sleep.'

'What is wrong, Pierre?' Dread tightened her stomach to a small, hard ball. She wondered what La Roque had said to make him this way.

'There is nothing wrong.' He sighed and turned away from her, to lie on his side.

She felt the sting of his rejection, and shivered. All of the warmth, of what had bound them together, had gone, and she did not understand why. Pride would not let her ask him again. She rolled to her side, close to the edge of the bed, and gazed out of the window.

At Telemos the moon had been a slim crescent, now it loomed huge and full outside, too big to be real, too bright for the night. So much had happened in those days in between. Her father was dead, his good name despoiled, and Josie's innocence lost. She had hated Pierre Dammartin, hated him more than she had thought it possible to hate, but somehow in their journey hate had turned to love. She could not say where, or how or even why. She should hate him still, but her heart was a traitor to all logic. And fool that she was, she had believed that he felt something of it, too, this ridiculous, accursed, forbidden love. But now…now she was no longer sure.

The ice crept from her feet up through her legs, from the tips of her fingers up through her arms. Josie did not shiver; rather she embraced the chill, praying it would soon reach her heart and numb the ache within.

Dammartin fixed his eyes upon the door, the wall, the crooked picture that hung upon it, anything in a bid to resist the temptation to turn to the woman who lay behind him. He could hear the soft sound of her breathing, feel her small movements as she curled on her side. Her faint scent of lavender water touched his nose. He tried to stay strong, to resist, determined that he, Pierre Dammartin, would not be so easily under the influence of any woman, but he could feel the insistent prick of guilt at the callous words he had uttered. And his mind was filled with her: whether she was hurting, whether she was cursing him, the sight of her standing by the door in her shift with the flimsy material revealing the protrusion of her nipples and contours of her hips. His skin tingled at the memory of that brief brush of her fingers.

Dammartin could resist no more. He rolled onto his back. 'Josie.'

She ignored him, lying there so still as if she were asleep.

He moved to her, curving his body around hers, warming her chill with his heat. His arm curled around her, anchoring her in, his hand finding hers and closing over it.

'Forgive me, Josie,' he said softly against her ear. He felt her hand move within his. 'I did not mean to hurt you.'

She turned in his arms, rolling round to look up into his face.

'I should not have spoken to you as I did.'

'You are tired,' she said, making excuses for him.

'No.' He shook his head. 'I am a fool…' he stroked her hair, gliding his hand down to gently cradle her face '…a thousand times over.' He lowered his face, and pressed a kiss to her forehead. 'There is something between us, Josie, you know that, do you not?' His lips lightly traced the line of her nose to place a kiss upon its tip. 'I have tried so hard to fight it.' His mouth reached hers and lingered so close above, his breath brushing warm against her lips. 'Harder than you can imagine.' Their lips entwined, her mouth responding to his with such sweet tenderness that he almost could not break the kiss to pull back and look deeply into her eyes. 'I want to kiss you and never stop. I want to love you for an eternity. I need you, Josie Mallington. I need you like I have never needed anyone.' His thumb caressed her cheek, slowly, sensually, conveying with that small movement what his words could not. 'But if you do not want this…if—'

She touched the tips of her fingers to his lips, cutting off his words. 'I need you too. I know I should not. It is against all sense, all logic, everything that is right. My father, and yours, and the war…'

He saw in her eyes the same agony, the same desperation and fight as were in his soul. And he knew that Josie was as powerless in all of this as he; that desire had made slaves of them both. Her eyelids briefly closed and she shook her head, and when her eyes opened again, she reached up and touched her lips to his in a single kiss as light as a butterfly's landing.

They were wrapped around each other, so close that Josie could feel the beat of his heart where her hand rested against his chest, strong and steady like the man himself.

She sighed.

'Josie,' he whispered, and one hand massaged a caress against her back where he held her, while the other tilted her face up until his mouth lowered to find hers. And he began to kiss her again, slowly, gently, filled with tenderness and love.

He kissed her and kissed her, the stubble upon his chin scratching her skin pink, until their mouths began to move harder and faster, and their lips grew moist and needful. The kiss was everything to Josie. It clouded the pain of the past and obscured the fear of the future. There was only here and now and Pierre Dammartin. Her heart was thudding, but not with fear. Desire flowed through her veins. Her breasts tingled with it. Her thighs grew warm with it. She wanted the kiss never to end.

His hands moved down to caress her breasts, his thumbs teasing across their pebbled peaks. The thin linen of her shift strained against their sensitivity as Josie arched, thrusting herself into his hands, aching for his touch, wanting more.

Then his hands were pulling at the shift's neckline. 'Take it off,' he whispered.

She sat up and did as he bid, as eager to rid herself of the barrier between them as he was. But when she lay back down, he caught hold of the blankets before she could cover herself again.

'Let me look at you. I want to see you, every inch of you.'

She lay there, naked and exposed as the dark smoulder of his gaze travelled over her. He reached to touch her breast.

'I—I wish to see you too,' she said, amazed at her own boldness.

He smiled at that and climbed from the bed to stand before her. The moonlight paled his skin, and revealed every detail of his tall, athletic frame.

Josie stared, amazed at how different his body was to hers. He was all hard and lean and muscular, nothing of softness, nothing of curves. Her eyes skimmed the breadth of his shoulders, the strength of his arms, the dark, flat nipples of his chest, down lower to the regimented pattern of muscles that sat in lines across his abdomen, and lower still…to the nest of dark hair and his manhood that sprang from it, so large and rigid. Her cheeks flushed hot and her gaze dropped rapidly down his strong muscular legs to his feet.

'Do I pass muster, Mademoiselle Mallington?' he asked with a wry grin.

She cleared the dryness from her throat, feeling her cheeks grow hotter still. 'I have never looked upon the male form before.'

'That I am glad to hear.'

Then he reached his hand to her and pulled her up to him.

They stood there, naked in the moonlight. And Josie no longer noticed the coldness of the room, but the contrast of his skin as it caressed hers, and how big and honed and strong he was. She traced her fingers up his arm, across the tight, hard muscle of his chest, up his neck to reach his jaw, feeling the dark shadow of stubble rasp rough beneath her fingers. Her hand crept farther up to lay gently against the scar that ravaged his left cheek.

He stood very still, his eyes glittering and dark in the moonlight.

Then, standing on her tiptoes, she reached her face up and kissed the top of the scar. One kiss and then another and another, tracing down the long line of the scar until all of it had been kissed.

From outside in the streets came the sound of men's voices, French, drunk, the clatter of their boots against the cobbles, and of women's laughter, deep and throaty. But neither Josie's nor Dammartin's gazes shifted. They stayed steady, trained on each other.

He moved his knuckles to gently stroke the outer edges of her breasts. She sucked the breath hard into her lungs.

'You are beautiful,' he whispered, the backs of his fingers thrumming against her taut nipples, 'so beautiful.'

He dropped to his knees before her and she gasped, feeling the excitement shimmer within her as his lips grazed the skin of her stomach. His breath was hot, searing a path up to her ribs. Her breasts were heavy with need, ripe for his touch. Her nipples, standing to attention, hard and ready within the cool night air.

She did not look, just stood there waiting, while in her mind she was urging him to do it, begging his mouth to suckle upon her. And as his mouth closed over one breast, his tongue flicking over its most sensitive tip, she sighed her relief. He sucked her and the warmth low in her belly ignited. She looked then, saw his head so dark against the pallor of her breast, and the sight of what he was doing to her caused her thighs to burn. Her fingers threaded through his hair, pressing him closer, inviting him to feast all the more.

But he pulled back, his dark smouldering gaze flicking up to hers, as his mouth slid lower, retracing its path to where it had started. She felt him hot against her stomach, his tongue circling around her navel before travelling on down. Josie gasped as he kissed the curled fair hair of her mound, his hands moulding to her buttocks, guiding what he wanted to his mouth.

'Pierre!' She gasped in shock.

But he was between her legs and she found herself opening instinctively to him. She groaned as his tongue stroked her most intimate of places, and the unexpected raw pleasure of it shimmied through her. He kissed her there and the need within her spiralled. He sucked her and the need stoked hotter and hotter until she was burning with it. His tongue flicked and licked at her and the need raged, unbridled and wanton, and she was panting and her legs were trembling.

He rose then, scooped her up into his arms and laid her on the bed, climbing over her and pulling the blankets to cover them both.

She felt his manhood against her belly, probing and firm, while elsewhere their bodies barely touched.

He stroked her hair, stroked her cheek, looked deep into her eyes and there she saw such love that it took her breath away.

'Pierre,' she whispered his name into the stillness of the night. 'Pierre.' And she knew only the depth of her love for this man and the depth of her desire.

He moved, and his manhood was between her legs, touching where his mouth had been, sliding with such slow enticement against her wetness. She wanted him. She needed him. Such overwhelming love could not be wrong. Her hips moved against his instinctively, sliding herself along the length of his shaft, gasping with the pleasure it wrought.

'Josie,' he whispered into her ear, and there was a pause before he thrust into her, filling her with himself. There was the smallest of pains, but he was kissing her again and their breaths mingled and their bodies were unified, and the pain was forgotten. As he began to move inside her, Josie knew that this was meant to be—nothing had ever seemed so right.

They were as one, a man and his woman moving together in the most intimate of sharings—a physical expression of their love, two souls entwined. With each thrust Pierre claimed her as his own. She writhed beneath him, feeling the pleasure riotous and wanton, knowing that this bond would bind them for eternity. She looked up into his face, and it was dark and shadowed despite the brightness of the moon high in the sky outside, and the intensity in his eyes was scalding. Someone groaned, moaned, gasped and she did not know whether it was Pierre or herself from whom the sounds issued.

She loved him, loved him absolutely, overwhelmingly. She clutched at him, moving faster with him, clinging to him, crying out his name for this merging of souls until, with one last thrust, all the barriers broke, and her whole being exploded in a myriad of ecstasy. Such bliss. Such euphoria. Such love. The joy of it pulsated through every inch of her being, every corner of her mind.

She was his, and he was hers. They were as one.

Josie could see that the strength of love transcended everything; all else was tiny in comparison with its vastness. Love was all. War and power and politics were as nothing. All that had been and all that lay ahead was, in that moment, irrelevant. She loved him; they had shared that love in a union of their bodies, and nothing else mattered.

They clung together in the darkness, even when Pierre arranged the covers over them that they might not grow cold through the night. She clung to him and there was no need for words. She did not think of the past nor of the future. There was only now, this precious moment with the man that she loved, and the glorious wonder of it. And eventually she slept.

Major La Roque sat up late. He had finished the best part of a bottle of brandy and it still did not make matters any better. It was all Josephine Mallington's fault. How he rued the day that they had chanced upon Mallington and the girl in Telemos. *Then* it had seemed like a godsend. Mallington's death should have freed him from the constant torment the past months had brought. But he had not reckoned on the girl.

What kind of madman took his daughter to war? What was she even doing there in that goddamn monastery? She should have been killed there, like her father. La Roque still did not understand how she could have walked out of the monastery alive.

Damn her, and the spell she had woven over his godson. Because of her, Pierre was asking too many questions. Because of her, Pierre doubted his own godfather's word. Jean Dammartin was dead, and La Roque's heart was still heavy with the grief of it, but at least there had always been Pierre. But now Pierre no longer believed Mallington's guilt and that knowledge shook the very foundations of La Roque's defences.

He stared at the empty brandy glass, tracing his finger slowly around its rim—such a delicate balancing act, just like life itself, he thought. He had involved Molyneux for Pierre's own good, trusting in his own instinct that the girl might cause trouble, but not for one moment had he imagined just what her presence might lead to.

Pierre should have been repulsed by her, he should have hated her as La Roque now hated her. But Pierre had wanted her, and now it did not matter how quickly he tired of bedding her. He could cast her aside tomorrow and it would be too late; the damage had already been done, the spectres raised.

La Roque unstoppered the bottle and emptied the last of the brandy into his glass.

There was nothing else for it, nothing else he could do. What damn choice did he have if he wanted to survive? The agony that he had endured in these months seemed trivial in comparison to that which lay ahead, but La Roque would bear it; he had to. It would be the best for them all in the end. All the risk had to be destroyed. He sat alone, sipping his brandy, and made his plans for tomorrow.

* * *

Dammartin woke, and for the first time in such a long time there was a contentment about him, a calmness, a warmth. He felt the weight of Josie's legs entwined in his and he smiled. Last night had been wonderful; this morning was wonderful; Josie Mallington was simply wonderful.

The light was still murky with the night, but there seemed to be a slightly golden quality about it, a strange brightness within the dark. He dropped a kiss to Josie's head and, taking care not to wake her, climbed from the bed. Fetching up his discarded jacket from the chair, he draped it around his shoulders against the chill and moved to stand quietly at the window.

At one side the sky was lit with a warm, golden hue, while across the way still lay the mid-inky blue of night. And as he watched the glow intensified and spread, warm and ethereal. Across the city the rooftops were covered with a glittering white frost, and from a few chimneys smoke curled wispy into the air. Dawn moved across the sky, lightening its blue, opening up a new day. A bird was singing, while others chirped, and it seemed to Dammartin the most glorious of mornings to be alive.

His mind slipped once more to the woman sleeping in the bed behind him, and his heart seemed to fill with joy and he found that he was smiling. If this was lust, it was like no lust Dammartin had ever known. La Roque might say what he would, but Dammartin had no intention of giving up Josie. He wanted to hold her in his arms for ever, to keep her safe from all harm, to make her happy. He smiled again at the thought of it.

'Pierre?' Her voice sounded sleepy and unsure.

He turned from the window and went back to bed,

snuggling into her, ignoring her protestations that he was cold.

'I will soon make you warm again, *ma chérie*,' he whispered against her ear. And he kissed her, and, with such gentle tenderness, loved her all over again.

The streets were busy with voices and footsteps by the time that Dammartin finally left the bed to hurriedly wash, shave and dress.

Josie was sitting up in the bed, the covers pulled high, hugging her knees. Part of her feared to ask the question, not wishing to destroy what last night and this morning had brought, but the other part knew that she must.

'Pierre...' She hesitated, before continuing, 'What did Major La Roque say last night that was so very bad?'

The blade within Dammartin's hand nicked the edge of his chin. *'Merde,'* he muttered beneath his breath, and pressed the towel to stem the blood.

'I am sorry,' she said, 'I should not have asked.'

Dammartin sighed. 'You have every right to ask, Josie, but I do not think that you will like the answer.' He finished scraping the beard growth from his face before splashing the water up to cleanse away the stubble-peppered soap lather. Only when he had finished and was drying his face did he turn to her.

'La Roque was only twenty yards from the man that shot my father. He is adamant that the man was Lieutenant Colonel Mallington and no other.'

'But you know that is impossible. You have read my father's journal. You know about the injury to his hand.'

'I am afraid that neither are conclusive proof of his innocence, Josie.'

'But you believed me before.' She threw aside the covers

and climbed out of the bed to stand there naked beside it. 'Are you saying that you no longer do so?'

Dammartin's gaze swept briefly down over her body. 'I think that your father did not murder mine, but—' his eyes came back up to meet hers '—the truth is, I can never be absolutely certain of it.'

The hurt welled up in her, gushing and disbelieving. 'Then you do not truly believe me at all,' she said, and all of the magic of the night and the morning shrivelled and died.

'That is not what I am saying, Josie.' He pulled the shirt on over his head, and lifted his breeches from where they lay on the floor.

'It sounds like that to me,' she retorted.

'I do not have time to argue with you over this, this morning. We will speak of it later, I promise.' He fastened the fall on his breeches and fetched his cravat and waist-coat from the chair.

'What of La Roque stealing my father's journals? What of his giving me to Molyneux that he might find the missing journal? Do you believe the truth of that?' She watched him, holding her breath, waiting for his answer.

'Josie,' he chided.

'Tell me,' she said from between gritted teeth.

She heard his sigh. He finished tying the cravat in place and looked round from the mirror. 'If La Roque had the journals, I would know of it. What need has he to lie? Your portmanteau was probably stolen and dumped without the journals ever having been recovered.'

'And Molyneux?' she demanded.

'You are a beautiful woman, Josie, and Molyneux can hardly keep his breeches up at the best of times.'

'That is not true; he is married with two small sons.'

He gathered his boots and sat upon the chair to pull

them hard upon his feet. 'Molyneux is not married, and as to children, who knows what he has left behind. He was spinning you a story, Josie, that he might crawl beneath your skirts.'

She flinched at his baseness. 'He was acting on La Roque's orders.'

Dammartin eased himself into his jacket, fastening each button with speed. 'La Roque may well have encouraged Molyneux's interest as he so disapproves of mine. He loved my father and sees…our friendship, as a betrayal.'

Josie looked down at her nakedness, to her breasts peaked hard with the cold, and the bloodsmears that stained the pale skin of her inner thighs. She had given herself to him, body and heart, and still he did not believe her. And she could have laughed bitterly at the irony of his talk of betrayal.

'You do not believe anything that I have told you,' she said, and could not hide the anger and hurt from her words.

'Chérie.' He came to her, pulling a blanket from the bed to wrap around her, rubbing his hands over her to chase away the chill. 'You misinterpreted what you overheard of La Roque's and Molyneux's conversation.' His hand stroked against her hair. 'Now get dressed before you are frozen completely.' He pressed a brief kiss to her lips. 'I am already late, I have to go, but we will talk of this later, yes?'

'No,' she said firmly, 'I do not wish to talk of it later.'

'I have not the time for this now, Josie.'

'No, for you have had what you wanted—my father's journal and my body in your bed,' she said bitterly.

The light fled from Dammartin's face. He stilled, just stood there for a moment and stared at her.

She had said the words to hurt him just as he had hurt her, and she could see in his eyes that she had done just that. But the feeling was not one of victory; it did not make her feel better; her own hurt was not lessened by the cruel retaliation. She opened her mouth to tell him that she was sorry, that she had not meant it, but he turned and was gone. The door closed behind him and his footsteps echoed along the passageway towards the stairs, leaving Josie more alone than ever.

Dammartin departed La Roque's office in a hurry, the small leather document wallet tucked securely within his jacket. He already knew which men he would select for the mission—those that were trustworthy, and fast, whose aim was true and whose courage was great…and Molyneux, of course, since Dammartin could not trust that Josie would be safe with the Lieutenant around.

He spoke to Lamont first, making sure that his sergeant understood why he was being left behind. 'There is no one that I trust more to guard her. Do this for me, my friend, and forgive me that I do not take you with me.'

Lamont nodded.

'Have a care, Pierre. The road to Valladolid is a dangerous one for any Frenchman, and I grow too long in the tooth to be taking orders from a new puppy of a captain.'

Dammartin smiled and clapped his friend on the arm. 'You will not be rid of me so easily, Claude. Keep the brandy ready for my return.'

They laughed, but both of them understood the risk involved in travelling through Spain with such a small escort.

'Ready the men. There is something I must do before I leave.' Dammartin made his way back up to his room.

Chapter Fourteen

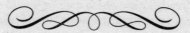

Josie was sitting in a chair by the window, bathed in sunlight and stitching a tear in one of Pierre's shirts when he arrived.

He came in, leaving the door open behind him and picked up his portmanteau. 'I am for Valladolid with an urgent message for General Foy. I have come to take my leave of you.'

Her heart plummeted at his words. The sewing was set hastily aside as she jumped to her feet. 'You are leaving now?'

He gave a nod. 'We are under orders to pass a letter to Foy before he departs for Paris.'

He could not go now, she thought, not when there was so much that she needed to say to him. She felt as if the rug had been pulled from beneath her feet. Her fingers touched to her forehead. 'How many men travel with you? Are there not bandits on the road?'

'Go to Lamont if there are any problems. Rosa shall keep you company during the days, and if you are afraid at night, I am sure that she would stay. All being well, I should be back some time next week.'

He was going and she was not fool enough to dismiss the danger of his journey.

'Molyneux, he comes with me, so you need not worry over him, but Ciudad Rodrigo is filled with men. Keep the door locked. Do not venture out alone.' He produced a purse from his pocket and threw it on to the bed. 'There should be enough money in there to buy yourself food, clothes, whatever you need.'

She looked at the purse, feeling her heart beating very fast, and then up at Dammartin. 'You are leaving no guard; you are giving me money and freedom. Are you not afraid that I will escape?'

'I can no longer hold you against your will, Josie. If you wish to leave me, I will not stop you.'

Their gazes met and held.

The sunlight glinted against the darkness of his hair and lightened his eyes to a clear warm amber.

She did not understand what this meant. She wanted him to want her. She wanted him to fight for her, to hold her in his arms and kiss her and love her as he had done so often. But everything had changed. Cruel words spoken in haste lay between them; cruel words and a lack of faith.

They looked at each other across the little room for a moment longer, and as he turned to go, she knew that she could not let him leave like this.

'Pierre.'

He stopped, looked back at her.

'The words that I spoke to you this morning, I...I did not mean—'

The shuffle of booted feet sounded outside the door, a man clearing his throat before he knocked.

Josie bit at her lip, all explanations and apologies left unspoken.

He gave a nod of acknowledgement. '*Au revoir*, Josie.'

And she wanted to tell him, wanted to shout the truth out loud to him, but the door swung wide and Lamont was standing there, his little black eyes watching them.

'Captain,' he murmured. 'The Major wishes to see you before you leave.'

Dammartin nodded. 'I am coming, Claude.'

One last look and then he turned and walked away, closing the door behind him as he went, leaving only the sound of brisk booted footsteps that receded into nothing.

Josie stood by the window and watched Pierre ride out with only twenty-five of his dragoons, knowing that there was a very real risk that he would not come back.

After he had gone she sat in the chair and stared out of the window, thinking and thinking some more, as the sun moved across the sky.

Only twenty-five men to secure his safety when Foy had taken twenty times that number. And she thought what he might face—Spanish armies, disgruntled locals, murderous bandits, all of whom had a reason to hate Bonaparte's men. The horrible stories of what they did to the French soldiers that they captured made her shudder. If Pierre were to suffer, if he were to die... She closed her eyes to the thought, unable to bear it. Such cruel imaginings to torture herself with, not knowing for days whether he was safe, whether he still lived.

She thought of their parting: awkward, stilted, with so many barriers between them. And she had not had the chance to tell him that she regretted her harsh words, that they were spoken only out of hurt and anger, that she had known that they were not true. He had gone carrying those same words with him, not knowing the truth that she loved him.

The sky stretched unending in a clear, pale blue silk, and as she stared at it, she knew that was her biggest regret of all. She loved him, and she had not told him so. She loved him, and he might die without knowing it.

He did not believe her, she reminded herself, but what was that in comparison to losing him? Whether he believed her or not now seemed of little consequence. Was it so bad that Pierre should have some measure of loyalty to his godfather? He had wanted to speak of it this evening, but Josie and his orders had ruined that. He was gone, and her heart had gone with him.

Dammartin scanned the surrounding rocks while his men rested and the horses took their fill from the stream. He swigged from his canteen, wetting his parched throat and leaned back against the boulder behind him.

'Anything?' he shouted across at the trooper who had been posted as lookout.

His man shook his head. 'Nothing, Captain.'

Molyneux approached, his face sheepish. 'Captain, I wonder if I might speak with you.'

Dammartin gave a slight nod.

'I wished to apologise for what has happened between us. One evening when I was visiting the women's tent, Major La Roque called me in and explained that he was concerned for you because of Mademoiselle Mallington. He is a most important man, and your godfather, and so when he asked me to keep him informed of matters concerning Mademoiselle Mallington, I could not refuse him. I was not permitted to tell you, sir, and for that I am sorry.'

'I understand the position you were put in, Lieutenant.' Dammartin stoppered his canteen and placed the strap across his body, fixing the container back into place by his hip.

Molyneux visibly relaxed.

'What did the Major offer you in return for your...help?' Dammartin's eyes met Molyneux's before the Lieutenant glanced away.

Molyneux cleared his throat and would not meet his gaze.

'Come, come, Molyneux, do not be shy. Tell me,' Dammartin said quietly, with the barest suggestion of a threat about the words.

'He offered me the girl.' Molyneux glanced fearfully up at his captain.

Dammartin frowned. 'Mademoiselle Mallington?'

Molyneux nodded. 'I would not have hurt her.'

'Just taken her against her will,' said Dammartin dryly. So Josie had not misunderstood. She had known exactly what was going on, and if she had been right about that... 'And the journal?'

Shock flitted across Molyneux's face. 'You were not supposed to know about the journal. The Major said—' He stopped himself in time.

'What *did* the Major say, Lieutenant Molyneux?' Dammartin's eyes narrowed.

But Molyneux just shook his head.

A hollow feeling of dread rose in Dammartin. 'La Roque was sending you to retrieve the journal from Mademoiselle Mallington by means of rape.'

'It would not have been like that. She trusted me. She would have given it over to me. I would have been gentle with her, for all that La Roque said I might do.'

Dammartin's lip curled, he glanced away, and gave a subtle shake of his head, and as he looked back, he stepped

forwards and landed his fist hard against Molyneux's jaw.
The force of the blow sent Molyneux sprawling.

'Stand up, Lieutenant.'

Molyneux got to his feet, dabbing a hand gingerly to
the blood that trickled from his lip. He did not cower, just
faced Dammartin squarely. 'I suppose that I deserve that.'

'When Mademoiselle Mallington came to me, what
then?' demanded Dammartin, thinking fast.

'The Major said you would soon tire of her, and then…'

'You would have her.'

Molyneux nodded. 'He wants the journal.'

Dammartin's face hardened. 'If he wants it so damn
badly, he is not going to sit and wait for us to come back
from Valladolid, is he? He thinks Josie has it, and he will
go to her to get it.'

'He would not—' Molyneux stopped, and his gaze met
Dammartin's.

'I think perhaps we both have underestimated my godfather, Molyneux.'

'But she just needs to give him the journal and she will
be safe.'

'She cannot give him the journal,' Dammartin said in
a cynical voice, 'when it is in my possession, can she? I
am going back to Ciudad Rodrigo. You must deliver the
letter to Foy.'

Molyneux stared in disbelief before he nodded.

Dammartin put his hand into his pocket to retrieve the
document wallet with its letter just as the lookout shouted…and the shots began to fire.

Josie was still sitting in the chair by the window when
the knock sounded at the door. Rosa, the thought flashed
in her mind and she went to let the Spanish woman in,
pausing by the door before she opened it.

'Rosa, is that you?'

There was a silence before the reply sounded.

'Mademoiselle Mallington.'

Josie recognised the voice and her scalp prickled with the knowledge of who stood there. 'Major La Roque,' she said through the wood of the door.

'Open the door, *mademoiselle*.'

She remembered that night crouched outside his tent, and of the words she had heard. She made no move, just stood there quiet and waiting.

The door handle rattled beneath La Roque's hand, making her jump back.

'I bring bad news of Captain Dammartin.'

She felt the sudden dip in her stomach at his words. It had to be a trick. La Roque would not come himself to tell her of anything. She glared at the handle, part of her willing him to go away, the other small part scared that he was telling the truth. Lamont would know, she thought, he would come to tell her of any news.

There was silence and as the minutes ticked by she wondered if La Roque was still out there. Maybe he had gone; maybe she was safe.

There was a wrenching sound, the splitting of wood; the door vibrated beneath its force. Josie backed away, her eyes scanning the room for a weapon, but it was too late. The door swung quietly open and La Roque walked slowly in. In his hand was the long knife with which he had levered the door to burst its lock.

He pushed the door behind him, closing it as best he could against the splintered frame. 'There is much we have to discuss, *mademoiselle*, and it so much easier to speak face to face, do you not agree?'

She could feel her throat grip tight to her breath, feel

her mouth dry in an instant. Her eyes looked to the knife in his hand.

'Do not let this worry you, at least not yet.' He slipped the knife inside his jacket. 'And you need not fear that the Spanish doxy shall interrupt us; I have ensured that she will be kept busy for some time.' He smiled, but his eyes were like ice.

She wetted her lips nervously. 'What do you want?'

He laughed. 'I like a woman that gets straight down to business.'

She backed away to stand by the window, her eyes flicking to the partly open door.

La Roque positioned himself between Josie and the door, blocking her in, covering the exit. 'I want Lieutenant Colonel Mallington's journal for Oporto.'

'I do not have it,' she said.

La Roque raised his eyebrows. 'Oh, but I know that you do, *mademoiselle*.' He looked at her with those pale eyes of his.

'You are mistaken, sir.' She forced herself to sound calm.

'Then where is it?'

She bit at her lip, feeling the fast trip of her heart within her chest, the thrum of her pulse in her throat, knowing that she could not tell him.

'It has to be with you as it was not with the others at the bottom of your portmanteau,' he said.

Her mind was whirring, frantically seeking a way to escape him.

'You are not surprised, I see, *mademoiselle*, by my knowledge of the journals. I wonder to whom you might have been listening.'

And for one awful moment she thought that he knew

of her eavesdropping…but that was not what La Roque meant.

'Did Molyneux tell you? He cannot think any higher than what hangs between his legs.'

She balked at his vulgarity.

'I want that journal, Mademoiselle Mallington.' His hand slipped within his jacket, and when it came out again, it was holding the knife. 'And I will do whatever it takes to have it from you.'

Her eyes widened. She backed away until her legs were pressing hard against the chair, her gaze frantically seeking a way she might reach the door; but La Roque stood between her and that route of escape.

'By the time that I have finished with you, *mademoiselle*, you will be begging me to take the journal from you.' He smiled and moved towards her.

One look at his face told her he was in deadly earnest, and yet still she could not tell him the truth, for she feared what he would do if he knew that Pierre had hidden the journal from him. 'I burnt the journal, Major La Roque, for fear that it would fall into French hands like the others.'

'A clever attempt, *mademoiselle*,' La Roque sneered, 'but I do not think that you would destroy the only evidence of what happened in Oporto that day.'

The silence hissed between them as the penny dropped in her mind. Her eyes met his. 'You know,' she said as if she could not quite believe it. If La Roque knew her father to be guilty, then why would she not destroy the evidence that could prove it was so. But La Roque's words revealed that he knew otherwise. She stared at him aghast as she understood the implication of his words. 'You know that my father was innocent. That is why you want the journal,' she said slowly, 'not to protect Pierre, but to hide the truth.' The sickness welled in her stomach at the realisation that followed, for there could be only one reason why La Roque wished to hide the truth.

Something of it must have shown in her face, for La Roque stepped closer. 'I see that you have guessed my little secret.'

'What secret is that, sir?' She tried to feign ignorance.

'Come now, *mademoiselle*, it is written all over your face.'

'I do not know what you mean.'

'Oh, but I think that you do,' he said, as his hand closed around her wrist. 'An English woman alone amidst an entire French garrison and not just any English woman—the daughter of one of the most hated men in all of France. It is hardly surprising that some loyal soldier shall take his revenge.'

She tried to pull away from him, but he squeezed his fingers and held her tighter. 'Pierre shall know what you have done.'

'No, Mademoiselle Mallington, he will never know.' He looked her directly in the eye. 'You see, I was not lying when I said that I brought bad news of Captain Dammartin.'

The fear was churning in her gut, but none of it was for herself. Her lips felt cold and stiff, making it hard to force the words out through them. 'What do you mean? What has happened to Pierre?'

'He will not be coming back,' he said quietly.

'How can you know that?'

La Roque just looked at her with his cold, dead eyes, and she knew.

Her legs began to shake with the dread of it. The breath was uneven within her throat, and her fists clenched. All of the pieces fell into place. 'It was you that ordered Pierre to ride to Valladolid with the letter for General Foy.'

'The letter that he carries is unimportant; it was merely an excuse to get him away from Ciudad Rodrigo.'

The chill was spreading throughout her body, and the pulse was hammering in her head. 'Why would you do that?'

'Why do you think, *mademoiselle*? Pierre and his men will be attacked by guerrillas. The letter will be stolen, and no French survivors left, no loose ends.'

'Oh, dear Lord!' She shook her head as if she could not believe what he was saying. 'Why? He is your godson, for pity's sake!' she cried.

She saw the pain crease his face. 'Do you think it does not kill a part of me to have to do this? It is like ripping out my own heart.'

'Then do not do it. Please!'

He shook his head. 'I must.' His mouth contorted and she could see the hostility blazing in his eyes. 'The fault is all yours, *mademoiselle*.'

She stared at him in horror.

'Everything was going so well until you came along. Pierre and his brother and his mother looked up to me. I took the role that had been Jean's: hero, father, protector. All of France respected me. And all because Jean was dead by the hand of the evil Lieutenant Colonel Mallington. Do you know how much Pierre hated your father? Do you know that in all of the months since Jean's death, Pierre thought only to look into your father's eyes as he killed him?'

'He believed the lie that my father had murdered his.'

'He did.' La Roque's mouth twisted up at that and the smile was filled with pain and bitterness and anger. 'Until Mademoiselle Mallington inveigled herself into his life and, with her charms...' he swept a glance down over her body '...captured him.'

The smile had gone and his expression was grief-stricken. 'Pierre is too like Jean. Once he was no longer convinced of Mallington's guilt, there was a very great risk that he would discover the truth. I have known Pierre all his life, watched him grow from a boy to a man. I love him as if he is my own son.'

'And yet you would kill him!' she cried.

'I have no choice!' She saw the tears well within his eyes. 'I could not let him know what I had done. Thanks to you, *mademoiselle*, he questioned my word. Everything between us has changed.'

It was she who had unwittingly signed Pierre's death warrant. 'No, you are wrong, sir. You are his godfather. Pierre looks up to you. He respects you. He does not believe my protestations of my father's innocence.'

'Indeed?' La Roque looked cynical. 'And yet he has kept you against all of my advice, Mademoiselle Mallington— the daughter of the man he is supposed to believe murdered his father. He craves you in a way I have never seen Pierre act over a woman. I begin to fear the worst—that there is more between the two of you than just lust.'

She felt the heat rise in her cheeks. 'Call off the attack, please. I am begging you. I will do anything that you want. I will give you anything that you want.'

'You will do that regardless, *mademoiselle*.' And when he looked at her, she could see the cold hatred blazing in his eyes. 'Besides, it is too late. What has been set in motion cannot be stopped. Indeed...' he glanced out at the sun's position in the sky '...the deed should be long done. There can never be any going back.' He smiled and it was filled with a melancholic bitterness. 'As you are so committed to revealing the truth, Mademoiselle Mallington, I will tell you a little truth that you do not know.' He leaned forwards so that his face was close to hers.

Her fingers gripped the chair behind her.

'Molyneux told me that you are unaware of the fate of your father's messengers.'

She grew very still.

There was a pause before he continued. 'They did not reach Wellington. We found them, and we shot them like the dogs that they were.'

Josie felt the words hit her like bullets. 'No,' she whispered. 'They were not caught.'

La Roque just stood there and looked at her.

'No!' she said again. 'You're lying; you're lying now just as you lied about my father.'

He smiled a small, icy smile that made her shiver. 'It is because of you that I have sent Pierre to his death, and broken my own heart and that of his dear mother in doing so. Now you will suffer as I suffer. I wish to God that you had died in Telemos that day, Josephine Mallington.'

The tears streamed silently down her face. Her father had sacrificed himself and his men in vain. The man that she loved was dead. She had nothing left to lose, and all of the fear left her, and her devastation was so great that it seemed to Josie that she felt nothing at all. She looked at the man who had started the whole cycle of destruction with the murder of his friend.

'Why did you do it? Why did you kill Jean Dammartin?' As she looked, she saw that hatred and fear had eaten away at him to leave only the shell of a tired old man who had killed those he loved best.

'Does it matter?'

She opened her mouth to reply, but the door suddenly thumped back hard, reverberating against the wall.

'Yes, it damn well matters!' said Pierre Dammartin as he strode into the room.

'Pierre?' Josie heard La Roque utter his name with incredulity.

She did not know how much of the conversation Pierre had overheard, and she did not care. She stared at him, not quite believing that he was really here in the little room with her, and not dead by La Roque's traitorous order miles away in the desolation of the Spanish countryside. She was unsure whether he was real or a ghost or a vision willed by her imagination. The tears were still welling in her eyes, dripping down her cheeks. She scrubbed them away, stared at him all the harder. The steel of his blade hissed as he drew it from its scabbard. Then he glanced over at her, his gaze meeting hers momentarily, and his eyes were dark and simmering with something that Josie had never seen in them before.

'Has he hurt you?'

She shook her head, not trusting her voice to answer.

He gave a tiny nod of acknowledgement, then turned his attention back to La Roque. 'Drop the knife.'

The knife clattered to the floor.

'P-Pierre, you should be on your way to Valladolid,' said La Roque. 'The letter for General Foy—'

'We were attacked by guerrillas and many good men were lost, but then you already know that, Frederic, do you not? Their leader squealed like a pig with my blade at his throat, and told me of the French major who had paid him to kill his own French dragoons.'

'The villain was lying. I would never—' La Roque began.

'Do not waste your breath,' said Dammartin. 'Now, Major La Roque, you were about to explain why you murdered my father.'

La Roque's face had turned ashen. 'I—I...' He seemed

to stumble over the words and looked at Dammartin beseechingly. 'You are mistaken—'

The sharp edge of Dammartin's sabre raised to point at La Roque. 'Your explanation, if you would be so kind, Major.'

La Roque moved his eyes from the blade to his godson. 'It is not as it seems.'

Dammartin just stared at him in stony silence. He did not utter one word. He made not one movement. Just stood there, with his blade pointed at La Roque, and his very stillness was more threatening than if he had slashed and shouted and swore.

'You would not kill me, Pierre,' said La Roque slowly, 'after all that we have been through together. A lifetime, your mother, your brother…'

Dammartin moved and the sabre blade touched ever so gently against La Roque's heart.

'Very well.' La Roque inhaled a shaky breath and gave a nod. 'I suppose that you, of all people, have a right to know.' He cleared his throat nervously and began to speak. 'I worked hard all my life, harder than anyone else I have known, harder by far than Jean, and as a result I was good at many things. Good, but never quite as good as Jean. It was always that way—as boys and as men. Jean always won the race while I always came second—even with Marie.'

'Leave my mother out of this.'

'I loved her, but it was Jean that she chose to marry, not me. He had the woman that I wanted. He had the sons that should have been mine. He had a bigger house, more money. He outranked me in the army. And then there was the Battle of Oporto when we were captured by Lieutenant Colonel Mallington. I saw the way that even his enemy looked at him—with respect, with admiration, as a friend.

Mallington barely looked at me at all. I knew then that beside Jean I would always be nothing, no matter how hard I tried.

'Mallington gave us our parole and we rode away. Jean was in front of me, as always, and...' he swallowed '...and—I shot him. I could not help myself. There was just one minute when the idea came to me, one minute to make a choice to change a lifetime.

'I had a chance to escape from his shadow, a chance that people might actually see me for once, and I took it. And I was right. Marie needed me. You and Kristoffe needed me.' He stopped talking and looked at Dammartin.

'I shot myself in the arm—a minor wound that amounted to nothing. You know the rest.' He stopped again. 'I am so sorry, Pierre.'

'Not half as sorry as I am.' Dammartin's voice was low and filled with deadly promise.

La Roque's face crumpled in entreaty. 'Forgive me.'

Dammartin gave a hollow, mocking laugh. 'You killed my father and sent me for vengeance against an innocent man. You lied to me and would have had my lieutenant rape Josie, and you think that I will forgive you?' Dammartin's lip sneered as he pressed the blade hard and made to slash.

'No, Pierre!' The words tore from Josie.

'You know what he has done, to your father and to mine, to you and to me. How can you tell me to stay my hand?'

'If you kill him, you will be court-martialled and executed.'

'I do not care.' His eyes, still focused on La Roque, were hard and ruthless. She saw how hard his blade pressed against La Roque's chest.

'But I do,' she said. 'I have lost everyone, do not make

me lose you too.' She paused. 'I love you, Pierre. I should have told you that this morning.'

He looked round at her and as he did so La Roque moved, throwing himself away from the blade and towards Josie. The Major wrenched her back hard against the front of his body and drew his sword.

'I think you might want to drop your weapons, Pierre,' La Roque said as he pressed the edge of his sword to her throat.

'Do not! He will kill you regardless,' she managed to shout before the cold touch of the blade became an unbearable pressure that threatened to choke her.

'Do it!' urged La Roque in a coarse whisper, and she gasped as he began to tilt the blade edge towards her skin.

Dammartin's gaze met Josie's, and she saw the agony in them and heard the clatter of his sabre and pistol hitting the floor. 'Release her.'

La Roque smiled. 'Kick them over here.'

Dammartin watched La Roque like a hawk watches its prey, his eyes locked on those of his godfather's, as he did as he was bid. 'This is not about Josie. Let her go.'

La Roque gave a chuckle. 'On the contrary, this is very much about Mademoiselle Mallington. She has destroyed everything for which I worked so hard.'

He began to walk towards Dammartin, driving Josie before him as a shield.

She could barely breathe for the blade, which seemed to press ever harder. He was going to kill Dammartin, she knew it, and there was nothing she could do, and still Dammartin just stood there, letting La Roque close the distance, and she wanted to cry out to him to run, that La Roque would kill her anyway. Dammartin must have known that, too, but there was nothing on his face save the cold hunger of a hunter.

Just as they reached Dammartin, La Roque threw her away, before he lunged with his sword at Dammartin.

She landed hard beneath the window. Her ears were filled with a scream and she did not know that it was her own voice that cried. Everything seemed to slow: movements, words, time itself as La Roque's blade headed directly for Dammartin's heart.

To Josie there was no way he could evade the death-blow and she was yelling, her eyes widening with horror, scrambling to her feet—all too slow, too useless. And just as she thought the blade would strike she saw Dammartin react, sidestepping to come in so close to La Roque that their faces were almost touching, jerking La Roque's wrist until the sword dropped to lie upon the floor. Then the two men were fighting, with fists and feet, kicking and punching, so that their blood began to splatter as each hit thumped home—flesh pounding against flesh, the sheer ferocity awful to watch.

Josie tried to reach Dammartin's sabre and pistol, or La Roque's knife where they lay, but the two men were moving around the room so much that she could not get to them. She glanced around for anything that could be used as a weapon, anything to help Pierre. But there was nothing. When she looked again, Dammartin was punching and punching at La Roque, harder and harder, until his cuffs were soaked with La Roque's blood, and La Roque lay limp upon the floor.

Only then did Dammartin look at her.

He stood there with his face cut and bruised and bleeding, and his coat torn and stained dark with blood, and in his eyes was such intensity that it took her breath away.

He came to her then, walking slowly, and, reaching down to where she stood, pulled her up to him. 'I did not believe you.'

'It does not matter.' He was alive, alive, and she was dizzy with the relief of it.

'I am sorry,' he whispered, and feathered kisses to the top of her head, her eyebrows, the tip of her nose. 'So very sorry, for you and for your father.'

She could feel that her cheeks were wet, and taste her tears mixed with his blood as his lips brushed hers.

'My love.' He caressed her face as he kissed her again and again, his eyes imploring her forgiveness. 'My sweet Josie.'

His arms wrapped around her, crushing her to him as if he would never let her go, as if he would merge their two bodies together.

'What he said about your father's messengers was a lie told to hurt you. We did not catch them, *chérie*.'

Josie clung to him, as he clung to her, and in his caress, in his kiss, in his very touch he offered her all of his comfort, all of her strength, all of his love, and she accepted them wordlessly, weeping silently against his chest.

They stayed that way until, at last, her eyes grew dry.

Dammartin summoned two men to carry La Roque from the room. Only then did he leave to set in motion the accusation that would tell the world the truth of La Roque.

The grey light of day had begun to fade by the time Dammartin returned to the bedchamber. He could see that the blood had been cleaned from the floor and walls and the room tidied.

Josie was standing by the window when he entered, just as she had been when he had left for Valladolid earlier that day. Only a few hours had passed, and yet, in that small time, everything that was important in his life had changed. Nothing was the same.

Her silhouette showed a slim figure; although she was

looking at him, the fading light cast her face into shadow. His woman. His love.

'It is done. La Roque is arrested. He is denying all, saying that you have driven me mad.'

'But he confessed.' He saw the worry on her face.

'Only to us.'

'There is my father's journal.'

'It alone does not prove La Roque's guilt,' he said.

'He cannot murder your father and just get away with it.' She stepped towards him, away from the window, and as she did so the dying light lit her face and he could see the outrage upon it.

'He will not get away with it, Josie. The provost marshal shall have the sworn word of Jean Dammartin's son of La Roque's confession. The Spanish guerrilla leader will point out the man who paid him to kill my dragoons and me'

'You brought him back with you?'

'I could not leave such good evidence behind. There is also your father's journal from Oporto, witness statements from my men that in Telemos your father could not fire a musket even when his daughter's and his own life depended on it, and...' he paused '...Molyneux's testimony of the Major's actions these past days.'

'Molyneux will stand against him?'

'Oh, yes. La Roque arranged for him to be killed along with the rest of us. That, together with the fact that he now understands exactly why La Roque was so determined to obtain the journal, has persuaded him most thoroughly. The evidence should convince a military court, but even if it does not, it is enough that people will know the truth of La Roque. All of France will know it and that, not death, is the greatest punishment for a man like him.' He smiled a small smile. 'Your father's name will be cleared, Josie.'

She looked at him and he could see the sparkle of moisture in her eyes. 'Thank you.'

'It is I who should thank you.' His eyes scanned hers.

'Then we are even,' she said, and her voice sounded husky. 'What will happen now to us...to me?'

'Your father asked that I keep you safe until I could return you to the British. I have failed on the former.'

'You did not fail—I am safe, am I not?'

Sorrow and regret weighed heavy upon him. 'I exposed you to La Roque, and...' he thought of his interrogating her, of his kissing her, bedding her '...my treatment of you has hardly been honourable.'

She sighed and shook her head. 'Pierre.'

'I should take you to Lisbon, give you into Wellington's keeping.' He walked forwards, only stopping when there was no space between them. 'And I will do it...if that is what you want.' He waited, and Dammartin was truly afraid. He felt the beat of his heart and the throb of the pulse in his throat. He waited because he loved her and it was her decision to make.

Her gaze clung to his. 'And if that is not what I want?'

He smiled and took her hands in his. 'Marry me, Josie.'

He saw the surprise and joy light her face.

'Marry me because I cannot face my life ahead without you, because I want you in my bed each and every night. Marry me because I love you, Josie Mallington.'

'Yes,' she said, and she was smiling with overflowing joy. 'I will gladly marry you, Pierre Dammartin.'

'I will speak to General Gardanne's chaplain in the morning; we will be married before the week is out.'

And then she was in his arms and he was kissing her, kissing her with all the love and tenderness that was in his heart.

He lifted her into his arms and carried her over to lay

her on the bed and as the sun set low in the sky, he showed her just how very much he loved her, again and again and again.

Afterwards, they wrapped the blankets around their nakedness and stood together in comfortable, sated silence by the window, looking up at the clear white disc of the moon and the glitter of the scattered stars.

Dammartin's voice sounded through the quietness. 'Next week, we march with the convalescents and the garrison of Ciudad Rodrigo to meet up with the main French army.' He paused. 'We are for Santarém. We are part of Massena's reinforcements.' The moonlight showed the planes of his face all stark and angular, and the gouge of his scar and the concern upon his face. She saw the intensity of his gaze. 'You know what that means, do you not you, Josie?'

'That you will be fighting against the British when you reach your destination.' She gave a small, involuntary shiver.

'My love,' he whispered. 'I know the position in which this places you.' He touched his hand to her cheek. 'It would be safer for you in England.'

'There is nothing left for me there.' She turned her face to kiss the palm of his hand. 'My place is with you, now. I followed the drum for my father, I will follow it the same for my husband. And if it is a different drum that beats, then so be it. That is all I can do for the man that I love.'

'*Chérie,*' he whispered, and kissed her.

And Josie thought that out of the darkness of war and enmity, out of revenge and jealousy and murder, out of sacrifice and loss, had come love, and that one thing alone shone as a light in the darkness, and with its joy, made all of the grief and the pain and the suffering bearable. Love alone was enough. She marvelled at the knowledge, and snuggled in closer to the warmth of Dammartin's body.

Epilogue

The sky was a cloudless blue that seemed to stretch to an eternity, lit by bright golden sunlight. Josie closed her eyes and felt the sun warm upon her face through the dappled shade of the trees. Up above, the birds were singing, and she could hear the droning buzz of the bees amidst the lavender, and smell the perfumed scent of the nearby roses.

She opened her eyes and looked down over the lawn to where a tall, handsome man was absorbed in playing with a small boy. Both the man and the boy had the same dark hair and eyes. The man's face was filled with love for his son and the sight of it made the happiness well up throughout Josie. The little boy looked round and saw her watching.

'*Maman, maman!*' he cried, and ran to her, clambering up on to her lap.

Her husband came, too, and sat down by her side, draping his arm across her shoulders, and dropping a kiss to her cheek.

'Pierre.' She smiled.

As he leaned in to kiss her again, a little wail began from the basket that sat on the bench at the other side of her. He smiled and lifted the tiny baby to him, stroking a finger gently against his daughter's soft downy cheek.

And Josie's happiness was complete.

* * * * *

REQUEST YOUR FREE BOOKS!

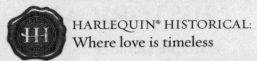

HARLEQUIN® HISTORICAL:
Where love is timeless

2 FREE NOVELS PLUS 2 FREE GIFTS!

YES! Please send me 2 FREE Harlequin® Historical novels and my 2 FREE gifts (gifts are worth about $10). After receiving them, if I don't wish to receive any more books, I can return the shipping statement marked "cancel." If I don't cancel, I will receive 6 brand-new novels every month and be billed just $5.19 per book in the U.S. or $5.74 per book in Canada. That's a savings of at least 17% off the cover price! It's quite a bargain! Shipping and handling is just 50¢ per book in the U.S. and 75¢ per book in Canada.* I understand that accepting the 2 free books and gifts places me under no obligation to buy anything. I can always return a shipment and cancel at any time. Even if I never buy another book, the two free books and gifts are mine to keep forever.

246/349 HDN FEQQ

Name	(PLEASE PRINT)

Address	Apt. #

City	State/Prov.	Zip/Postal Code

Signature (if under 18, a parent or guardian must sign)

Mail to the **Reader Service:**
IN U.S.A.: P.O. Box 1867, Buffalo, NY 14240-1867
IN CANADA: P.O. Box 609, Fort Erie, Ontario L2A 5X3
Not valid for current subscribers to Harlequin Historical books.

Want to try two free books from another line?
Call 1-800-873-8635 or visit www.ReaderService.com.

* Terms and prices subject to change without notice. Prices do not include applicable taxes. Sales tax applicable in N.Y. Canadian residents will be charged applicable taxes. Offer not valid in Quebec. This offer is limited to one order per household. All orders subject to credit approval. Credit or debit balances in a customer's account(s) may be offset by any other outstanding balance owed by or to the customer. Please allow 4 to 6 weeks for delivery. Offer available while quantities last.

Your Privacy—The Reader Service is committed to protecting your privacy. Our Privacy Policy is available online at www.ReaderService.com or upon request from the Reader Service.

We make a portion of our mailing list available to reputable third parties that offer products we believe may interest you. If you prefer that we not exchange your name with third parties, or if you wish to clarify or modify your communication preferences, please visit us at www.ReaderService.com/consumerschoice or write to us at Reader Service Preference Service, P.O. Box 9062, Buffalo, NY 14269. Include your complete name and address.

Harlequin® Special Edition® is thrilled to present a new installment in USA TODAY bestselling author RaeAnne Thayne's reader-favorite miniseries, THE COWBOYS OF COLD CREEK.

Join the excitement as we meet the Bowmans—four siblings who lost their parents but keep family ties alive in Pine Gulch. First up is Trace. Only two things get under this rugged lawman's skin: beautiful women and secrets. And in Rebecca Parsons, he finds both!

Read on for a sneak peek of **CHRISTMAS IN COLD CREEK.** *Available November 2011 from Harlequin® Special Edition®.*

On impulse, he unfolded himself from the bar stool. "Need a hand?"

"Thank you! I…" She lifted her gaze from the floor to his jeans and then raised her eyes. When she identified him her hazel eyes turned from grateful to unfriendly and cold, as if he'd somehow thrown the broken glasses at her head.

He also thought he saw a glimmer of panic in those interesting depths, which instantly stirred his curiosity like cream swirling through coffee.

"I've got it, Officer. Thank you." Her voice was several degrees colder than the whirl of sleet outside the windows.

Despite her protests, he knelt down beside her and began to pick up shards of broken glass. "No problem. Those trays can be slippery."

This close, he picked up the scent of her, something fresh and flowery that made him think of a mountain meadow on a July afternoon. She had a soft, lush mouth and for one brief, insane moment, he wanted to push aside that stray lock

HSEEXPI1111

of hair slipping from her ponytail and taste her. Apparently he needed to spend a lot less time working and a great deal *more* time recreating with the opposite sex if he could have sudden random fantasies about a woman he wasn't even inclined to like, pretty or not.

"I'm Trace Bowman. You must be new in town."

She didn't answer immediately and he could almost see the wheels turning in her head. Why the hesitancy? And why that little hint of unease he could see clouding the edge of her gaze? His presence was obviously making her uncomfortable and Trace couldn't help wondering why.

"Yes. We've been here a few weeks."

"Well, I'm just up the road about four lots, in the white house with the cedar shake roof, if you or your daughter need anything." He smiled at her as he picked up the last shard of glass and set it on her tray.

Definitely a story there, he thought as she hurried away. He just might need to dig a little into her background to find out why someone with fine clothes and nice jewelry, and who so obviously didn't have experience as a waitress, would be here slinging hash at The Gulch. Was she running away from someone? A bad marriage?

So…Rebecca Parsons. Not Becky. An intriguing woman. It had been a long time since one of those had crossed his path here in Pine Gulch.

Trace won't rest until he finds out Rebecca's secret, but will he still have that same attraction to her once he does?
Find out in CHRISTMAS IN COLD CREEK.
Available November 2011 from Harlequin® Special Edition®.

HSEEXP1111

brings you

USA TODAY Bestselling Author

Penny Jordan

Part of the new miniseries

RUSSIAN RIVALS

Demidov vs. Androvonov—let the most merciless of men win...

Kiryl Androvonov

The Russian oligarch has one rival: billionaire
Vasilii Demidov. Luckily, Vasilii has an Achilles' heel—his
younger, overprotected, beautiful half sister, Alena...

Vasilii Demidov

After losing his sister to his bitter rival, Vasilii is far too
cynical to ever trust a woman, not even his secretary Laura.
Never did she expect to be at the ruthless Russian's mercy....

The rivalry begins in...
THE MOST COVETED PRIZE—November
THE POWER OF VASILII—December

Available wherever
Harlequin Presents® books are sold.

www.Harlequin.com

HP13023